Praise for Chandra Prasad's *Death of a Circus*

Death of a Circus gives us not only the roar, the glitter, and the chills and thrills of an early twentieth century circus, but also a vivid understanding of the tawdry, dangerous, filthy, and human inner workings of the big top. This is the story of one black drifter who literally rises to the top of the circus world as the greatest, most inventive tightrope walker on earth. Fittingly, the language of *Death of a Circus* is acrobatic, sinewy, and daring.

—Polly Whitney
author of *This Is Graceanne's Book* and *Farewell, Conch Republic*

Death of a Circus is a compelling story of people on the edges of society—circus workers, thieves, prostitutes, and impoverished hobos—which grapples with the heart of American identity through its exploration of social mobility, the formation of celebrity, U.S. race relations, and sexuality.

—Janet M. Davis
author of *The Circus Age: Culture and Society Under the American Big Top*

Prasad walks a fine line between realism and fantasy in her construction of circus life. But she walks this line gracefully, with nary a misstep. Her vivid characters live not just in the center ring spotlight, but also in the shadows of the circus backyard. They've come from wildly varied pasts, and carry with them unique fears, phobias, and fascinations. The result is a volatile mix under the big top, and a story loaded with color, compassion, joy, and heartbreak.

—James Foster
former editor of *The White Tops*, official magazine of the Circus Fans Association of America

Chandra Prasad is a writer of merit and daring, weaving language and story together in a manner that is uniquely modern, even as it echoes early twentieth century traditions.

—Don Massey
author of *A Matter of Degree: The Hartford Circus Fire & The Mystery of Little Miss 1565*

DEATH OF A CIRCUS

DEATH OF A

CIRCUS

CHANDRA PRASAD

RED HEN PRESS | Los Angeles, California

Book design by Mark E. Cull
Cover design by Erin Mary Greene

ISBN-10: 1-59709-024-7
ISBN-13: 978-1-59709-024-7
Library of Congress Catalog Card Number: 2006922893

The City of Los Angeles Department of Cultural Affairs,
Los Angeles County Arts Commission
and the National Endowment for the Arts
partially support Red Hen Press.

Published by Red Hen Press
First Edition

ACKNOWLEDGMENTS

My deepest and most heartfelt thanks to those who have been instrumental in helping to guide this book into print: Vinod K. Rustgi, M.D., Rosalie Siegel, Mark E. Cull and Kate Gale, Radha and Sue Prasad, and not least of all, my wonderful husband, Basil Petrov.

DEATH OF A CIRCUS

PART ONE

• CHAPTER ONE •

NEW HAVEN, CONNECTICUT: 1912

Lor Cole ran along the shores of the Quinnipiac River, bucket in hand, leaving in his wake footprints that filled with briny water then disappeared. He scarcely noticed the odor of low tide: the rank intermingling of dead fish and drying seaweed. He was happy simply to be near the water and all its parts: the creeks, the sound at the edge of the skyline, and especially the rivers—Quinnipiac, Mill, and West—whose mouths fed into New Haven Harbor. Here, at the confluence of river and sea front, he delighted in the splash of spray and the slip-sliding of waves curling toward the shore.

When given a chance to roam the beach, Lor ordinarily wiled away time watching the sleekly lined sloops and sharpies. But today he had a task to complete: his mother had ordered him to fetch oysters. The oystermen always spilled some of their catch on the beach after shuttling between the beds. Lor plucked his first find from the sand, momentarily fascinated by the gleam of shell and the promise of flesh inside. Even though he was a child, he knew how much depended on this tiny animal: the food at his family's table, the passing of money, the very architecture of the town. Indeed, so many shells littered the area that the sea captains on Front Street used them as the base of their houses.

Within a half-hour Lor had filled the bucket. He smiled with anticipation, for now he could do as he pleased, even idle. His mother wouldn't be home until midday. In one of the many tidal pools that dotted the area, he watched a seastar wrap its body around an oyster, then slowly pull it apart with suckered tentacles. Later, Augusta Cole would take a less sophisticated approach to opening the oysters in the bucket. She'd use a hammer and square cracking block to loosen the shell, then she'd pry it open with a knife. Sometimes Lor helped, but he disliked the ritual: the splintered, broken bits, the fetid splash of brackish juices.

Lor was so busy combing the sand and dreaming that he scarcely noticed the girl. She looked to be his age, six or seven, with petal-like corkscrews of yellow hair encircling her head. She had white skin, the kind his mother had warned him of. By turns, she stared at him, then at the ground. He ignored her.

Unable to capture his attention, the girl hissed between a gap in her teeth, "Little boy, look at this!"

Lor steered his gaze toward the harbor. He hoped the girl would stop trying to communicate with him, but she continued to call until he could tolerate it no longer. Grudgingly, he made his way to her side.

"A fish—big as a whale!" the girl exclaimed. "Right in this puddle."

Up close, the girl's eyebrows pressed together with simian results. Her nose formed a mocking snub. Her lips, rosebud pink, lingered open. Lor didn't trust her. Nor did he believe she'd found a whopper of a fish in so small a tidal pool. But she insisted with conviction, and the prospect, however remote, of seeing something out of a fisherman's legend enticed him. He imagined himself bragging later to his best friend, Opal, who would stare at him with eyes that looped around him like a lasso. He'd tell his older brother, too, only Woodrow never believed his stories. The two siblings shared a fractious relationship, brought on by Woodrow's unfounded yet stubborn conviction that Lor was in some way responsible for their father's death. Mr. Cole had passed within days of Lor's birth. What everybody else supposed to be unfortunate coincidence, Woodrow understood as providence.

"It's there. I swear it," the girl promised.

Lor suddenly remembered a story he'd once heard about whales, how they could swallow a person whole. He imagined himself living out the rest of his life in the dark, humid cavity of a whale's belly, then shuddered. He looked around, worried that his mother would find him somehow. Dallying was bad enough. But she'd surely paddle him if she caught him with a child such as this.

"Don't mingle," Augusta had often warned. "Let the whites stay with the whites."

Anxiously, Lor stepped away from the girl's soiled eyelet dress and peered into the green-black water below.

"The fish was here a second ago," she professed. "It bobbed to the surface. It was going to jump."

Lor knew to leave, but the lure of a fantastical sight kept him rooted. He waited with the girl, their heads level under the sunlight, oysters and the rest of the world secondary to the possibility of a flop of a tail, the shimmer of scales, maybe even the glassiness of an eye. How long they waited Lor wasn't sure. It would have taken a seismic catastrophe to interrupt them. And that's exactly what happened.

The hand on his shoulder was bone-thin, but strong, capable of sending him flying—and his bucket too. When he crashed to the ground, the oysters fell around him like a shower of hailstones, round but sharp-edged, nicking his skin as they descended. Pain seared his elbows and knees, but he dared not move. Maybe whoever had thrown him would think him dead and leave him be. Yet the same rough hand grabbed for him again. Not his shoulder this time, but his hair. He yelped in pain as he felt a thick hank being twisted from his scalp.

Lor looked up; his tears blurred the image of his assailant. His lips quivered uncontrollably. He blinked until the person more clearly materialized—a woman, harried, petite, and lean, with a face that would have been pretty if not for its pockmarks. Lor couldn't believe she'd been the one to hurt him, until he saw her expression. Proud and defensive, exactly like Augusta's. Clearly, this warrior was the girl's mother.

He recoiled as she moved toward him a third time. Yet she halted before she reached him. Lor watched her look not at him, but at the clump of hair in her hand, which was dark and bristly. She was disgusted, and Lor realized that this disgust was exactly what might save him.

Wanting to disappear, he pulled his knees to his chest, wrapped his arms around his head. His eyes didn't stray from the woman. Like him, she'd been collecting oysters. These she stored in the well of her apron. Miraculously, even through the tumult, her harvest had stayed intact. Still, Lor was sure she would try to steal his oysters too, though they were scattered. He fought to speak. He wanted to say that she should leave, that he'd done nothing wrong. But his tongue felt like a stone in his mouth and he could manage not a word. Maybe the girl would explain. Surely she would tell her mother that they'd been playing, that they'd only wanted to see the fish.

The girl, however, sobbed hysterically. At first, Lor thought her mother's attack had triggered her distress. But Lor saw in her eyes, in those predatory orbs crowned by a single deceitful brow, that the girl was satisfied with her mother's actions. And though her little lips were swollen in mock pain, Lor saw a corner upturned—a fraction of a smile, meant for only him to see, gone even before it had formed.

There had been no fish.

• • •

Lor saw he could not win, not against both of them, so he abandoned the oysters and ran. He ran for only one purpose—to get home to his mother. He imagined hiding in her thick, rustling skirts. She would pull him onto her lap, tend to his wounds, kiss each scrape and bruise. Then her energy would convert into rage. She'd take another look at his patch of exposed scalp and swear revenge. Lor welcomed his mother's potency. If anyone could protect him, it was Augusta Cole. Fervently, he wished for her to be back from her errands.

When Lor arrived home, panting hard, sweat and blood oozing down his limbs, he sensed her presence. He always could. Sometimes he heard her shoes reverberating against the pine floorboards, smelled the brisk scent of her skin, listened to the swish of her clothes. But other times he simply felt her, the way, sometimes, he could feel someone looking at him from behind.

He didn't call to her. In fact, for reasons he couldn't explain, he didn't announce himself at all. He simply crept toward Augusta's bedroom, the only room in the tiny house with a door: space sealed off from prying eyes. The door wasn't entirely closed. A crack of light peeped out, enticing him, beckoning him to peer though. His trepidation mounted.

He pulled open the door carefully so it wouldn't squeak, mindful that Augusta might be napping. But inside, she was all motion—and not alone. A man, a stranger, wrapped his arms around her, kissing on her fervently. He had gray hair, sparse at the crown, and skin like the wrinkled ivory pages of an old book. He unbuttoned his shirt then lunged for Lor's mother, sending them both careening onto the bed.

Augusta let out a girlish giggle Lor seldom heard. She protested as the man kissed her neck, but her pleas were weak, insincere. Eventually, she opened her pouter pigeon blouse, revealing what seemed to Lor a most unholy sight: bare breasts—areolas like saucers, nipples wide as wine corks and ruddy as madder lake.

Instinctively, the boy understood what his mother and the man were doing, although he didn't know the name for it. He'd seen dogs behaving this way, and sometimes the boys in his class talked about the zealous, sweaty positions men and women assumed at night.

Unnerved, Lor thought of his father, who still kept watch over the house, if only in spirit. How horrified Mr. Cole would be to see Augusta in such a predicament. Lor couldn't understand. How many times had his mother called men like this the enemy: an unscrupulous, loathsome breed?

He felt frozen, in need of relief, but in no way ready to confront his mother. He was no longer certain she would comfort him. Indeed, how could she defend him from the enemy when she had her arms wrapped around one?

Bitterly, he closed the door. By then, the sounds of their passion drowned out the creak of an unoiled hinge and Lor's own violent sigh. A fresh fountain of tears sprung from his eyes. He wanted to run away, but feared venturing far from home—what if the woman from the beach was still looking for him? In the end, he climbed into a nearby tree and let the branches cradle him like so many arms. Here, in the soft whistle of leaves, he decided never to talk about this day, not to anyone, not even Opal. He would try to forget the anger too. But unlike the image of his mother and the man, which had already faded in a choke of hazy disbelief, his fury had sharpened. It cut into his heart, deeper and deeper, until at last, with dazzling precision, it left a hole.

• • •

Augusta Cole was an open-minded woman, as open-minded as they come. But she was also fastidious. She liked her dresses neatly pressed and her hair carefully pinned. Augusta Cole always arrived at social gatherings equipped with small tokens of her appreciation: a bouquet of fresh flowers from her garden, a spice cake, the secret and much coveted recipe to her rum raisin bread, an elaborately embroidered quilt square, her favorite prayers neatly printed on little cards. She always smelled of talcum powder and bleach, fresh scents—as if she herself had just been laundered, squeezed of impurities, and hung out to dry. Her cheekbones were sharp, much like her tongue, which she had trained to sound demure even when it yearned to scold and slash.

Augusta arrived half an hour early to every engagement, particularly services at the Dixwell Avenue Congregational Church. She favored the early service, and the second row, where she could more diligently observe the ushers, Father Hopewell, and the replica of the crucifixion. She would never have admitted it, but she liked to stare at the pale, forlorn Jesus, his wrists and ankles nailed down and dripping blood.

Augusta's husband had died quickly, but she hadn't been surprised. She'd always suspected he would leave her prematurely. It had been in his nature to be unreliable. Despite his broad physique and easy laugh, he had been delicate: quick to get sick, easily rubbed down by worry.

Her husband had been a good man, never around very much, but maybe that's why she'd been so fond of him. She tried not to think about him much, unless the boys asked her questions, which they often did. *What was he like, Mama?* Never mind that. He was like any other man. *Did he whistle? Did he like to go fishing?* Can't say I remember. *How did you meet—*

when did you know you loved him? It was so long ago. God, give me the strength to live in the present.

She'd lived in the present from the moment he'd passed, in fact. Circumstances had demanded a new strategy for survival. Mr. Cole had not left her any money. And though Augusta was an exacting woman, some might even say a finicky woman, she'd been forced to make changes. Taking lovers for money was one.

At first she'd adopted an open approach, accepting even objectionable men, so long as they could pay. White gentlemen comprised the bulk of her batch. They fancied themselves explorers, the first to conquer uncharted lands. But it wasn't merely her novelty that excited them. It was the fact that they believed themselves to be trespassing on society's dictates, on their wives' greatest fears, on the very order of the universe. Yes, Augusta thought, it was the deviance that drew them.

Augusta's lovers came and went, out for the thrill then back home again, except for Alonzo Biddle. He ambled into her life and stayed put. Augusta considered herself fortunate to have aroused his jealousy. Alonzo couldn't stand the idea of sharing her, so he made sure he didn't have to.

Their arrangement was simple. Alonzo came around the house a couple times a week. He pulled his coat collar around his face whenever he approached, although the Coles did not have any close neighbors. He feared the gossip. God forbid his family, which included a wispy-frail wife and several young girls, be exposed to salacious rumors. Augusta worried too. She managed to keep Woodrow and Lor away from home during most of their trysts. But she supposed the occasional lapse wouldn't matter. Children so young would forget.

Alonzo ran a prominent bronze and silverware shop on the east side of town. He lived in an enormous house that was three tiers high, like a wedding cake. But no wedding loomed on Augusta's horizon. He'd spelled out the terms of their arrangement from the beginning: Augusta mustn't speak of their encounters, she mustn't communicate with Alonzo's wife and children, and she mustn't expect him to have a hand in rearing her own brood.

Fortunately, these dictates didn't matter much to her, not when he gave her money to buy new boots for her boys. Never had she been more grateful than when purchasing those sturdy leather pairs, extra-thick for New England winters. She bought sailor suits too, and a new corset for herself.

There were other benefits aside from the money. Alonzo didn't mind tending to the occasional repair. His laugh rang hearty and smooth. His love talk was as comforting as her homemade cordial. Best of all, Alonzo didn't behave like a husband, nor she like a wife. She didn't placate him, do the things that women are expected to do for men: press their clothes, soothe their egos, fill their stomachs, play mother, angel, and maid. In fact, being a mistress—aside from its filthy connotations—was an ideal arrangement. Augusta only wished it wasn't a sin.

"Mary, Mother of God, forgive me for giving myself to a man other than my husband," Augusta whispered. But under the covers, Alonzo was a tempest, and that was God's honest truth.

She hadn't imagined herself carrying on with him for months, never mind years. But life is a hurried affair. Much of the time it just blows past, leaving a wake of swirling dust and leaves.

These same conditions accompanied Alonzo's funeral on October 4th, 1913. It was a nippy-in-the-knickers autumn day. The trees had exorcised their leaves, leaving barren branches. The ground felt damp, although Augusta's shoes were good and solid—she had her lover to thank for that.

Alonzo lay in his coffin, in a burrowed-out ditch of half-frozen ground. It wouldn't be long, Augusta supposed, before the worms began to burrow through the veneer and wood. She shuddered uncomfortably, deciding there and then that she would be cremated when her time came. She couldn't stomach the notion of her clean body rotting away.

The mourners resembled one another: a sea of expensive overcoats, fur muffs, and snide hats. But Augusta identified Alonzo's wife through the homogeny. She was the one who fought for control and lost, surrendering herself to body-wracking sobs and wringing hands.

She lacks my fortitude, Augusta thought. No wonder Alonzo had come calling.

Augusta stood well behind the mourners. It was colder here, and darker. The wind blew ferociously and there was no communal body heat. Nevertheless, Augusta had vowed she would never reveal herself to Alonzo's wife, and she certainly wasn't going to do so now. Not on his last day.

The wife suddenly doubled over in grief. Someone put his hands on her shoulders to make sure she didn't fall. Augusta's disgust waxed. What did the wife have to cry about? She would have money, land, and security; each of her girls, a bountiful inheritance.

Augusta sniffed at the woman's self-absorbed hysterics. Augusta might not have the world, but she did have blessings—her sons, for one. Each was handsome, strong, and capable, not like the pale paper dolls surrounding Alonzo's wife. Then there was the sum Alonzo had left her—not formally in his will, but discreetly, privately, when he'd first learned of his illness. That sum, Augusta knew, would last through a few more seasons, a few more pairs of boots.

• CHAPTER TWO •

"Steady, Lor. *Steady*," called Opal Hinely, a pretty twelve-year-old with ribboned hair. She watched as her best friend, who was also twelve, climbed the soaring maple tree next to the house of Mr. and Mrs. Benjamin LaRue, a wealthy couple who—fortunately for daring children—seldom looked out their windows.

Lor's task was daunting. He had to shimmy up the bulk of the mammoth trunk, swing himself onto a branch, and walk its perilous length. The branch appeared sturdy and even, except for a few snaky turns. Eventually it dipped close to the widow's walk atop the LaRue's towering house. Lor would be able to jump to the safety of that walk—if he didn't fall first.

He was only ten feet above the earth, but already his gaze was fixed upon the challenge. Skyward, the maple's glorious autumn foliage rustled in the cool air. Orange, yellows, and russet-reds draped against a backdrop of sky. It was a sight spectacular enough to make him heady.

For years the children had crept across every dangerous surface they could find: the ridgepole on Old Man McFaddan's roof, the fallen tree that spanned a stream near Lor's own humble home, the whitewashed fence that wound itself around All Saints Chapel, the long planks of wood in the shipyards, the tracks of the New Haven Railroad.

To date, their hardest challenge had been rigging nautical rope across a narrow point of the Mill River, a shallow stream flowing between Fair Haven and New Haven. Getting across had required tremendous effort on many fronts. Opal and Lor had had to position the rope so that it was slack enough to accommodate their weight, but tight enough to resist dangerous sways and wobbles. Tying the knots, securing the rope to nearby trees, and reinforcing it with wooden stakes had taken an entire day.

"We'll do this when we're grown," Lor had shouted jubilantly as he attempted his first steps across. "Do you hear me, Opal?"

"I do," she'd called back nervously. "Close that big bazoo! Concentrate!"

"We'll walk between mountains. From one city's bell tower to the next! People everywhere will know our names."

"Hush, Lor. Pay attention!"

He had fallen, of course. Smack into the river, where he quickly hit the silted bottom, thereby twisting his ankle. That had been the last time Opal had completed a challenge before him. In fact, it had been the last time she had agreed to attempt one at all. Before, the thrill of their dares had surpassed the possibility of danger. But in recent months Lor had upped the ante, daring feats of preposterous difficulty with devil-may-care panache. Opal had removed herself from contention, and caution wasn't the only reason for her withdrawal.

"Now he can have the spotlight all to himself. And isn't that what he wants?" she thought. But these were words she could never speak aloud.

"Where next?" Lor called down. A good twenty feet high in the maple tree and puffing like a dragon, Lor was close to his goal, but on the wrong side of the trunk.

"Work yourself around. Take the right side," she shouted.

The descending sun mirrored the vibrant hues of the leaves. Glints of light, like shards of glass, pricked her eyes. Opal lifted her hand to her forehead, salute-style. Still, her vision of Lor was blurry, dreamlike. She wondered if she would have to get glasses like her father, pop-bottle thick and bookish.

Using the tree's gnarls and knobs as handholds, Lor pivoted around the trunk. He slipped his hands around a branch and curled his ankles around it too. A moment later he was swinging back and forth like a monkey.

"Stop being a scooch," Opal scolded. "Boost yourself up."

Lor grinned, but pulled himself onto the branch, then rose, the balls of his feet firm on the bark beneath him. The vista ahead made him dizzy and he clung to the trunk as if it were a life buoy. The widow's walk wasn't far. He wouldn't have any trouble getting there if he could crawl on his hands and knees, but this wasn't the strategy he and Opal had agreed upon.

Meticulously, one hand at a time, Lor released his grip on the trunk. He placed his right foot forward, concentrating on the destination, rather than on each step. His attempts at walking everything from ropes to ridgepoles had taught him that studying each step was the surest way to stumble. He must eye his target, breathe evenly, raise his hands from his sides like he were a bird taking flight. Only then would he reach the end, almost without thinking, supernaturally, as if coordination and confidence could enable a person to soar.

From below, Opal squinted, fearing—simultaneously hoping—that she would see the branch shake or bend. Even a surefooted walker might doubt himself, lose faith, stagger and lurch. But the branch remained frozen. Only the setting sun shifted position.

From her vantage point, Lor's body became a series of lines, his strong, slender limbs extensions of the branches. A silhouette against a smoldering dusk. Opal shuddered. She wondered how the air could be so cool with the leaves aflame and the sky afire.

Up in the heavens, Lor's footing became increasingly confident. He reached the part of the branch that dipped near to the widow's walk. Triumphantly, he climbed over the low iron railing.

"Like walking a pirate's plank—and living to tell about it!" he shouted.

What a funny sight Lor made perched on the widow's walk, Opal thought. So happy a figure where a lonely woman ought to be standing, waiting with hands clenched for her husband to return from sea. Opal's father had told her stories of women waiting years, whole lifetimes, for their lovers to come home to them. Their looks faded. Their eyes became worn with the waiting. Their hope transformed from necessity to burden. Life stalled and only memories survived. Opal, who was told frequently that she was far too serious for a child so young, shook off the thought.

But it lingered, as did the vision of Lor dancing quick-footed against the sunset.

• • •

To climb down the widow's walk, Lor decided upon the LaRue's rose trellis. The challenge of scaling down such a precarious fixture alarmed Opal. Swiftly, she crept across the lawn to the side of the house. If necessary, she decided, she would catch him herself.

The LaRues never did have much luck growing roses, despite the behemoth trellis they had installed. Lor was relieved he didn't have to worry about thorns. He did, however, fear the fixture would dislodge from the side of the house, leaving him scrambling mid-air.

With the same dexterity he had displayed on the maple tree, Lor climbed halfway down the house. At that point Opal noticed a lamp flickering inside the LaRue's house.

"I think they're home," she hissed.

The punishment for two colored children trespassing upon the property of wealthy folks would be harrowing, at best. Opal worried they would be thrown in jail for life. Lor worried the LaRues would tell Augusta, who would first thrash him with a belt, then freeze all his privileges, including these climbing adventures.

He picked up speed, his descent increasingly erratic. A piece of rotted wood gave way underneath him. He hung like a flag, flailing as he struggled to find another roost.

"Jump, Lor," Opal insisted. "You're not far from the ground."

He looked down. The security of earth seemed far away, but he had no choice. Closing his eyes, he dropped. His knee buckled when he hit the ground, but he could stand, possibly even walk, if he could bear the burden of pain. He bit down on his lip to keep from screaming.

"I thought you were gonna catch me," he grumbled to Opal.

Opal didn't reply, instead grabbing her friend by the hand, pulling him along; together, they fled as fast as they could. It was a long way from New Haven proper to Lor's house in the rural sprawl of Fair Haven.

Although Opal didn't look back, she was sure she heard the front door open and angry adult voices in their wake. Twice Lor had to stop to rest. He was glad night had descended, and it was too dark for Opal to see the tears dribbling down his cheeks.

When they finally reached his house, something about the homey smell of dinner—oysters battered in homemade beer—soothed his wary soul and aching leg.

"I'm home, Mama," Lor called. "I've brought Opal too."

Augusta was in the kitchen cutting biscuits. She kissed her favorite son wetly on the forehead.

"Where have you been?" she scolded.

"Opal's," he lied.

"Is that so?" Augusta asked Opal.

"Yes, ma'am."

"You two are awfully dirty," she observed, plucking leaves and bits of bark from Lor's hair. "You'd think Opal lived in a treehouse."

"We were playing outside, Mama."

"Is that so?" she repeated, then went back to carving biscuits out of a sheet of dough. "If Opal's going to stay, I'll need more potatoes. Go fetch some from the cellar."

Lor made a funny face at Opal behind his mother's back.

"And take a lantern!" Augusta called absently.

The door to the cellar was outdoors, built into the side of the house. Lor and Opal plodded outside slowly. Neither enjoyed going to the cellar, least of all at night, when the musty gloom of the place reached ghoulish proportions. To Lor, the cellar was the dampest, creakiest, most macabre place in existence. He was terror-stricken whenever he had to go there. He would rather have crossed the Mill River a dozen times in a row, blindfolded. One couldn't see in the basement—not really, just enough to detect vague shapes and outlines. It didn't matter if one went night or day, with or without a kerosene lantern. Without the benefit of good light sight was of little use. The children therefore relied on their other senses—smell most of all. And how many scents the cellar held: salted pork, wet fur, dug-up ground, over-ripe vegetables, rodent droppings, turpentine, vinegar.

Cautiously, Lor and Opal made their way down. The stairs were comprised of corroded boards, held in place by rickety beams. Descending, Lor felt exposed. He half-expected a troll or goblin to grab his ankle from behind—pull him into the triangular underbelly of the staircase, where spiders knitted cobwebs thick as yarn.

When both children had made it to the landing, Lor quivered. He lifted the lantern. Its flickering light made monsters of ordinary objects: a jumble of walking canes, sweet sausages dangling from the ceiling, rows of canned vegetables and preserves, a bicycle with twisted spokes. And these were only the objects the children could identify. There were so many other things—intangible, morphing, peculiar things—things that Lor was sure were breathing the same air as he, waiting to pounce.

Instinctively, he moved nearer to Opal, until their thin shoulders brushed. At the same moment that Lor trembled in fear, a sense of exhilaration crept up his spine. The cellar was a repulsive place. But right then, it had a new effect on him: stimulation. Indeed, he began to experience the same euphoria he felt while balancing. The blurriness, the filmy air, the subterraneous odors—everything combined into an ardor Lor had not experienced before. His breathing quickened. Blood pounded like a drum inside his head. Without entirely realizing what he was doing, he faced Opal, then ran a tentative hand along her flat, coltish frame.

"What're you doing?" she whispered.

"Shhh," he said and put his mouth on hers. The kiss didn't feel right. It was not at all how Lor had imagined it would be. He didn't know what to do with his tongue or how to move his lips. These actions didn't come naturally, as Woodrow had joked they would. Even so, the sensation was deliriously moist, rich, and strange.

Suddenly, Opal clutched his seeking hands and pushed them aside. She took a step back. For the first time, through the pale light of the lantern, Lor could see. He breathed shallowly, distressed, wondering what the repercussions would be.

Opal had already smoothed out her rumpled blouse and collected herself. Now she searched through the potato sack. She pulled out two oblong specimens and stuffed them into her pockets.

"Let's go," she announced, having decided to ignore what had just happened. Or rather, to hide away the unsettling details until later, when she was alone and could sift through them with a meticulous hand.

• • •

Lor's attraction to the female sex had been long budding, yet he knew it had blossomed in the cellar, there with Opal. As Lor edged into adolescence, girls became his premiere interest. He admired them all: nurses, shopkeepers' daughters, domestics, schoolgirls, seamstresses. Some days he skipped school just to watch the soft whish of female bodies hurrying by. His favorite spot was Wooster Square, where the girls passed like a parade, a line of light and luster, cherry lips and sashaying hips.

He admired them all, but in time, his heart stopped for only a few. Why had his scope narrowed? He remembered every time he touched the spot on his head. There, the little girl and her combative mother had drawn the battle line. There, the hair now sprouted in sparse, irregular whorls: a physical reminder that some people considered him tainted.

Lor sought the very girls who reminded him of that incident: pale, brazen, and suspicious.

If he'd searched his soul, Lor might have realized that he wanted to replay that scene by the tidal pool, this time with a different ending. He wanted to prove that he was worthy of the most unlikely affection.

But Lor never considered the origin of his inclination. He thought only of its emotional wallop as he walked down the street, eyes darting clandestinely down the length of a comely blonde. He was surprised when she returned his interest, slyly, but unmistakably. She edged close as they passed. Close enough for Lor to catch her rosewater scent, to feel the heat their bodies exchanged. Instantly, his face warmed. An energy seized him. He wished he could speak to her, impress her somehow, but he knew that that was out of the question. That girl—she'd made him think of all the things that were just out of reach. That same day, he wandered in circles, arriving finally at the New Haven Railway Station. For an hour he watched the trains come and go. Mostly he watched the passengers aboard. He stared at their faces in the small, soiled windows, imagining their final destinations, places far away. Closing his eyes, he tried to see himself in a window too. But just as he visualized himself as someone important, someone with a place to go, a voice broke through.

"Boy, what're you loitering for? You lookin' to fence?"

Lor opened his eyes to see a railway worker with eyebrows that formed irate question marks.

"You have a ticket?" he asked.

"No, sir."

"You waiting for someone?"

"No, sir."

"Then you best skedaddle, before I have you removed."

The man took a step closer. Lor could feel the stern press of his body, the finality of his uniform. He tried to walk away, but his legs betrayed him. His knees weakened and his feet rooted to the floor.

Irritated, the railway worker pushed Lor's shoulder, hard enough to rattle him. Lor staggered back, unable to catch himself. Awkwardly, angrily, he stumbled away, back to where he'd come from, stuck in his dreams with no ticket in hand.

• • •

Sometimes Augusta had trouble believing her boys were grown. She remembered all too vividly fussing over Lor's scrapes, bruises, and blunders when his adventures with Opal had turned into misadventures. A hundred times she'd poured iodine over his battered knees and watched it weep orange rivers to his ankles. A hundred times she'd plucked errant slivers from his flesh with her own fingernails.

"Stings!" he'd complain, when he was out of Opal's earshot and childish whimpering could replace manly bravado. But Augusta had never told him to end his crazy pursuits. *Just to be careful. For Lord's sake, be careful.*

Although these outlandish boyish impulses were over, Augusta did not sigh with relief. Now she had other things to worry about: her sons' economic security for one. Fiercely, she prayed for their prosperity, for only well-situated young men could provide for their mother.

When Woodrow found work as a carpenter, she kissed him on both cheeks and cried in joy. He'd been fortunate to learn the trade: most artisans refused to take colored apprentices. In New Haven, as throughout the country, nine out of ten blacks became menials.

She'd wanted Lor to learn the profession too, but Lor's lackadaisical disposition seemed at odds with steady work. Too often he wasted his time on imaginings and half-cocked schemes. Tolerant of Lor's wistful nature, Augusta didn't mind supporting him. She would do so for as long as she could. But she feared the day when she could tend to him no longer.

Augusta's remarkable and perhaps unwarranted forbearance was no coincidence. Her affection for Lor was tied to his uncanny resemblance to herself. He had inherited all of her best characteristics: self-possession, poise, charm. She recognized herself in his smooth mannerisms and arresting features. Augusta's youngest turned heads. His trail was always littered with

compliments. He wasn't an exact replica—for Augusta lived for her sons, while Lor lived for silly dreams—but he was close. And though she tried, Augusta could never stay cross at him for long.

There was another reason that Lor eclipsed Augusta's heart—and that was her conviction that he would not go unnoticed, that his life would be marked by greatness. Augusta had thought this from the very first, which was why she had called her second son Lor, a slightly blasphemous name that made people wonder if she'd indulged too liberally in her homemade cordial.

Soon after Woodrow's apprenticeship began, Augusta's eldest married a humble and loyal girl, a little on the plain side, but Augusta couldn't complain. At least Woodrow wasn't attracted to flashy girls. Augusta harbored a strong dislike for those city fluffs in tight skirts and high-heeled shoes. They tended to loiter on Grand Avenue at night, sneaking sips of alcohol, puffing cigarettes, and flirting with any lad who ventured past. Unfortunately, these were precisely the girls who drew her younger boy. In time, Augusta's motherly fretting turned into full-fledged anxiety. She did what she could to warn Lor.

"Stay away from those tarts. People aren't meant to be mixed," she said. "Blood blended is good as blood spilled."

She wanted to keep him clean, to maintain the family purity. Strange that purity would be the last thing on Augusta's mind when she fell ill. The local doctor called her symptoms typical of consumption, the great white plague.

Lor had heard of this disease: tuberculosis. The local Gaylord Sanitarium had been founded to treat it. That's where Old Man McFadden's wife had gone when she'd taken sick. Her husband had hoped her stay would be short. But she'd never come home. Lor thought maybe he could send his mother too, but the quack said Gaylord didn't accept Augusta's kind.

Lor, who was now a young man of seventeen, considered the options. Neither he nor Woodrow could afford to bring Augusta to a real doctor, despite Woodrow's income. All they could afford was this irregular physician, who brought with him a case full of small, unlabeled jars. From one of these jars, he smoothed a peach-colored jelly over Augusta's throat and chest. He said the disease most often affected the lungs. Little did he know, in Augusta's case, it had already spread to her kidneys, brain, and bones.

"Keep her outside," the physician advised. "Don't breathe the same air."

But how could Lor keep his mother outside when a chill might creep through her skin and into her blood? Against the doctor's wishes, he carried her to bed and swaddled her in blankets. Even so, Augusta's condition persisted. The quack prescribed more jars—some containing ointments for the flesh, others containing pills and strange-smelling herbs. Lor wondered if these medicines, administered in such minute quantities, could interrupt the sweeping progression of his mother's disease. There were so many ailments to combat: wheezing, coughing, aches, fatigue, and delirium.

Yet miraculously, after several months and several dozen jars, Augusta began to feel better.

By then, Lor was assessing his own future. Watching his mother deteriorate so quickly, he started thinking about his own life, and especially his childhood, when he had balanced high above the earth. How exhilarating those moments had been! His boyhood had been full of wonder—a series of escapades. As an adult, he was no longer allowed adventure. But how he yearned for it still!

With his mother's health on the upswing, Lor decided it was time to leave New Haven. He had always known he would walk an unconventional path: singing, dancing, perhaps even acting. And he'd always known he would leave his little world in Connecticut.

I'll go to New York City, Lor decided. He'd heard that talent scouts flooded Broadway each year to prowl for promising amateurs. Maybe he'd be discovered. Maybe he'd be scooped up and dropped onto the stage—with a bang! Then, boy, he'd have the world by its coattails!

But the attention—the intoxicating sound of applause—would have to wait.

Augusta had been overdoing it. She had long worried about money, even with men like Alonzo helping out. And she had always engaged in activities that would bring in a few extra coins: selling fresh eggs at the local market, making candles and soap, knitting blankets, sweaters, mittens, and the like. After her first bout of consumption, though, she worked as if each day were her last. Maybe she'd seen it coming. The way the coughing crept back, this time accompanied by bloody phlegm. The way a light stroll left her short of breath.

Lor again summoned the irregular physician. But this time there was no hope in the doctor's eyes. Once more, he advised Lor to keep his distance. But he couldn't, not when everyone else had taken leave of Augusta. Woodrow's bride was expecting and she refused to let her husband anywhere near the infection.

The doctor prescribed the same medicines, but this time they did nothing to halt the disease. Within weeks Augusta Cole's mind had clouded. Her appearance became grotesque: face gaunt, skin sallow, eyes drowning in their own vinegar juices. It was as if a witch had invaded her body, staking claim on all that was once proud and wholesome.

"Consumption—appropriately named," the doctor muttered. "Consumes the organs, it does."

It was his duty, Lor believed, to be by his mother's side. But for how long? A week, a month, a whole year? He started to grow resentful. And why shouldn't he? He had already decided that his destiny lay elsewhere.

He might have felt more sympathy had the shriveled woman in the bed resembled Augusta. But this woman was a stranger. Never would Lor's mother have muttered such strange, salacious words. Never had her fingernails been yellow-pricked with decay. Never had she alluded to the deeds done between dirty linens: secrets of the flesh, acts of lust and heat, desire best buried.

Worst of all was the fact that Augusta didn't recognize Lor anymore. She certainly did not see him as her son—she understood him only as a man.

"Come closer," she whispered one evening. He could smell her breath, putrid-sour on his cheek. "I want to see your face."

"What is it, Mother?" Lor went to brush stray hairs from Augusta's forehead, but found he could not touch her.

"Oh, I see what's going on. I see it clearly."

"See what?"

"The white girls—they're drawn to you," she told him. Her watery eyes rolled under their lids. "Can't say I'm surprised, handsome as you are."

"Please, Mother, you need to rest."

"Nonsense!" Augusta declared, struggling to sit up, but falling back quickly. "They flounce about without a care, so fancy in their bright dresses," she continued.

"Who does?" Lor asked.

"The white girls—the devil's daughters! You'll want to crawl close to them. You'll want to know their secrets. I'll tell you one: they've like bitches in heat!"

Lor shoved his chair back from her bedside. He wondered from whence these evils had sprung. He wondered what he could do to quiet them.

"They'll lure you, those girls," Augusta continued, her voice having taken on a preacher's zeal. "You'll want to serve them, again and again, until your body aches. Servitude: how familiar a concept! To be inside them, filth inside purity. That's the myth. It is the white girl who is foul! It is she who will trap you!'

At that, she looked Lor squarely in the eye and an ounce of reason returned to her expression.

"Opal's the right girl for you," she proclaimed. "Don't forget that."

"All right, Mama. Be still, be calm."

The sickness was rotting her from the inside out, Lor knew. Her brain was perishing—sure as oil dances on a griddle.

"Hush, go to sleep now," Lor whispered every night until the eve of her death. That was the night he lost patience with her—and with death's tardiness. The doctor had long ago ceased making house calls. Woodrow hadn't visited in two weeks, although he lived less than a mile away.

Lor pulled the pillow from beneath his mother's head. She was sleeping, her breathing raspy and garbled. Pressing the pillow over her face, Lor counted. One hundred seconds. And when he was through, his heavy heart lightened. In his mind, he had but taken something that was already gone.

• • •

Nearly a month had passed since Lor's mother had died. While sorrowful, those closest to Augusta were glad the disease had finally ended its brutal reign. Nobody thought to question the unnaturally blue sheen of her face. Or why, even in the repose of death, her hands seemed clawed in resistance.

In some ways, Opal had mourned for Augusta more than Lor or Woodrow. Opal's experience growing up had been the converse of Lor's: her mother had died young and she'd been tended to by her father. Indirectly, she'd come to view Augusta as a surrogate mother. Secretly, she'd hoped Augusta had looked upon her with the same tenderness.

Just now, Opal was taking in clothes from the line. Lor watched her nimble hands pluck garments from wooden clothespins. She folded them into perfect squares and stacked them in a wicker basket. She bundled socks into knots, neatly separated the boys' underclothes from the girls', draped her father's good Sunday shirt on a hanger, wrung out bits of fluff from her sisters' dark stockings. And all the while, the sun glinted in her hair, creating a halo about her face.

They both had news. This much Lor could tell by the way Opal carried herself: shoulders back, belly out, her face aglitter with pride.

His cap sitting roguishly off-center, Lor leaned against a willow tree that grew near the line. He grinned as he watched the girl he'd known for almost as long as he'd been alive.

Lately, he'd seen less of Opal. He'd been too busy caring for Augusta, and before that, too busy furtively observing the girls in town. Once in awhile, he'd returned to her doorstep. They'd even made love a few times, awkwardly, amid amateur giggles. But in Lor's mind their paths had already diverged. Whenever he and Opal reunited, nostalgia—rather than real affection—prompted their connection.

"Why are you smiling?" she asked him.

Lor scratched his head. "I'm trying to remember how you looked when you were little."

"Got fleas?" she teased.

But he brushed off her joke. "What do you think that means—that I can't remember?"

"You've seen me month to month, year to year. I've changed gradually."

He took a toothpick from his pocket and twiddled it between his thumb and forefinger. "Maybe," he granted. "But all the same, I wish my memories were sharper."

"What do you need your memories for? You're not going anywhere."

Lor smiled again, this time a little uncomfortably. He hadn't yet told her about his plans to leave. How he was going to make it big. Maybe in a few years, when he'd established himself, he'd come back for her. Then again, he couldn't be certain.

He watched her cautiously. Even though she was still young, Opal showed a worldliness beyond her years. Her face was a map, vividly contoured and angled, crescent-shaped lines at the corners of her mouth, eyes still uncharted. A small scar marched jaggedly across her left cheek, the remnant of one of their long-ago quests. It caused her beauty to be asymmetrical, yet somehow more enchanting.

Because the two had known each other since infancy—and indeed, had been inseparable for many years after—townsfolk tended to compare them. It was commonly thought that the more conspicuous Lor had outdone Opal, but that wasn't so. She had simply retreated to a quieter time and place. Here, where judgments were gossamer whispers, she shielded herself from the one truth that left her crumbly as sandstone. She'd given her love to someone who didn't much care.

"You used to have the skinniest ankles," Lor recalled. "That much I *can* remember."

She adjusted her skirts, pulling them straight around her well-curved calves. The calico fabric ruffled in the breeze. She smiled evasively.

Lor was becoming frustrated. What was it that she had to tell him? He wanted to know her news before he revealed his own. Historically, Lor had been able to read Opal. After all, he'd had a lifetime of practice. Yet, something had lately changed—his sense of mastery over her state of mind.

"What is it? What's going on?" he asked finally.

"The midwife told me my ankles would swell. No more tree-climbing, I reckon."

And there it was. Her maturity had trumped him. She'd become a woman before he'd become a man.

In shock, Lor made his way to her. He fell to his knees and pressed his head to her belly. His arms wrapped about her waist. Her flesh felt cool and distant beneath her clothing. Opal's youth had gone, but where had it fled? Lor realized it had tunneled back into her body, where it would christen another.

"I didn't want you to know so soon," Opal whispered. "Not until I was sure."

Lor kept his head buried. He wasn't even aware of the grimace on his face, of the frustration that ultimately took control.

"Opal," he said, tilting his head upward.

His eyes appeared delicate. She avoided them, knowing how easily she fell prey to their skills.

"I've got to go. You know I've got to. I don't see myself settled down. Not now. I've still got so much to do—the world to conquer!"

His theatrical performance should have infuriated her. But Opal heard the chime of his boyish enthusiasm, and this endeared him to her. With eyes diverted, she purposely studied the ordinary things around her: the way the last hanging shirt flapped in the breeze, how some of the willow's knots resembled faces.

"Opal," Lor pleaded, desperate for her approval. "I've thought about leaving for a long time now. I want to travel to new places—maybe get my name in the papers. I can't do that if I roost!"

She turned away then. There was still work to be done and she moved as before, deftly and sure. She folded a handkerchief, watching it diminish into half its size, a quarter, and then an eighth. She folded it fiercely, as if to reduce it to nothing.

"If you leave now, don't come back for me. I won't wait."

"I will come back," he countered, his ambivalent tone betraying that intention. "As soon as I've traveled a fair bit, as soon as I've done what I need to do."

"And how old will our child be then?"

The sun had disappeared completely. Its last, feeble rays shone with a cheerless cast. Opal had taken all the clothes from the line. The ropes looked bare and sterile, the metal rigging only a skeleton. The picture would have appeared bleak, save for the luminous couple in the foreground.

Lor, still on his knees, watched her. He had the sudden sensation that his body was small, like a boy's, and that Opal's had grown majestic. It was with this feeling of minuteness that he left her, more determined than ever to find grandeur.

• CHAPTER THREE •

NEW YORK CITY, 1918

Cirella Flannery and her three sisters, all younger; one brother, still an infant; and mother lived in a loud, cramped, chaotic tenement building on New York's West Side. Theirs was an Irish and German neighborhood along the Hudson River. It was an unremarkable place. Cirella's father, Seamus Flannery, used to say the only peculiar thing about it was that Irishmen and Germans drank together in peace.

Seamus Flannery was a first-generation American. For many years he had found steady work as a factory hand in and around the city. He had provided his family with a decent, modest life—until recently, when he had taken off without warning, leaving the rest of the Flannerys to fend for themselves.

He had left no clue to his whereabouts. And certainly no note, since he had never learned to read and write. But the fact that he had taken all his clothes indicated that his decision was premeditated and permanent.

Mrs. Flannery waited several days for him to return. She stuck to her regular schedule: forcing the girls out of bed at dawn, preparing a meager breakfast for them, shooing them off to school, doing chores and scrounging about for work. But on the fourth day of her husband's absence, something inside her capsized. Horrible realizations hammered her brain: Seamus was gone, she had almost no means of supporting five children, and she hadn't a clue what to do. Catherine Flannery's life was so off course from her childhood ideal, which had included an unhurried life in the green pastures of Galway, that she found herself unable to get out of bed that day. She remained under the lone, shabby cover until Moira, her youngest girl, plopped her crying baby brother onto the bed.

"No school today, Mama? It's a holiday?" the little girl asked.

Eyeing the two small children with distress, the newly widowed Mrs. Flannery sat up. She ran her fingers through the graying knots atop her head. Most of her children had taken after Seamus, whose hair was so red it reminded her of the fires of Hades.

If she'd had only herself to mind, Mrs. Flannery might have stayed in that bed for the rest of her life. But with so many brats scurrying about, she hadn't time for self-pity. For their survival, she must get up.

"Why aren't you dressed?" she scolded Moira. "Put on your things this instant, or you won't live to see your next holiday."

The Flannery's living space didn't afford much privacy. Certainly not enough for Catherine to wallow in solitude. Originally, their house had been built for a single wealthy family. But it had been reconstructed in 1840, and twice thereafter, as subdivided tenement quarters. Each time the house underwent renovations, the rooms became smaller, and light and ventilation more scarce. To ensure profits the landlords crowded in as many tenants as possible. The three-story structure was now packed to the brim with fifteen families. They were jammed into the musty attic, the damp basement, the subbasement, the re-routed hallways, the odd-sized crannies, nooks, and closets. A whole family inhabited the garret on the second floor. Two families split the ample-sized dining room on the first. A single man had recently rented the shed adjacent to the house, which measured eight feet by eight feet. Everybody shared space with rodents, lice, cockroaches, and fleas.

Such living conditions were commonplace—as commonplace as vanished husbands. In these tumultuous times, men frequently left town. The perennial search for work kept some away. They tramped up and down the East Coast in search of casual labor, often taking on new mistresses and families along the way. Others turned to the sea. The shores marked points of debarkation, but also of entrance into new opportunity.

The ships and ports seemed bereft of the very things that drove men away: nagging wives, household responsibilities, brats and more brats.

Had Seamus Flannery run off with sailors? Catherine doubted it. Her husband lacked a sailor's vigor. In fact, he seemed to lack vigor of any kind. No, Catherine could more easily envision him drinking too much ale, staggering onto a merchant's ship, and floating inadvertently to parts unknown. Perhaps he had already forgotten what he'd left behind. The bottle had dulled his memory a long time ago.

Moira reappeared, clad in a simple frock and wool leggings.

"Where are your sisters?" Catherine asked. She was still in bed, her son cradled in her arms. He had fallen asleep and looked so soft and delicate, she was loathe to move.

"They're not ready, Mama."

Setting down her slumbering son, Catherine climbed to her feet. She crossed her arms over her considerable chest.

"Cirella, Mattie, Mildren!" she shrieked. With Moira in tow, she approached the small room where all four girls slept.

"Yes, Mama?" Cirella answered sweetly. The girls looked ready for school, thank heavens for that. But there was a funny smell in their room, one Catherine knew well. She yanked Cirella by the ear.

"Open your mouth," she demanded. The foul odor of tobacco floated on Cirella's breath.

"Again!" Catherine cried. Of all the children, Cirella had the reddest hair, a fact her mother often and irately repeated.

"We're late, Mama," the girl retorted, evading Catherine's venom and heading full-speed for the door. The other girls followed behind like ducklings. Among the children, Cirella was the undisputed ringleader.

If she weren't in such an awful mood, Catherine would have delighted in making the offenders eat soap before school. But she had too much on her mind, and too much work to do.

Mrs. Flannery's household occupied two rooms, including the bedroom she and Seamus had shared and the girls' room. Half of the former was curtained off to divide it from a small makeshift kitchen. With her children's constant jesting, quarrelling, and playing, there was no free space in the tenement and hardly enough room for their few pieces of furniture.

Catherine tried to keep the place clean, but it wasn't easy. Her girls tracked in filth from the muddy streets. The plaster walls crumbled. During the cold season the chimney clogged and regurgitated charred smoke. One of the two windows was broken, and despite multiple requests to the landlord for repairs, it remained an exposed passage into the outside world. On chilly nights, the icy wind blew through the tablecloth Mrs. Flannery had used to plug up the frame. The gusts caused ashes from the stove to scatter. On stormy days, the rain also blew through, wetting the feather beds. These problems only added to Catherine's usual domestic challenges: spilled slop pails and chamber pots, burns from the stove, torn clothes.

With the girls finally out of the house, Catherine set about her chores. Dandling her son in her arms, she decided first to visit Mrs. Greer, an elderly widow who lived on the first floor. Mrs. Greer enjoyed playing auntie to Catherine's brood. Daily, she lent linens, brought over armfuls of kindling, and shared rainwater so Catherine need not make extra trips to the street pump. In Catherine's eyes, Mrs. Greer was the only wholly dependable person on this earth.

"More like a parent than my own mother ever was," Catherine frequently told her.

Mrs. Greer opened her door and ushered Catherine inside. Mrs. Flannery handed her baby to the older woman and promptly flopped on a chair. She hooked several locks of hair behind her ears and sighed miserably.

"What is it, dear? Seamus?"

Having been invited to divulge, divulge is exactly what Catherine did. Her woeful tale of abandonment lasted exactly an hour, and culminated finally in a flurry of financial worries. Though Seamus had always earned the lion's share of the family income, she had contributed too. Amid her makeshift housekeeping, she found time to stitch shirts for one of the nearby clothing shops. On sunny days, she washed extra laundry for anyone who would pay. But these tasks brought in a mere pittance, not nearly enough for a family to live on.

"Have you thought about taking in a boarder?" Mrs. Greer asked. "I know a nice young man. . . . "

"With four girls ripe to enter womanhood, I shouldn't consider it!"

"Well then, you have no choice. You must pull the eldest girls out of school and send them to work."

"But Cirella and Mattie are children yet!"

"These are hard times," Mrs. Greer acknowledged, with a finality that caused Catherine's tears to halt.

That same day, Catherine made inquiries. She hoped the girls could be hired as domestics—perhaps to a wealthy family. But nobody wanted two young girls without experience. In the end, her daughters pursued a more common option: scavenging. They set off in search of saleable junk.

Cirella didn't complain when her mother informed her of her new duty. School hadn't agreed with her anyhow. The boys were always diverting her attention. Scavenging would at least enable her to be out and about. She knew how to do it too: she had watched other children forage. As for Mattie, she was happy simply to be with her older sister, away from the watchful gaze of their mother.

The two gamines set out early in the day, Monday through Saturday, just after sunrise.

They spent much time on the waterfront. Here they foraged for scraps of cloth that had fallen off the bales of docked packet ships. The girls could sell it to junk dealers. The dealers in turn sold it to manufacturers, who converted it into shoddy—the same cheap, ready-made material that comprised much of Cirella and her sisters' wardrobe.

On lucky days the docks were littered with spilled cargo and precious litter: tea and coffee from open barrels, salt and cornmeal seeping from torn sacks, bits of rope that could be shredded for oakum, an unraveled spool of lace, a tin of saffron, and once—a whole bolt of yellow silk that Cirella managed to wrap clandestinely in her coat.

While Cirella mostly scouted for big finds, Mattie rummaged for odds and ends. On the shores, along the cobblestones and dusty roads, she uncovered cogs and bolts, chips of china, the sharp triangles of a broken window. The sisters would stuff these items into a gunnysack, haul them to a glassmaker or iron founder, and barter for the highest possible sum. Cirella took it upon herself to conduct each sale. Most of the craftsmen and junk dealers were men and they responded well to her charms. Beautiful, with a doll's heart-shaped face, Cirella was easily recognizable about town for any number of reasons. The most notable was her hair: a preternatural beacon of light.

Men followed Cirella with a wanton gaze. She quickly learned to reroute their attention in advantageous directions. A coy wink or half-smile could usually bring her twice the return on any item. Promises to visit later in the week, to sell more trinkets or maybe just to flirt, also yielded rewards. Cirella divided her time more or less equally among the line of secondhand shops that wound around the waterfront. Here, doting merchants threw in little extras for their favorite customer. *It is raining? Please, take one of our umbrellas. Pretty lass, care for a bottle of lavender water?* On any given day, she might leave with a crimping iron, pincushion, hat pin, even a bracelet or ring.

But it was going on dates that eventually became Cirella's most productive means of commerce. On these outings Cirella quickly learned several crucial lessons: some men had money and others did not; some men spent on women, others on the racetrack; and some men—quite a few men—couldn't resist redheads.

Through trial and error, Cirella began to weave together the prototype of her ideal bloke. He was wealthy, preferably middle-aged, for young lads were too capricious with their affections. He adored her. He lavished her with gifts and money. But he was not a marital prospect, certainly not. Cirella didn't want the responsibilities, the scolding, the lifestyle that her mother had chosen. Most of all, she didn't want to move beyond fondness. Love's wretched sisters—vulnerability and abandonment—already brushed too close.

• • •

For a long time Cirella didn't mention these dates to her mother. If she came home late, well, she had worked hard all day. Wasn't she entitled to a little fun?

But by her fifteenth birthday, Cirella no longer lied about her romantic frolics. She didn't sneak out of the house; she left without apology. Indeed, she even told her mother where she was going and whom she intended to meet. Catherine, who by now had picked up a penchant for tobacco herself, felt powerless in the face of her daughter's self-assurance.

"I shouldn't feel bad, should I? I can't be minding five children all the time, can I?" she asked Mrs. Greer one afternoon.

"No, my dear. You certainly cannot."

Cirella was practically a woman now, anyhow. Better to free up the reins and hope her daughter had enough sense to find a rich man, Catherine thought.

Of course, on the streets, where rakes, hustlers, and trollops abounded, all mothers worried a little. Catherine just prayed none of her girls would end up pregnant. In Ireland, a beau would be held accountable should trouble arise before marriage. But these were different times. And New York was a different place. Catherine could only imagine what rowdy pastimes went on at the shooting galleries, penny arcades, oyster houses, and dance halls. Of all her daughters, Cirella was closest to inviting trouble: gonorrhea, rape, or worst of all, another brat. But still, it was hard to hold her back, to demand that she succumb to control.

"I earn the most money of all the girls," Cirella complained. "And almost all my money goes to the household. You can't tell me what to do! I left school for you."

How could a mother reply? Catherine could not—not with a clean conscience.

Most girls in Cirella's station, young and working class, went to the Bowery for amusement. A wide and frantically-paced avenue running along the island's East Side, the Bowery was the very embodiment of blue-collar culture. Trimmed with workshops and manufactories, it was a thoroughfare for cheap goods, home to the butcher district, and stage to all kinds of public amusements. Here, shop girls, seamstresses, and domestic servants mingled with craftsmen, artisans, tailors, and sailors.

The Bowery was a place where girls came to find beaus of the same social class. Which was exactly why Cirella avoided it. Instead, she took to Broadway: the Bowery's wealthier counterpart.

Why, Cirella thought, should she endure the salty tedium of barroom brawls when she could find a male escort who would take her to fine eateries, museums, horse races, and the theater?

Broadway was a poor girl's dream. Cirella spent hours window shopping, picking fineries she would surely buy if she had more money: silk chemises, lace handkerchiefs, gilt buckles, ornate hats. One evening, as she eyed rich pastries in the window of an especially expensive restaurant, a man approached her. His eyes twinkled as he smiled, asking her if she would join him for a walk along the promenade. He introduced himself as Mr. Tristan Thompson. Cirella recognized the name at once. It dripped off his tongue with well-heeled aplomb.

"Of course," she agreed.

Mr. Tristan Thompson wasn't the first man who had stopped to speak with her that evening. But he was the most promising. And what man wouldn't stop, she thought smugly? Cirella was no longer the street urchin of her youth, clad in secondhand clothes of plain color and design. No, with the money from scavenging and her many male benefactors, Cirella now dressed in style. Tonight, she was the very picture of high fashion. A boneless corset accentuated her bosom and waist. A hobble skirt, the hemline slashed scandalously at mid-calf, hugged tightly around her hips.

Mr. Tristan Thompson smiled down at her. His breath smelled of peppermints. A prickly peach fuzz covered his jaw. She took his arm as they walked the promenade, casually observing other couples and the raucous crowds at the theaters. The scene was a colorful panoply. But Cirella was only too glad to leave it when Mr. Tristan Thompson suggested walking back to his residence. On the way there, she pointed out a brooch in a shop window. He promptly bought it for her.

After that night, Cirella and Mr. Tristan Thompson agreed to meet again. Quite soon, they met every few nights, sometimes in public, sometimes in seclusion. Mr. Thompson bought her two silk nightgowns and a nightcap for their private meetings. He also gave her money—lots of it. He swore he loved her and wanted to marry her.

"But I have a wife already," he admitted.

"Don't worry, darling," Cirella responded. "I'm in no rush. No rush at all."

Months later, her mother found one of the nightgowns stuffed inside Cirella's pillowcase. She demanded to know who had purchased it for her.

"Mr. Tristan Thompson," Cirella replied.

"Your behavior will land you in a brothel," Catherine declared. "I have half a mind to turn you in to the authorities before you ruin your good name."

"Tristan is my steady, mother."

"Is he going to marry you, that's what I want to know?"

"I hope not," Cirella revealed, and upon realizing her error, covered her mouth with both hands.

In the end, a policewoman, not her mother, brought Cirella to Juvenile Hall. The policewoman had noticed with great alarm a girl standing with an older man outside a dance hall. The girl ogled her companion and kissed him in a most unladylike manner. In fact, it was in these exact words that Cirella was later described in a police report. The officer also made mention of Cirella's temper, which was "fiery as her untamed hair, which is in certain need of combing."

Cirella's arrest was by no means unusual. In urban areas across the United States, legions of reform workers and police officers patrolled the streets between the hours of 3:30 and 11:30 p.m. They looked for "suspicious-looking girls," especially those "in danger of jeopardizing their morality and womanly propriety." Or so decried the literature they carried. Found in typical adolescent haunts such as movie theaters and amusement parks, these girls were apprehended, scolded, and brought back to their parents. If arrested more than once—or found engaging in particularly indecent behavior—they were placed in a juvenile detention centers.

This was in fact Cirella's fourth arrest. The officer, Mrs. Prue Van Waters, felt a combination of relief and vindictiveness when she finally towed away the misfit. Prue Van Waters didn't know if the work of the state was to protect female sexuality or to police it. But she did know that Cirella was a delinquent. Any girl who engaged in pre-marital intercourse was. Maybe the new economy was to blame. After all, it had created new and untested rules of female conduct. Girls were no longer bound to domesticity, but out in the workforce—and in public. They were wage-earners, not children. They were staying out late smoking cigarettes and drinking hard liquor. Most importantly, girls were breaking a centuries-old tradition. Instead of being passed from their parents to their husbands, they were enjoying something America's founding fathers had never intended for women. Freedom.

• • •

Before the judge, Cirella appeared unrepentant. She didn't think she was headed for moral ruin, she argued. And if she was, moral ruin wasn't as bad as it was presumed to be.

What did she think about her obscene language and bawdy behavior, the judge demanded? Had she considered the consequences of her rebellion upon her poor, abandoned mother and impressionable siblings? The court awaited an answer.

"I've never thought about it," Cirella admitted, arms akimbo.

And then there was the matter of her health tests. The juvenile detention center served as both a temporary home and a place for medical diagnoses. A physician and psychologist examined each of the detainees to determine bodily damage. Female inmates, whether they had been apprehended for thievery or truancy, had to undergo compulsory pelvic exams too.

Lying on a table, her legs spread, skirts and underclothes bunched around her waist, Cirella demanded to know why.

"I need to determine if you have any diseases," a male doctor informed her. "And there is the matter of your purity. Are you pure?"

"What does that matter?"

He probed her private parts with a cold metal instrument.

"The hymen is destroyed," he stated blandly, as if he were reporting on the weather. "Have you been practicing self-abuse?"

"Self-abuse?"

"Have you engaged in sexual intercourse with a man—or with yourself?"

"What does that matter?" Cirella repeated.

The doctor remained calm. Only his furrowed brow conveyed annoyance. He saw dozens of girls like Cirella every week.

"Have you ever been pregnant?"

"No."

The doctor's furrows deepened. "You understand that abortions are illegal, don't you?"

"Yes, doctor. But I think you've made a mistake."

"Oh no, there can be no mistake. I see the evidence plain as day."

In fact, Cirella had had an abortion over a year ago. Worried that she'd wind up in a predicament like her mother's, she'd asked a local woman to perform the procedure. The woman was neither a doctor nor a midwife. She was simply known in the neighborhood as someone who could get girls out of trouble.

The procedure had been bloody—more dangerous than Cirella realized. Sedated with a dark herbal brew, she remembered only the tools: long prongs and thick wire. She had lost consciousness midway through.

Just now, Cirella closed her legs and sat up. With mounting exasperation, she challenged the doctor: "You speak with indignation, but you have no right. *You* will never be saddled with children!"

The physician carefully recorded this correspondence. Later, he added his notes to Cirella's other court documents. Various probation officers questioned the girl's friends, neighbors, and family members in order to assess the cause of her delinquency. In terse words, Catherine Flannery described her daughter's troublesome lifestyle as well as her own inability to control it.

Why, one probation officer asked, hadn't she channeled the girl's misguided sexual energies into respectable domestic pursuits?

"Will you look at the color of her hair?" Catherine demanded.

Ultimately, the court determined that Cirella should be committed to a reformatory until the age of eighteen. Good behavior notwithstanding.

• CHAPTER FOUR •

It is well known that feeble-minded girls are likely to become the root of unspeakable debauchery and licentiousness. Their loose moral standards pollute the lives of other youths in the community. Moreover, these same girls disseminate in a wholesale way the most vile and dangerous of diseases, and in so doing, permanently poison promising boys on the threshold of manhood.

With arms crossed and legs uncrossed, Cirella was watching a film called the *End of the Line*. The opening title sequence declared production by the Social Hygiene Division of the United States' Committee on Protective Work for Girls. As the film played, Cirella recognized the script—it came straight from pamphlets that had been distributed to her by stern-faced volunteers and reformers. They had a knack for picking her out on the street, as Officer Prue Van Waters had.

Problem girls are likely to be found idle in conversation with boys on Main Street and various social venues. The most promiscuous girls may be found loitering until late hours, many times drinking alcohol and smoking cigarettes with young men. The public dance hall, in particular, is a source of unsurpassed evil. Its air of license, its dark corners and balconies, its tough dancing, and its heavy drinking are infamous for weakening the moral inhibitions of susceptible females.

Cirella suppressed a yawn. It was mandatory to watch sex delinquency films at the New York Industrial School for Girls. They were mostly the same: government-endorsed propaganda meant to frighten girls into chaste behavior. Cirella and her fellow inmates liked to joke about the reform school's "movie nights." "Where's the popcorn," quipped one girl, Jill. "Who's gonna neck with Miss Great Fannie?" ribbed another, in reference to one of the reformatory's more ample-bottomed guards.

Cirella would have to watch many more such films if she stayed her full term at The Prison. Fortunately, she had already planned an escape. No chance she was going to waste her precious time letting zealots trick her into thinking she was a national threat.

How does this tragedy happen? Most often, girls become misguided as a result of maternal neglect. The Committee on Protective Work for Girls recommends close supervision and guidance of young girls during adolescence. This can be achieved only when mothers and educators give girls proper care, which calls for plain diets, plenty of sleep, little mental strain, regular exercise, and careful instruction in sexual hygiene. Girls must be taught about sex with an emphasis on motherhood rather than on the sex relation itself.

Jill threw a small paper wad at the back of Miss Great Fannie's head.

The good mother must be a thrifty and capable housewife, in possession of stable moral standards, and with time and energy to give to the needs of her children. Unfortunately, we have entered an era in which some mothers are working during the day, just when their girls are most in need of strict guidance and control. Without mothers to instruct their daughters on the primacy of marriage and motherhood, many girls are succumbing to moral downfall. And it isn't just neglect that is fueling this calamity. The structure of many households also poses a problem. Too many wayward girls are living in tenement buildings and overcrowded residencies. A cramped living situation encourages a lack of privacy and brings on the loss of self-respect, modesty, order, and neatness.

Jill threw another wad. This one landed in Great Fannie's lap. The matron swiveled her elephantine neck, but her gaze burned into the wrong offender.

"I didn't do it. Honest!" spoke the accused.

Having sex outside of marriage leads to more than sexual delinquency. It is also associated with disease. Take for example, Cora, a sixteen-year-old who chose to engage in sexual behavior with a beau. Cora's immoral decision has subjected her to gonorrhea and syphilis. It has also contributed to the propagation of defective and unfit offspring.

The correctional facility was supposedly a place of rehabilitation, but the nickname—The Prison—was apropos. The girls were forced to perform heavy domestic labor throughout the day. If they were lazy about their work or resisted orders, they could expect any number of punishments: a restricted diet of bread and water, solitary confinement, strap whippings, even hosings with cold water.

Cirella had heard of other centers where girls were trained in clerical work, sales, and manufacturing. One of the inmates spoke of a reform school that had student body meetings and outings to plays and concerts. Cirella didn't know where this fairy tale school was, but it certainly wasn't anywhere near the New York Industrial School for Girls. Here, the only memorable communication between inmates and guards involved a belt and a bare bottom. Lights went out at 9 p.m. Morning exercises in the dusty yard started at 6:30 sharp. More than once, Cirella had picked a roach out of her stew.

She couldn't stay—that was for sure. But leaving wouldn't be easy. She would need to break out of The Prison the same way she'd entered it: through a man. Cirella could think of only one prospect.

The reformatory had a laundering deal with several New York City hotels—it was hard work for the inmates, but good money for The Prison's administrators. Twice a week, on Wednesday and Saturday afternoons, a wagon pulled up to the Center to drop off soiled sheets and towels and to pick up freshly cleaned loads. The driver of the wagon was a man named

Fritz. Men were forbidden on the premises, but Fritz was allowed to drive past the gate to do the loading and unloading. He performed this work in a cargo area located beside the institute's kitchen. As he lifted and lugged sacks of linens, the girls on kitchen duty watched from a small, screened window. Through a rare loophole in supervision, this window was the only barrier separating the deliveryman from the detainees.

Fritz wasn't handsome. He had missing teeth and a cauliflower ear, perhaps from a childhood accident. But his hairy chest all but burst forth from his unbuttoned shirts, which featured the name "Fritz" embroidered across the front and "Hanson's Delivery Service" on the back. His arms were ropey with muscle. Most importantly, he was the only sign of testosterone for miles—except for pictures of moony-eyed film stars that some girls kept hidden under their mattresses.

It didn't take long for Fritz to become a star attraction. Just the sight of his big black boots and wide stride generated female frenzy. From the window, the inmates waved, whistled, and cooed. One girl went so far as to stand on the windowsill and pull the hem of her skirt over her head. Shy and reserved, Fritz seemed embarrassed by the attention.

The kitchen of the New York Industrial School for Girls was huge, with side rooms for storage and refrigeration. Its only manager, Miss Plunkett, was the eldest member of The Prison's staff. She had grown absentminded with age, more grandmotherly than guard-like. Consequently, she never noticed that the girls became hot-faced and combustible two afternoons each week. She never noticed that Cirella played a game of Rapunzel, standing by the window and letting the wind blow through her hair whenever Fritz was in sight.

Of course, it wasn't Fritz Cirella was after; it was his wagon, which had a covered back and ample space to hide.

Cirella knew that to get Fritz, she would have to make the other girls back off. She couldn't bribe them: she didn't have anything they would want. She couldn't tell the girls she was in love—that kind of sentiment didn't hold water around here. She couldn't even agree to do their share of the work: the shifts were well monitored by guards like Miss Great Fannie.

In the end, she decided to tell the truth to the fifteen inmates who shared dishwashing duty every afternoon.

"I'm gonna make Fritz fall in love with me so that I can crack out of here. Any of you rat and I'll stuff your mouth with slut's wool," she announced, as the girls scrubbed pots and Miss Plunkett snoozed on a chair in the corner.

For girls who were accustomed to adventure, life in The Prison was one long exercise in boredom. Cirella was giving them a chance at amusement. The last thing they wanted to do was turn her in.

"How can we help?" asked Jill.

"Just stay out of my way," Cirella instructed.

The following Wednesday, for the first time ever, the girls steered clear of the window when Fritz came to exchange the linens. He looked around, bewildered by the silence. Where were the girlish squeals? But in the window he didn't see the usual hoard of oversexed adolescents. He saw only one face: sweet and pink-cheeked. A face framed by the reddest hair he had ever laid eyes on.

The girl beckoned him to the window, but of course he couldn't go. They were trouble, these inmates. Perhaps not dangerous, but trouble all the same. He'd noted their cheap talk and fluttering eyelashes. He could only imagine what went on underneath their uniforms, which hung like sacks over their limber young bodies. He wondered what the girls said about him. Were they speaking in earnest when they cooed his name from that window, or were they making fun? He longed to know, for these San Quentin quails stayed in his mind long after he pulled off the lot.

The redhead's face was lovely, so pale and smooth-skinned. His own wife had a mole on the tip of her nose that seemed to grow each year. Fritz shuddered. He began the task of uncovering the tarp on the back of his wagon. The mountain of linens loomed.

"Pssssst," came a whisper from the window. "Fritz. Psssst."

Fritz wheeled around, a sack of sheets slung over his shoulder. The redhead was waving to him. He shook his head. What would his wife say if she knew he was being beckoned by this creature? Keeping his head down, he hauled the sacks out of the wagon as quickly as he could. But the redhead's gaze bore into him. His anxiety reached a level of fever.

"Leave me alone!" he hissed.

The girl giggled. Such a face, my lord, such a face. Lips berry-dark, bruised, like they'd been kissed too many times. Barrels of freckles and just the right age: a woman-child.

"Scared of a girl?" she called out. But Fritz had already slinked back to the wagon.

Between Wednesday and Saturday, Fritz spent considerable time thinking about the redhead. He worked six days a week, twelve hours a day, and had dozens of clients throughout the city. Still, every other destination was beginning to seem like a stopover on the way to that screened window. In the pocket of his overcoat, Fritz kept a picture of his wife. He pulled it out. The mole on her nose had indeed grown. Could photographs change, reflecting the years? No, of course not. Fritz shook his head and stuck his wife back into his pocket.

"Giddy . . .up," he instructed his two brown mares.

When Saturday arrived and he again approached the New York Industrial School for Girls, he felt like he was drawing closer to calamity. She was there exactly as he'd imagined she would be. He wondered what it would be like if they were alone together. A girl like that wouldn't be a cherry, oh no. She'd probably had her first man at age twelve. All that experience—she'd be a real charity girl.

The distance had made his fantasizing seem safe. But now, parked beside the kitchen, Fritz didn't feel so well. He thought he could smell her hair in the breeze. Cinnamon and nutmeg. Why was it that women seemed more accessible when they were far away?

The screen between them felt like the curtain of a confessional, Fritz the sinner rather than the pardoner.

"Fritz, that's your name, isn't it?" the girl called out. Fretfully, he looked around. Where were the guards? His teeth rattled. He shrugged "yes."

"I'm been watching you work, Fritz. You're an awfully strong man. Just the kind of man a girl needs." She paused. "Don't you want to come closer to the window, Fritz?"

He shook his head dumbly.

Cirella giggled. "Oh, it's all right. I won't bite."

He looked around again. The coast seemed clear, but his head certainly wasn't.

"That wasn't so bad now, was it?" she asked, once he had approached. "I'm Cirella."

"Pretty name," Fritz managed to blurt.

"Nice of you to say." Their eyes locked. "I'm lonely in here," she whispered, several seconds later, her lips close to the screen.

"You are?"

"I need you to help me."

Fritz battled against a swell of doubts rising in his chest. She signaled for him to lean closer. He pressed his face to the screen until he could feel her breath. Just like he'd imagined, she smelled of spices.

"Please help me get out of here," she said, a tear slinking down her cheek. "I can't take it much longer. The things they do to me—you can't imagine!"

Fritz's eyes widened in horror.

Cirella peeled back her sleeve, revealing an angry-looking welt across her forearm.

"I got this because I forgot to make my bed," she whispered.

He couldn't believe his eyes. Cirella was only a girl, a stone's throw away from childhood. How could she be treated so cruelly? And in America—the most dignified place in the world? It was an outrage.

"I'll help you," he told her.

"You will?"

"Yes."

"Today—oh Fritz, can I leave here today?"

"Cirella," he said, savoring the sound of her name. "It won't be today. I'm not ready. I have no plan."

Sulkily, she looked at her burn. "If not today, then when? Each day in this place is an *eternity*."

The little world he and Cirella had created around themselves was beginning to unravel. If he didn't get out of here soon, someone would surely see. And then there would be no more correspondence, never mind an escape.

"On Wednesday I will have a plan," he promised her. "Wait for me here."

"How do I know you'll come through?"

Fritz fished around in his pocket. Next to the picture of his wife, he had tucked away a small package. He had bought it on Wednesday, immediately after his first encounter with Cirella. Now he pulled it out and slid it through a small tear in the upper corner of the screen.

"What is it?" she asked, her mood brightening.

"A gift," he said. "Something to make you remember that I keep my promises."

The gift was a silk scarf—a luxury item at The Prison, where such trappings were strictly prohibited. Cirella tied it around her waist, out of sight. She loved the softness of the fabric against her skin. But more importantly, she loved that Fritz was already, in no small way, attached to her. She had seen in his eyes what had taken Mr. Tristan Thompson's months to develop: a cross between prurience and passion, something wholly unsinkable.

"I've got him," Cirella told Jill after Fritz had departed. "He didn't even put up a fight." The other girls began to rally around, eager to hear Cirella's news.

Jill smirked. "What did he think of the burn?"

"Oh, you! It worked fine, but you didn't have to make it so big. It hurts like the dickens!"

Cirella turned a worried head toward Miss Plunkett, but she was still fast asleep, her snores audible over the clanking of metal utensils, the splashing of water, and the girls' chatter.

• • •

In the days that followed, Fritz thought about Cirella's plight and of nothing else. He was committed to rescuing his ladylove—and reaping the carnal rewards that would follow. But the process would be dangerous.

And if they got caught, he would be thrown behind bars for the first time, she for the second.

After revising his plan several times, Fritz decided the most basic escape route would be the most effective. He would arrive at the detention center on Wednesday, as usual, to do his job. Then, just before leaving, he would cut the screen away with a pocketknife, and hoist Cirella down from the window. From there, they would make a dash for his wagon. He would tuck her in the back, beneath piles of linens. Then would come the hard part: exiting the scene. He didn't know if they should rush out, thereby alarming the security guards, or leave without haste. If they were lucky, nobody would notice that Cirella was missing until hours after the escape. Then again, if someone witnessed her climb out the window, he wouldn't have time on his side. It would be a race between how quickly his mares could gallop and how promptly the correctional facility could shut its gates.

The following Wednesday, early in the morning, Fritz spent a quiet moment in church. He crept in, dipped his index finger in holy water, and made the sign of the cross: touching the forehead, heart, left side, and right. Then he pressed his hands together so that his fingers pointed toward the heavens, like a steeple.

Fritz knelt on a pew in the back of the half-empty church and prayed. He prayed to the Lord to help him save Cirella from the evil forces that had burned her arm. He prayed for a quick escape—one free of mishaps. He prayed for his wife to forgive him for leaving her. He prayed for that mole to stop growing. He prayed for the feelings between himself and Cirella to stay true. He prayed for his future, which had never been in peril until now.

A few hours later, Fritz pulled onto the grounds of the New York Industrial School for Girls. He didn't even look at the window until after he had finished hauling the linens. When he did dare a peek, he noticed that Cirella had already cut through the window screen. Perhaps he had overestimated her helplessness.

"Fritz," she called to him in an anxious whisper.

"Darling," he answered. "Climb up to the sill. I'll help you down."

Cirella nodded and hoisted herself up with the help of Jill, who pushed her from behind. To the girls' dismay, Miss Plunkett was awake. However, she had wandered presently into the storage room, out of sight.

"We'll have to hurry," Cirella murmured, as he grabbed her by the waist. "They'll find out any second."

Fritz took her hand and pulled her to the wagon. Inside the kitchen, the girls were cheering loudly.

"I wish they'd shut up. Don't they have any sense?" he asked her.

"Why do you think they're here?" she responded.

After tucking her into the back of the wagon, he pulled the linens over her body, until only her head bobbed among the colorful sacks. Then he pulled the tarp over the back, settled into the front, and snapped the reins. He drove off the grounds in a roar of flying hooves and unsettled dust. So much for a subtle getaway.

So far, so good, Fritz thought, as the horses galloped down the street. The guards had even tipped their hats on his way out. The plan was almost complete. If he kept his wits about him, they might even make it. Pushing the horses to the brink of capacity, Fritz drove until he reached the heart of the city, smack into the hustle and bustle. He stopped abruptly on Adams Street, a small, mostly deserted dead-end.

Fritz climbed out of the wagon, tears welling in his eyes. But he wasn't crying because Cirella was free. These were tears of sadness, the kind that spring during difficult farewells. Fritz removed the blinders from his mares. He patted their heads and stroked their soft, damp muzzles. They nuzzled his hand affectionately.

"I have to let you go," he told them. "Hiding two is bad enough. Four's impossible."

He couldn't keep his wagon or the horses—not when the authorities were probably already trolling the streets. Nor would he and Cirella flee the city. That's exactly what the police would expect them to do.

Fritz uncovered the back of the wagon and pulled Cirella out from under the sacks. He told her about his plan to stay. There were advantages to New York. The city was chockablock and disorderly. No one paid attention to other people's business. As long as they kept low, their chances of apprehension would be minimal.

Fritz helped the fugitive pile her hair under the scarf. He told her to keep her head down, not to speak to anyone or make eye contact. She nodded and took his hand. He noticed that her fingers were chapped and peeling—from work or from one of the institution's primitive punishments? He shuddered in disgust. Thank God he had saved her from that hellhole.

"Where are we going?" she whispered.

"Where we can rest."

They checked into a cheap inn under an assumed name.

An hour later, the floor of Fritz and Cirella's room was littered with sheets, blankets, pillows, and clothes. They had made love quickly, turbulently, with little finesse. The girl now slept, bare-breasted, a sheet wrapped around waist. Fritz watched her chest rise and fall with methodical grace. She appeared to be rolling in and out of a dream, her interludes of consciousness clouded with drowsiness.

Fritz's skin was still moist with sweat: the heat of their encounter had raised the temperature of the room. His mind remained thick, but he was contented. Turning, Cirella rested her head on his thigh. She draped a pale, graceful arm over the side of the bed.

Since their escape, Fritz had been waiting for words of commitment to escape her lips, but she hadn't said a thing.

"Her affection will come," he told himself.

Suddenly, Cirella tilted her head. Her hair shifted, each lock vivid as a peacock's plume. Her eyes rolled open slowly, a drowsy seduction.

"You know what I crave?" she purred.

"No," he replied, hopeful.

"Chocolates! I haven't had them in years. We could never afford them because we were so poor. My love, do you think you could be brave and buy me a box?"

"Now?" he stammered.

"*Right* now."

He twisted one of her curls between his fingers, realizing she was impossible to refuse.

"Very well," he agreed.

Fritz slipped out of bed and dressed. He donned his hat, a wide-brimmed number that cast a shadow over his face. He felt like a mobster. But now that they were on the run, he would have to get used to the style.

At the nearest store, Fritz fiddled in his pocket for his wallet. He checked his back pockets too, but realized he had left his money in the room. The wallet had probably fallen out of his pants when Cirella had yanked them off—with a practiced hand, he had noted.

"Can I give you an IOU?" he asked the shopkeeper. The clerk shook his head.

Not one to protest, Fritz hurried back to the inn. He would find his wallet, apologize to Cirella for the delay, and make another trip. He felt no sense of impending calamity until he returned to the room and found the door ajar. A sense of emptiness struck him with a wallop. Had she gone to look for him? That would have been dumb—they had only one key. Had the police somehow discovered their location? Already? He was sure he hadn't dropped a clue.

"Are you there?" he called softly.

When no one answered, he pushed open the door. Tiptoeing into the room, he called her name. "I must have forgotten my wallet," he told the empty air. Cirella was nowhere to be seen. Nor were her clothes, which had been scattered about like bright-colored gift wrappings only minutes earlier. He searched half-heartedly for his money, but with a defeated spirit, realized he would never find it.

No gratitude. Not even a note. Fritz sat on the bed for several minutes, wondering if the situation were as dire as it seemed. And indeed, he realized it was.

• • •

Once on the street, Cirella ran. Aside from bamboozling men, running was her second best talent. Her knees kicked high, her feet flew off the cobblestones. She loved the way the wind cooled her fire-spiked hair. She ran a considerable distance, until her hamstrings throbbed and her knees tingled. When she finally stopped to look around, she realized she was in a section of the city she didn't know.

"Gee whiz," Cirella sighed, whistling between her teeth, but she was unafraid. She tied the scarf around her throat. The vibrant fabric rippled in the breeze and she laughed as she thought of Fritz, and his deformed ear, and his naïve belief that she loved him.

"A more foolish man I've never met," she said aloud.

Although she didn't know where she was or where she intended to go, Cirella knew that she had no intention of sleeping on the streets—nor in any sort of discomfort. Months on The Prison's stone-hard, sweat- and urine-stained mattresses had been punishment enough. She had money—the thick wad she had swiped from Fritz. And she could hustle up more if need be. Curious, she fished around the wallet and found the odds and ends of Fritz's life, among them, a picture of an ugly woman with a rather bulbous beauty mark on her nose.

She wondered if she were Fritz's girl—or his wife. "Whatta match they make," she giggled.

Fritz's warnings about staying out of sight vanished from her mind. Cirella had already moved on, happy to be free and on her own again. There was a skip in her step as she traipsed about. There were better things to think about than being an outlaw. Her clothing, for one. Fritz, who had said she couldn't be seen in the stiff uniform of the correctional facility, had bought her a cheap, decidedly unbecoming frock. Although Cirella was hungry, and weary to boot, right then she desired most a more stylish wardrobe.

She studied the clothing of the girls who passed. Females in this part of town seemed different—and Cirella knew why. She knew how they afforded their provocative attire. She knew what they sold. Yet they had none of the broke-down desperation of the typical neighborhood floozy, the girl who'd gone astray and never found her way home. Cirella could see this as they stared at her, almost confrontationally, with none of the false modesty Mrs. Flannery had tried so hard to instill in her daughters.

"Poor Mama," Cirella laughed, thinking of Mrs. Flannery's love of obedience. Her laugh was sharp-edged, however, for memories of her mother now conjured as much resentment as they did fondness. If not for Mrs. Flannery's insistence on her daughter's delinquency, Cirella could have avoided incarceration. Try as she might, Cirella did not understand why her mother had betrayed her. She might not have been a well-behaved daughter, but she had never been disloyal—not like her father.

"Forget Mother," Cirella told herself. "I don't need to draw a bead on her any longer."

Cirella continued to wander until something made her halt—a girl wearing the most wonderful dress. The frock seemed spun of gold, of sunlight. Although the color was befitting of a queen, the style was entirely modern: shoulders drooping recklessly off the shoulders, everywhere ruffles and ribbons. Cirella was in love.

"Wherever did you buy it?" she asked the wearer, whose little face peeped above an expensive choker.

"That's no business of yours," the girl chided.

Cirella, who was used to tough talk, took the comment in stride. "It's only that I admire it."

The girl sniffed, then turned up her nose in annoyance.

"Was it very expensive?" Cirella prodded.

"It doesn't matter. I've got money to pay for nice things."

"From your papa?"

"No!" the girl scolded. "I earn my own wages." She had a child's mouth filled with small milk teeth. Cirella realized that the girl, despite her rouge and painted lips, was only Mattie's age.

"I haven't got time to dally with a dock rat. You better be on your way," she told Cirella.

"But I haven't a place to go."

The girl's eyes filled with sympathy, but only halfway. Around these parts everybody had a sad story to tell.

"Where are your parents?" she asked Cirella.

"Don't got any."

"Where are you going to sleep tonight?"

"Don't know."

"Where did you sleep last night?"

"In the doorway of a bakery," Cirella said, playing her fib with a stiff upper lip. "But the shopkeeper chased me out with a stick at dawn."

The girl looked around anxiously. Her little teeth clacked together. She reached into her purse and pulled out a quarter. "Here, take this. Buy yourself something to eat."

Cirella took the offering, but money wasn't what she wanted.

"Now be on your way," the girl declared. "I'm meeting someone."

Cirella shivered, her eyes coated with mock tears. She began to walk away, then returned. Her instincts told her the girl had more to offer.

"Say, could I stay with you for a spell? I can't afford a flophouse, even with this." She extended her palm, the silver circle an offering of friendship. "You can have it back—if you want."

Just then, the girl noticed the unsightly burn on Cirella's arm. She had a few of her own, now mostly scars, from the days when her father had come home angry. She never knew why—maybe because all his days were the same, always hard and always long. She didn't quite trust this strange girl, who had the face of a starlet, and perhaps, the dramatic flair of one too. She worried that she was a cold-decker. Then again, there were hundreds of girls in legitimate trouble—girls whose bodies were burned by men, girls whose parents had deserted them, girls who spent vulnerable nights on doorsteps.

She took Cirella's hand, but left the coin. "Come with me. You can spend one night where I work." She tilted her head boldly. The redhead noticed again the soft traces of childhood on the girl's face. Those traces would be gone in a year, Cirella knew.

"Where is that?" Cirella asked.

"Don't ask questions you well know the answers to," the girl replied. "In fact, it's better if you don't ask questions at all."

• CHAPTER FIVE •

1922

Lor was southbound, traveling away from Connecticut's dairy pastures, tobacco fields, firearms and ammunition factories, and of course, its oyster-laden shores. He didn't have a map, so he followed the New Haven Railroad, whose main line operated all the way from Boston to New York City. Occasionally, he veered off course. On the roads, he tried to hitch rides. But he'd caught only one. Travelers were reluctant to pick up a colored man.

Three days had passed since his departure from New Haven. The soles of his shoes had worn through at the toes and heels. The undersides of his feet felt tough as pounded leather. He hadn't slept regularly, never more than two hours at a clip. He'd tried to steal winks in the train stations along the way, but someone inevitably chased him out. Nevertheless, when he first caught sight of the urban sprawl of New York City, all the bother seemed worthwhile.

For a boy who had never been out of New Haven, New York was The Land of Canaan: a whirlwind of activity, irresistible and infinite. Here was every kind of person, every shade of skin, so many languages—Lor couldn't tell one from the next. The density of the population astounded him. He couldn't walk down the street without dodging and darting around the swarms. At first, he felt discombobulated. He excused himself when he brushed into others, like Augusta had taught him. But he soon realized that New York was for the steely, not the apologetic.

To fit in, Lor became like the others. He walked purposefully, with eyes fixed forward or sometimes up toward the sky. He couldn't believe the height of the buildings. Some of the office and commerce facilities surpassed forty stories. He stole into one of the tallest, the Woolworth Building, and rode in a contraption called an elevator. What a marvelous device! A little room that could carry people up and down with the pull of a lever.

Lor rode the subways too. Unlike New Haven, with its limited trolleys, New York had its own internal train system. It could carry people anywhere, from the Battery, to Harlem, to Third Avenue in the Bronx. The trains also extended into Brooklyn, with elevated lines on Myrtle Avenue, Adams, Fulton, and York Streets. Lor rode up and down the city, three or four times in a row, gazing out his window. He had never seen so many signs: *New and Used Bookstore. Piping Hot Coffee. Get Your Cold Soda Here! Ice Cream Sodas/New Flavors Daily. Our Bread Is Always Baked Fresh! Beauty Salon. Ladies, We Give Manicures! Best Shoe Shine Here. On Sale: Cigarettes. Fresh Grilled Sandwiches: Buy One Get One Free.*

When he tired of riding the railcars, Lor set out on foot again, determined to walk the length of the city from Broadway, starting at Bowling Green, through the retail shopping district at 10th Street above 23rd, back to Seventh Avenue to Central Park. Lor explored every region, but it was Harlem that he liked best.

Here was something Lor had never seen before, something he later heard called the "black Bourgeoisie." Colored men and women dressed like whites, in the latest fashions, purchased brand new. Here were poor blacks, just like in New Haven: janitors, factory hands, and domestics. But Lor noticed something else: a middle class. These blacks lived in respectable brownstones and held respectable jobs as bookkeepers, accountants, draymen, hackmen, teamsters, dressmakers, nurses, and midwives. Lor had never seen anything like it—colored people who spoke as if they'd gone to school their whole lives, whose manners were as impeccable as the crisp white shirts the men wore under their suits.

And there was more. Lor wouldn't have believed it if he hadn't seen it with his own eyes: the upper echelon of colored society. He wished he could tell Augusta about it. Colored people who were doctors, lawyers, ministers, businessmen, and professors. Colored people who had their own clubs and restaurants and music and theatres and dance halls. Pride permeated the place. It was apparent in the sway of the ladies' hips, in the excited voices of the young men on the streets, in the gloss of the hairstyles and the snap of the clothing.

Black Harlem, Lor knew, was on the verge of something great. He wanted to stay for as long as he could, but then he got sidetracked.

Lor wore his savings, all the money he had, in a rawhide pouch around his neck. Augusta had left him a nice sum. He didn't want to spend it all at once, so he dipped into it sparingly. He ate inexpensive foods: brown bread, local vegetables, beans, hard tack. But he began to feel weary and his stomach yearned for home-cooked meals. He knocked on tenement buildings with "Rooms to Let" signs. He checked into cheap lodgings. Although he knew he would later regret it, he went to restaurants and feasted on beef stew, broiled fish, and boiled potatoes. He bathed almost daily, even though clean, heated water was expensive.

The weight around Lor's neck lightened. He was in no mood to pay for further luxuries. But in this vast city he could hardly avoid the prostitutes.

They were everywhere: strolling the boulevards, beckoning from windows, plying their wares on street corners. The streetwalkers were the most obvious: eyes roaming, breasts like the rolling tide. The wenches were slightly more discreet. They inhabited what were called "cribs," long series of narrow rooms, each with a door and window opening directly onto a street or alley. Finally, there were the bawdy house girls: the high-end product of a low-end market. Most bawdy houses had been built specifically for the sex trade. Madams monitored their girls' progress through countless peepholes. Every room had a front door and backdoor for controlled access. Massive pocket doors connected individual rooms. These could be slid into and out of recesses in the doorway walls. When these doors were open, the rooms were large enough for parlor parties.

Closed, the doors created the private rooms necessary for business. In the bawdy house, every room had a window facing the street. By these windows the prostitutes sat, observing the world beyond, occasionally tapping a hatpin against the pane to attract attention.

How there had come to be so many hookers in New York City, Lor didn't know. He suspected most were immigrants. Despite a wave of anti-immigrant hysteria, the great war had brought hoards of foreigners to the American shore: Croats, Serbs, Poles, Russian Jews. Even now, steamships sailed into the harbor daily, dumped their anchors into the silt, and unloaded passengers. The red brick buildings of Ellis Island, on the New Jersey side of the Hudson, saw thousands of people a day—including many young girls. Lor didn't think it was a coincidence that New York's parlor houses were also made of red brick.

Although he resisted, Lor could hold off no longer. He set his sights on a particularly pretty girl. He didn't know if she were an immigrant. All he did know was that his resilience had crumbled.

This wanton, pale and tender, sat by the second floor window of a popular West Side bordello. She had a beautiful face. More importantly, she had a taunting bosom. Lor knocked on the door. A few seconds later, he was ushered in.

Inside, they were draped everywhere. Breasts: large and ripe, snooty and vexing. Some were clothed. Others peeked at him mercilessly. Lust—tense and sandy—ground hard.

A few of the girls winked at him. Two walked over and introduced themselves as Isabella and Jasmine. Stage names, Lor wondered? He smiled nervously, not having the slightest idea how one ought to behave in such a place. Just as his nerves began to fray completely, a third woman approached. She was older and malodorously perfumed in a licorice scent. Her bottom protruded like a jetty. The beauty mark she had drawn on her cheek had smeared. Lor hoped she wouldn't proposition him.

"How may The House of Delight assist you?" she asked.

"I noticed a girl on the second floor. A redhead," he explained, his voice low. He realized, with no small relief, that he was speaking to the madam.

The woman nodded, then noticed Lor's tattered shoes.

"We're glad to have your patronage, sir, but we're an upscale house—and sometimes, beyond the means of certain people."

Lor wasn't troubled. He suspected that a brothel was one of the few places where all men stood on equal ground—provided they had enough money. He shook the pouch around his neck tellingly.

"Pardon me, sir! It's my duty to give everyone fair warning. I hope you understand."

"Of course."

The madam's gaze lifted. She studied his face, eyes aglow with approval. "I'll see if the girl you request, Cirella, is available. She's one of our busier girls. You'll see why, I'm sure."

With fleshy arms outstretched she ushered him to an overstuffed chair. "Please sit," she insisted before bustling away.

Waiting would be pure pleasure, Lor thought to himself. He watched the women flitter by, a waltz of curves and crevices, easy favors and luminous possibilities. He saw heaps of hair drawn up with tortoiseshell combs, tresses long down smooth backs.

Minutes passed, but Lor scarcely noticed. He came to attention only when Cirella arrived. Licks of fire curled about her face, the burnish of flame alighted her cheeks. He rose to greet her, but felt compelled to sit again. Something pressed him down. Perhaps it was Cirella's balmy presence. Or maybe it was his mother's warnings, still raging from the grave.

White women: whores by trade and by nature! Their waists might be cinched and their bosoms ripe. But their skirts cover the truth. Crusty, rusty female parts. Bright pink flowers blooming with the stench of desire!

"What is it?" Cirella asked him. He rose again, determined to stave off this guilty wave. She slipped her hand in his and the warmth of her skin soothed him.

"Nothing. Just nervous."

"Never been in a place like this before?"

"Yes—of course. Well, truthfully—no."

Cirella giggled. "Either way, we'll see to those nerves."

She led him upstairs to a strange red room. The red walls had tiny ridges like the texture of a washboard. Plush red furniture lounged along the walls. Even the rug was red. If he lifted a corner, Lor wondered, would the floorboards pulse crimson too?

A massive bed presided from the center. With its oak trimmings and giant pillows, it was certainly inviting. But Lor found it vulgar too. The sheer fabric over the canopy reminded him of cast-aside silk stockings. The sheets crackled with the heat of too many bodies. Cirella took her hand from his and sat at the corner of the mattress.

"What's your name?" she asked.

"Lor. And yours?"

He considered sitting beside her. He imagined sliding his fingers over the delicate slope of her back. But he could scarcely manage words, never mind actions.

"Cirella." She patted the space next to her, but he looked away sheepishly. "You look like someone who's traveled a long way," she told him.

"You're looking at my shoes, aren't you? Your madam was concerned about them too."

"Oh, I'm not surprised. She wants to keep this place respectable—an impossible feat!"

"Have you been here long?"

"No, not very. I was in a private school. But we didn't get along, the school and me. There were too many rules and instructors—and I had to wear a uniform. So I left. I like being on my own."

"Me too," Lor agreed. "Are you from New York?"

"Born and bred. New York's a rough place, but I'm good at watching out for myself."

"I bet you are," he replied, finding the courage to look her in the eye.

"What about you, Lor? How do you make your living?"

He shrugged uncomfortably. "I don't make a decent wage. I'm after something else."

"Yes?"

"I'll sound funny saying—it's just a dream."

"Ain't nothing wrong with dreaming."

"Fame," Lor said finally. "I want fame." He hesitated, surprised by his own candor. "Do you find it strange—that someone like me would say such a thing?"

Again, Cirella motioned for Lor to sit. This time he heeded her.

"I've heard stranger secrets from my clients," she responded. "But in the end, they all want the same thing."

"What's that?"

"To be adored."

Facing him, she removed his hat, then unbuttoned his vest and shirt, her hands resting lightly on his chest. Finally, she released the pouch from around his neck and tossed it aside. It lay vulnerable on the bed, fixed in Lor's gaze but beyond his reach.

"And what do *you* want?" he returned.

Cirella was surprised. Men were usually interested in her only in so far as she could please them. Although Lor didn't notice, she immediately softened. The first seed of longing, of bittersweet ache, took hold in the loam of her heart. Its presence made her uneasy, for she was used to space, wide-open and empty.

"I want what you want," she admitted, glassy-eyed. "Do you find it strange that someone like *me* would say such a thing?"

"Not at all."

"A man came up to me on the street a few days ago," she continued. "Said he would pay me if he could take my photograph for a magazine. Said I have 'a glow.' Maybe it was just flattery. I didn't trust him. I walked away. Now I wonder when my next chance will come."

"Soon, I trust."

Cirella smiled gratefully. She began to unhook the bodice of her dress. Casually, she exposed one of her breasts. Lor noticed that the nipple and areola were patently red. Had she painted those too? To him, her beauty was defined by extremes: the marble-white of her skin and the blaze of her hair, her frankness and her unknowable history. Watching her undress, he became nervous again. Before he knew it, his head swam with doubts. But these were not of Augusta's doing. They were entirely his own. He wondered why he was here, no closer to fame than he'd been in New Haven. He wondered why he was wasting his time seeking momentary pleasure when there was so much work to be done.

"What did you have in mind?" Cirella asked, her intention clear.

Rather than reply, Lor stood up. Hastily, he gathered his belongings from the bed.

"Where are you going?"

But Lor didn't have the faintest idea. Anywhere that would bring his hopes in line with reality.

"Please stay," she insisted. "We can talk if you want. I could understand you—if you let me. We're alike, after all."

For a moment, he hesitated. His hands trembled, so eager they were to explore the richness of that hair, the heavenly contours of her body. But his mind was made. Without explanation, he dashed out the door, navigated his way through the maze of corridors, then downstairs, where he darted around the madam.

"Did you pay, sir? I said, 'did you pay!'" he heard her shout.

Later, when he was far from The House of Delight, he wished he had thought harder about that question—about money and where he kept his own. Lor had walked a full hour around the city before realizing his error. He opened his pouch. He thought he might treat himself to a decent night's sleep. But what awaited him was a handful of marbles.

• CHAPTER SIX •

Penniless, Lor had grown filthy as an ash pan, his handsome face buried under soot. If Augusta could see him now! She'd take a bar of her homemade soap of lye and cooking fat and scrub him down good, then make him eat the rest as penance.

His workpants, vest, and socks were coated in crud. The buckle on his belt, once a silver-white gleam, had rusted over. The few slack-threaded buttons that remained on his shirt now hung precariously.

He hadn't started his trip with a fortune. But the small bag of money had seemed like a fortune to him. Now that it was gone, Lor had fallen into a gloom he couldn't shake. It was unlike anything he had experienced before. A vague but drenching black. It wasn't the feeling that he had gone astray. It was the conviction that he was going nowhere.

Life had seemed easier when he'd first started off. Then he'd been looking for only one thing: to discover his potential. In New Haven, he'd already been categorized. He was Augusta's son, Woodrow's brother, Opal's companion. Never had he been his own person, allowed to test his limits.

But now that he was on his own, he realized he wasn't as strong as he'd thought. Perhaps he had overestimated his ability to adapt. Perhaps his gifts—grace, dexterity, and stamina—weren't as formidable as he'd hoped.

His gait, too, had deteriorated. He no longer strutted, but moved with haggard, cautious steps. He kept his head down. His eyes shied away from the curious glances of passersby. Women no longer stared at him with coveting eyes. In fact, if they noticed him at all, it was with fear or pity.

It was time for a change, thought Lor. He decided to return to New Haven to restore his self-esteem, to eat a few good meals, to rest in a clean bed rather than on hard hearth. Of course, home wouldn't be the same without Augusta—and he'd have Opal and the baby to contend with. But there were other things to look forward to. Stability, for one. Maybe Lor could spend a few months working with his brother. He needed to earn back the money he'd lost. And he sure as hell needed a new pair of shoes.

Despite this anticipated respite, Lor didn't feel relieved. After all, he had departed with so much: a head held high, a sack full of money, aspirations untarnished. Now he was crawling back on hands and knees. He feared his already cracked composure would shatter entirely when folks began to talk.

I told you he'd never last. Augusta's youngest was always so fickle.

Look what's become of Mr. High and Mighty. He carries the stick now, don't he!

Days after he departed New York, an exhausted Lor finally arrived in his hometown—in the New Haven train yard, to be exact. Just as his energy started to fail him completely, the sky succumbed to a plumb-colored dusk. There was no one around, not the superintendent, yardmaster, section hands, or number dummies. A sudden rumbling in Lor's belly reminded him it was suppertime. Everyone must be home dining with their families.

In front of him lay a complicated system of tracks. All of it was low iron. Starting with the throat, the tracks spread out in diverse directions, like branches from a tree trunk. Each offshoot boasted a different purpose: repair work, storage of cars and freight, the assembling and dissembling of trains. Lor was familiar with the train yard because he had spent time here as a youth. On weekends, he and Opal had walked along the rails to practice balancing. The possibility that a train might pull onto the restricted tracks—or that the yardmaster would spot them and start hollering—had only heightened their excitement.

Tonight, in the entire yard, only two trains were present. One was a Unit Train, a freight train consisting of hopper cars for carrying coal. The other was a most welcome sight: the Bringlebright Circus train. Lor slapped his hands together gleefully. He realized he had come home just in time to see the circus. Or was he too late? The wagons were already loaded on the flats. An eerie stillness permeated the air—not at all like the kinetic pomp that normally accompanied the circus into town. This wasn't a train newly arrived, Lor realized, but a train due to depart.

A pang of nostalgia wheedled its way through Lor's memories. As children, he and Opal had watched the Bringlebright circus roll into town every year. "Circus Day" was a local holiday equivalent to Washington's Birthday or even the Fourth of July. Amid the drudgery of daily life, it was a day of celebration punctuated by fantastical displays: the joeys with their funny wigs and red-and-white faces, the pitchman crying ballyhoo outside the sideshow, the roustabouts preparing the groundwork for the dangerous Carpet Acts. The smell of hotdogs permeating the air, mingling somehow sweetly with the thick stench of animals.

Even the train itself was a spectacle, Lor thought, as he stared at it now. Its advertising cars were rich, moving billboards. A finely executed circus scene adorned each one: perchpole acrobats jumping through the air, a convoy of elephants standing tail to trunk, showgirls smiling atop bowing horses. Along the top of each advertisement waved a replica of Bringlebright's emblem: a blue and green flag.

Seeing the train and feeling as if he were in familiar company, Lor sat down on the tracks. He sat a long time. Eventually, dusk seemed far away and the dawn quite near. Voices hummed in his ear—nearby voices.

Circus folks, Lor reckoned.

Quick as a wink, he formed a plan. He would join them, he decided. Join the circus. He might not be able to make it in the regular world, but why not here, where performers were measured by talent, where a clown had as much chance of Center Ring celebrity as a beautiful showgirl?

Lor looked behind him, at the snaky sprawl of the train. Although he knew differently, he imagined that its wood and steel frame wound on for miles. The train had probably traveled coast to coast, seen every state in the union three times over.

It's certainly done more traveling than my tired, tatty shoes, he thought. Wouldn't it be nice to travel by rail for once?

Aloud, Lor whispered, "Yes, I believe it would."

• • •

From the tensions he had observed between townsfolk and circusfolk—or gillies and kinkers, as the two groups were more commonly called—Lor knew he wasn't on welcome ground. He also knew that circus trains traveled on a tight schedule, often with pre-dawn arrivals and departures. He wasn't sure how much time was left before Bringlebright was nothing but a choke of steam en route to its next destination.

Still sleepy from lack of rest, Lor struggled to his feet. He slapped at his pants, hoping to coax out the dust that had accumulated. He succeeded, for billows rose forth. He spat on his hands, rubbed saliva on his face, then brushed off the grimy residue with his shirtsleeve.

So much for making a decent impression, Lor thought grimly.

He didn't even have the prostitute's marbles anymore. He'd traded them with some savvy street Arab for a slice of bread. Resourcefully, Lor grabbed some rusted screws from the ground, then stuffed them into his pouch.

No use publicizing my poverty, he thought.

Lor crept closer to the voices. He saw that they emanated from several broad-shouldered men who sat about a hundred yards from the way car, in an empty section of the yard. They wore coveralls and work boots. They were sizeable, scruffy fellows—not exactly the type of men you were likely to see doing acrobatics in leotards. Must be roustabouts, Lor realized. Even through the dim light and distance, Lor saw that at least one of them was colored, like him. A stroke of luck, he wondered? Although he had never felt an immediate kinship with other blacks on account of heritage alone, others embraced the connection.

Summoning his courage, Lor approached the workhands. They sat around a fire playing cards. Juxtaposed against the featherly flames, they seemed to loom. Be cordial, Lor reminded himself. He hoped not to befriend the roustabouts, but rather to gather more information about Bringlebright itself. He wanted to know how the circus found its performers, and how those performers were hired as full-time wage-earners. He wanted to know whom to approach about becoming a star.

"Howdy, gentlemen," he said.

The eyes that greeted Lor's, however, were anything but pleasant. This was a mean crew, Lor understood immediately. One of the men, the fiercest, had tattoos running along the full length of his arms. His sleeves were rolled up to the biceps. Lor squinted at the tattoos through the smoke and cigarette haze. Bare-naked ladies, he realized! When the roustabout flexed his muscles, the ladies' legs spread scandalously.

The other roustabouts were only slightly less intimidating: a slack-jawed redhead with creepy, beetle-black eyes; a fat guy with lumpy jowls; a Spaniard with a veiny birthmark streaked across his nose; and the black man, sturdy and unsettling, except for his neat, carefully trimmed mustache. Some time later Lor would learn their names: Rusty, Fat Stan, Spider, and Bar None, respectively. All were large—larger than Lor—and infinitely worrisome.

"The name's Lor. Lor Cole. Mind if I play a hand?" he asked. He was conscious of their eyes on his face, his clothes, his shoes. Instinctively, he tried to make eye contact with the mustached man, hoping to capitalize on their commonality. But Bar None wasn't in the mood to make friends. He deferred response to the tattooed man. This ruffian, Lor soon realized, was the real boss and appropriately named Legman Jack.

"Get lost, stranger," Legman replied, returning his attention to the cards in his hand. They were playing a game Lor didn't recognize. To be sure, he didn't know a thing about cards.

"I lost all my money to a hussy," Lor continued, trying to stoke the fires of sympathy. "Should have known better than to get mixed up with a redhead."

"Hey mister, why don't you take your flapdoodle and scram," responded Bar None. "We got no time for chit-chat. And besides, if some chick took all your money, what d'ya intend to gamble with?"

Lor was failing at his mission. Moreover, he was risking physical jeopardy simply by being there. It was time to act, time to make an impression. A positive one, he hoped.

He shook the pouch. A magical sound, something like the clink-clank of money, filled the air.

The roustabouts didn't respond to politeness, but they certainly appreciated an extra player with money to lose.

"How much you got there, kiddo?" Spider asked.

"Enough," Lor replied.

Spider glanced at his friends' faces. Only Legman cast a disapproving look. No one from The Outside was going to get a better reception than that.

"Have a seat," Spider announced. "We're playing poker. I expect we don't need to teach you the rules."

It only took a minute for Lor to realize that if Legman was the master, Rusty was the dingleberry. Although none of the men were anything close to amiable, the heavy-set fellow seemed the most benign.

He tried to engage the roustabouts in polite conversation. He asked each where he was from, did he have a family, a girl? But they responded with only brusque retorts. The roustabouts were serious gamblers—serious about taking his money. Or at least the money they thought he had. No interruptions permitted. Quite soon, Lor realized he was ass over teacups.

"You sure waste a lot of words, kid. Didn't your ma teach you manners?" jousted Bar None.

"My mother's dead," Lor replied flatly. At his fingers, spread like a peacock's behind, lay a jack, a two, a nine, and a pair of eights. Was it a good hand, he wondered? A bad one? Hastily, he plucked the two and the nine and threw them, face down, onto the crate table.

"Two," he told the dealer. Legman took Lor's cards, then sliced a pair off the pile.

"No wonder," Bar None replied. "Any mother with a son as dirty as you would roll over in her Chicago overcoat."

Lor chuckled humorlessly. He was tempted to toss back a salty reply, but he needed to concentrate. Already, they'd played a few rounds. During this time, Lor had worked on unraveling the game. Nevertheless, he remained daunted. Cards of the same suit, especially face cards, seemed valuable, he'd ascertained. A hand containing two or more of the same cards—say, a nine of clubs and a nine of diamonds—also appeared lucky. When in doubt, Lor thought, he would throw his low cards into the discard pile and keep the faces and aces. He didn't know if this strategy were correct, but he felt somewhat relieved to have a strategy at all.

Bidding was another matter entirely. In this case, Lor's tactics involved little more than increasing the previous bidder's sum by a nickel or two. When he had no face cards in his hand, he passed altogether. Simple as this method was, it struck Lor as absurd. He had no money, after all, just metal bits. He could only hope that no similar bit of say, shrapnel, would pummel his heart when the roustabouts caught wind of his deceit. Mercifully, the players didn't put their money on the table. Legman was tallying the wagers with pencil and paper.

After several more rounds Bar None yawned. Like the plague, the yawn spread from player to player. Lor started to panic. The moment they ended the game, he would have to pay up. According to Legman's handiwork, he owed a grueling sum: seven dollars and forty-five cents.

"I could play all night," Lor said, hoping to buy time.

"Shut up, pigpen," Legman muttered.

"We're gonna turn in soon, boy," Spider added.

Legman dealt another round of cards. Lor fanned out his hand. To his surprise, he had three aces—in hearts, spades, and diamonds, plus a seven and a queen. A trio of power, he thought. He had to bite his lip to keep from smiling.

Before now, Lor had understood the term "poker face" simply as a figure of speech. Tonight, however, he understood its context. To have a poker face meant to tie back emotion, to still all expression. Even the imbecilic Rusty disciplined his shifty eyes. His gaze remained fixed on his cards, which he held guardedly to his chest.

There was no way he could lose, Lor thought gleefully. Here was a chance to earn back his money before the roustabouts discovered he was a fraud. Who knew? Maybe he could even come out ahead.

Confident that nobody else had as promising a hand, Lor pulled two cards—the seven and queen—and set them on the table. He didn't look at his cards as he conducted this exchange. Nor did he glance at the two fresh cards Legman dealt him. He didn't think he needed to.

'Round and 'round the bidding went, always clockwise, starting to the right of the dealer. Four times 'round, then five. Fat Stan folded. A long whistle escaped his lips as he threw down his hand. Six times. Bar None and Spider folded too. The bids grew ever steeper. These were bids for rich folks, Lor thought. Not for lugs paid meager wages for grunt work. Of course, Lor had no idea what other means of making money these men had. Quite frankly, he wasn't sure he wanted to. At the eighth round, when the bid topped ten dollars, the dimwit Rusty also folded. He did so with a slamming of the cards and a curdling of the blood.

"I suppose it's just you and me, pigpen," Legman said, staring at Lor.

"Suppose so."

"You gonna keep raising the bid?"

"No, I call," he said, mimicking the word he'd heard the other players use. For the first time since making the roustabouts' acquaintance, he felt something close to comfortable. He hadn't discovered any information on how to join the circus, but he hadn't been battered either. Considering his situation, he was coming out ahead.

"Gentlemen," Fat Stan announced, making a trumpet with his hands. "Show us what you've got!"

Legman threw down his hand.

"A flush," Fat Stan commented. "Not bad."

With a pang of worry, Lor wondered if a flush beat three aces. No, it couldn't, he reasoned. Legman's spray of clubs was not nearly as majestic as the sight of his hand.

As if reading his concerns, Spider told him, "You better have somethin' good there, bigshot. You'll need a full house—or better yet, a straight flush."

A full house? A straight flush? Lor might as well be in another country listening to an unknown tongue. Quite suddenly, his newfound ease evaporated. The nagging feeling that he was close to being scalped returned. He'd been foolish to convince himself that three aces were valuable simply because they *looked* valuable. His hand might be a winner. Then again, it might be the crap end of the stick.

Lor had forgotten completely about the two cards he had never picked up, the two cards on the table that the other players surreptitiously eyed. He was never to know that one of them was a fourth ace.

He lay down his fate—having no idea what it was. Quickly, he scanned Legman's face. Unabashed delight.

"Double or nothing?" he pleaded, desperate.

Legman shot him a dirty look.

"You think I'm a fool? I'm done for the night. And you, my friend," Legman emphasized, "need to turn over that pouch."

He could run, Lor thought. He probably should run. But the thought of outpacing five fit fellows—when he was already bone-tired—left him pessimistic. He could fight. Sure, and Rusty was a genius.

The roustabouts pounced on him while he was in the midst of indecision. On the ground Lor gritted his teeth. His leg, which the roustabouts had twisted behind his back, hurt the worst. He dared to move it back into position, but Rusty and Spider kept him pinned.

"Even if you got to New Haven's stem," Legman chortled, "we'd of gotten you. And we'd of gotten *this*." At the reference to the pouch, Legman reached down and tore it from around Lor's neck. Lor tried to stave him off, without success.

Legman emptied the contents onto the ground.

"What the hell?" he fumed. His foot hovered precariously over Lor's face.

"Listen," Lor said delicately, "You got me by the shorthairs. There ain't much I can do."

Legman motioned for Rusty and Spider to break Lor's arms.

"No, wait. Stop! Listen, I have a proposition for you!" Lor cried desperately.

"You got ten seconds," Legman replied.

"I can't give you the money—not yet. But I can make a deal with you. You guys are pushing off soon, right? You ever heard of a man standing atop the train as it travels?"

"Of course," Rusty replied, "it's called 'cooning it.'"

"Shut up, Rusty," Bar None interjected.

"Well, what about this: I promise to stand on top of your train—the entire ride from here to..."

"Boston," Bar None verified.

"Right! Chances are, I won't make it—so you won't have to worry about killing me. And even if I do, I surely won't be in one piece."

"What's in it for me?" asked Legman, still angry.

"Amusement, entertainment, the chance to see a man make a fool of himself."

"Seems like you've already accomplished that," Legman Jack retorted. But the other roustabouts were excited about the dare.

"C'mon, Legman," Spider chided. "It'll be a laugh."

"What if some brasshead sees?" Legman cautioned.

"They won't see squat."

"Where on the train would you stand?" Legman asked Lor.

Fat Stan interjected: "Maybe he should stand on a glory."

Legman glared at him. "A glory? What're you talking about? All our freight cars are jam-packed."

"Well then, I'll stand on the caboose," Lor chimed in.

"That ain't no good. The hoghead'll hear you. He's got an office back there," Legman complained, beginning to cede.

With the roustabouts' hands clasped around his wrists, Lor walked along the procession of cars. Eventually, he picked the most stable-looking structure. It was an extraordinarily large and heavy wagon—and these attributes made it safe, or at least he thought they did.

"The hippo den?" Spider asked in awe. "You know what you're picking, shit-for-brains?"

Lor's eyes widened. He hadn't known it was a hippo den. In fact, he wasn't even sure he knew what a hippo was. Even though he had seen the circus many times and recognized the creatures on sight, the actual names—elephants, hippos, giraffes—were too exotic to remember.

He hoped Rosie was a soft and fuzzy creature.

"Of course I do," Lor replied.

Spider chuckled and slapped him on the back. He knew what Lor didn't. It's one thing to stand on top a train, but quite another to stand on top a wagon that's tied down to a flatcar. Aboard a wagon, the momentum of the train is exaggerated, enhancing each jolt and jostle.

With a less-than-gentle push from the roustabouts, Lor climbed atop Rosie's home. An incredibly loud and annoyed grunt erupted from under him.

"Easy there," Lor murmured to the animal, which remained out of sight in the shadowy interior. Lor lay, belly-down, on the top of the wagon. Even in this position, he could feel the shifts and shuffles beneath him. The hippo knocked her head against the ceiling. Lor could feel the thuds, as steady, but more thunderous, than his heartbeat.

The roustabouts gathered into a nearby boxcar. They barely squeezed their burly bodies into the interior, which was stockpiled with stands. Like all of Bringlebright's canvas, pole, and prop wagons, this wagon had lateral slits on the upper half of each of its sides. Inside the boxcar the roustabouts used these slits as windows. From their vantage point Lor was clear as ice.

"You moving up there? Stay still, you jackass," Legman chided. "We're *watching* you."

"You hold on there, buddy," Spider cheered to Lor. "I got a dollar you're gonna make it through Providence!"

If Lor didn't fall off the train from the rocky ride or from Rosie's angry snorts, the roustabouts discussed, he'd surely suffer another way. The train could derail. Lor could get caught by a cinderdick. The train might pass beneath a low underpass.

"Then Lor will lose his head!" Rusty giggled excitedly.

In the time before the train's departure, the roustabouts kept busy making bets. A nickel that he'd lose an arm. A dime that he'd lose an eye. Legman wagered the highest, still upset that he'd been jacked.

"Don't try to find a foothold," Legman warned Lor.

Once the conductor got a clear board signal from the dispatcher, the train let out a scream of steam. Within five minutes it had moved from the yard tracks to the main line. The engine nose dived into the horizon. The through trackage was free and clear, allowing the locomotive to coast in bursts of rapid-fire speed.

How long he lay on the hippo den Lor didn't know. He didn't have any sense of time, only of the wind rustling up the back of his shirt, and of the animal that let its annoyance be known from below. Eventually, the whoosh of escaping steam filled his ears, punctuated by the staccato clickety-clak-clak of the train against the rails.

Lor lifted his head, intent on watching the train's progress. Once the locomotive reached the main tracks, it quickly picked up speed. It was now or never, Lor thought to himself. If he had learned anything during all those years of balancing on ridgepoles, ropes, and roofs, this was his opportunity to prove it.

Ever so carefully, he climbed to his feet. He kept his knees bent and his feet splayed. This stance, that of a swordsman, was the most stable. With one foot forward, the other back, and heels perpendicular to one another, Lor crouched low. Better to absorb the momentum of the train, better to avoid the awesome power of the oncoming wind.

Lor knew the roustabouts were watching him from the window slats. He paid them no heed. He couldn't hear their boos, hoots, cuts, and cracks. But even if he could, his concentration wouldn't have wavered. Lor had forgotten what it was like to balance. His was the body of a dancer: a medley of balance, harmony, and strength. He extended his arms, crucifixion-like, and there they remained. The wind ripped through his ragged clothing. But neither nature's exhalations nor the force of the engine could upset Lor's equilibrium. He was steady, fluid. A man more comfortable in the air than on the earth.

His cloudy mind cleared. All his nagging worries—the moneyless pouch, the gamblers eager to tear into him—ceased. He felt nothing less than divinely conceived. The tears that ran down his cheeks felt like a christening. How had he forgotten this thrill?

The roustabouts whooped and hollered, flabbergasted by Lor's skill.

"Judas Priest!" Spider cried out. "He threw you for another loop, Legman."

"Hate to agree," retorted Bar None, "but Lor's done this before. He's not even shaking up there."

"A natural," Fat Stan added.

"The rat bastard," Legman muttered.

Lor felt much like a bird, light and free and a child of the sky. Maybe that is why he got it into his head to fly.

As a boy, he had fallen many times. He had accumulated scrapes, bruises, a dislocated elbow. Augusta had tended to his broken fingers with homemade splints fashioned from popsicle sticks. Concerned as she was, she had never told him to stop. Maybe she had known what Lor had long suspected: he didn't need to fall. Not if he believed he would be carried. *Transcendence.*

When the train suddenly started to slow, Lor lunged into the air. For an instant, the wind swept him high and his body felt weightless. But when the instant ended, he recoiled. He wrapped his arms around his head and prepared for collision. Reality pelted him from all sides. He hit the ground already rolling, body in a ball. He turned one somersault, another, then a third and fourth. He would have kept rolling, if he hadn't stretched out his legs and dug his heels into the ground. The pressure was enough to tear his bedraggled shoes clean off his feet.

When he finally came to a standstill, Lor checked himself to make sure he wasn't dead. He knew he wasn't because of the pain. His head pounded like rain against stone. With great effort, he forced himself up. He stared at the slowing train and suddenly remembered all he had survived: an angry hippopotamus, five surly men, and a jump from a moving train.

A little lump on the head is nothing, he thought.

He couldn't see the roustabouts—they were still hiding in the boxcar. But he was sure they could see him, even from this distance. He waved at them impishly.

Moments later, the train pulled to a halt. Lor worried that the ruffians would jump to the ground and chase him down. He started to run, but heard someone call to him.

"Stop, stranger. Stop right there! I've got something for you."

Lor paused long enough to look over his shoulder. If one of the roustabouts had anything for him, it would surely be a knuckle sandwich. But the person who had called to him wasn't a roustabout. Lor wasn't sure what he was—a hallucination perhaps. He wore a strange suit, striped like a zebra. The man had hopped off the cab and now wildly gesticulated. What a funny sight he made: arms flapping frantically.

Although the striped man seemed faraway, his voice was as clear as if he were standing at Lor's side. Few people have the power to project so well: it is a learned skill. Lor shook his head, amazed that he hadn't recognized the fellow immediately. It was the ringmaster of the Bringlebright Circus, for heaven's sake! He had heard that voice at least a dozen times in his life. This was the voice that introduced death-defying acts, that encouraged the audience to laugh and cheer, that tantalized waffling patrons with promises of a grand spectacle.

Step right up and see the most enthralling and splendiferous show ever to take place under the big top!

As a boy, Lor had squirmed in anticipation of that voice. But now that he was all grown up, its captivating tenor was more than advertising; it was hope.

Lor walked back to the site of the stalled train.

"We should lock you up, son," the ringmaster said, once Lor had reached him. He twirled the curlicue end of his waxy mustache.

"Why don't you then?" Lor asked.

"I would 'cept I saw for myself that you've got balls. And Lord knows wire-walkers are hard to come by. We must lose three of you guys a year to gravity! I said to Gus—he's the conductor, see?—I said, 'Gus, stop the train! I gotta find out who this mystery man is.'"

"Well, here I am."

"Yes, here you are," the ringmaster said, eyeing Lor. "I see there's not much to you. Thin as a reed and dressed like a hobo. But we can fix that.

Yes sirree, here at Bringlebright, magic's been known to happen! But that's not the point. The point is, we've got a job for you, son. Barnacle's the name." The ringmaster extended his hand cordially.

Lor shook it carefully, not yet sold. He had to play tough. After all, these were troubled times. He remembered his misadventures in New York all too lucidly.

"You want me to join the show as a wire-walker?" Lor asked.

"Well, not quite," the ringmaster replied. "To jump straight from the streets to the majestic heights of the circus is quite a leap. And I ain't no fairy godmother. The fact is, boy, you've got the talent—and possibly the looks, somewhere under all that dirt. But just because I'm the owner of Bringlebright doesn't mean I can catapult a no-name into stardom. You must understand—Bringlebright's a place of opportunity. A place where the right person can show he's got the right stuff. We promote initiative and drive. But first you must prove yourself."

"Prove myself?"

"Yes, son, you could say the circus is like the military in structure. There are the privates. Then the sergeants, the lieutenants, the captains, the majors, the colonels, and finally, the generals. Can a private suddenly become a general simply because he's talented? No sirree. He must *work* for it. With his bare hands and chops. He must *fight* for it—with everything in his being."

"What are you saying exactly, Mr. Barnacle?" Lor asked.

"Son, if we take you on, you'll have to start at the bottom like everyone else. I thought we'd employ you as a roustabout at first—just to see what you're made of. Then, if you impress us, well, the sky's the limit!"

Mr. Barnacle continued to twirl the end of his mustache. The morning light was still faint, but the ringmaster's bold attire seemed to cast its own illumination.

Lor was eager to take the job—any job—but he had to know that he was moving in the right direction. If he wasn't, he might as well stay in New Haven.

"How do I know you won't keep me down—the ranks, that is?"

"Son, I won't kid you and say the world's a fair place. But as I said, I'll give you a shot. You think I'd stop this train for just anybody? Ask Gus—I haven't stopped this train for *a single soul* in ten years!"

Suddenly the ringmaster pulled out his pocketwatch and grimaced. "Look now, I ain't got much more time to waste. No more chit-chat. You in, kiddo, or are you out?"

Lor shuffled his feet. He studied the ringmaster's timepiece. It was gold with beautiful red stones around the edges. Rubies, Lor wondered? He wasn't sure; he had never seen a ruby before.

"How much is the pay?" Lor asked.

"Seven dollars a week. A teeny bit on the low side . . . "

But Lor had already made up his mind. Seven dollars a week—seven dollars more than he had on his person. Seven dollars closer to owning a watch like the ringmaster's. Seven dollars nearer to walking the skies. Seven dollars to achieve the fame he knew he was destined for.

"All right, Mr. Barnacle. I accept your offer."

"Good night! That's wondrous!" responded the triumphant ringmaster as he put his arm around Lor's soiled shoulders.

"Lad, we'll load you in with the roustabouts for now. I suspect—judging by your predicament on top the train—you've met some of them already."

• CHAPTER SEVEN •

The train ran on a tight schedule. There was no time to waste—no time at all. Quick as a firefly's twinkle, Lor was aboard the Bringlebright train, heading north to Boston. After the brief, fantastical moment since the ringmaster had invited Lor to join the show—and Lor, in an equally fantastical moment, had agreed—the roustabouts had scampered out of the boxcar and back to their crum cars. Their sudden movement sounded no alarms. The train's abrupt stop had caused more than a few circus members to stagger out of their cars in curiosity.

When Barnacle told Lor he would share his sleep quarters with two veteran roustabouts, Jack Hall and Stan Hooper, Lor didn't even blink. Everything was happening so quickly—reaction time seemed like a privilege.

His old friends were waiting for him when he arrived. The door slammed shut as soon as Lor stepped inside. Although the interior was dim, Lor could make out Legman's wide, crooked grin. Fat Stan chortled until his jowls shook. The train started rolling again and Lor wondered whether he would need to make another jump.

"So glad you could join us," Legman said.

As Lor's eyes adjusted to the gray light, he noticed how truly filthy his living arrangements would be. The crum car wasn't a whole car, but rather, a compartment. The bunks were soiled and smelled of feces. Sawdust blanketed the ground, which was no doubt home to mice and other assorted guests. Evidently, Fat Stan and Legman didn't care much for housekeeping:

cigarette butts, empty beer bottles, playing cards, girlie magazines, and chicken bones littered the already cramped interior. Lor kept his back to the door. His entire body felt itchy.

"We'd kill you right here, 'cept Barnacle seems to have taken a liking to you. It would be a shame to get on his bad side," Legman announced matter-of-factly. Lor did not doubt his sincerity.

"What's a matter there, friend?" Fat Stan chimed in. "You not happy with your royal quarters?"

A three-tiered bunk rested against the wall opposite the door. Ignoring Fat Stan's question, Lor asked which bed was free.

"What d'ya mean? Ain't nothing 'free' here," Legman responded tartly. "This is the U.S. of A.—you gotta work for things. It's first come, first serve, pigpen. That means we get the bunks, and you get the floor."

Lor was too tired to argue. And besides, he doubted he would make much headway. Right now, he would be lucky to pull off a few winks without getting whacked. He took off his ratty coat and rolled it into a ball, intending to use it as a pillow. Then he sank to the floor. The sawdust, although foul-smelling, felt surprisingly comfortable against his weary body. Legman and Fat Stan watched him with amusement.

"Comfy?" Stan asked. "Anything else we can get you? Maybe a nice busty girl with good hands?"

Legman roared with laughter. "Don't listen to him, pigpen. Everything that comes out his mouth is applesauce. We know you'd much rather have a boy in here—with good hands *and* a firm ass."

"Yeah, just wait 'till choosing day. Then you'll get your pick," Fat Stan clucked.

"What's 'Choosing Day?'" Lor dared to ask.

"Oh, so you're alive then?" Legman chided. "Wouldn't have known you're so quiet. By the way, we pee on that floor."

"Boy," Fat Stan said, edging in, "'Choosing Day' is the best day we've got in this joint. The management don't know about it, 'cause if they did, we'd get thrown out.

"On that day," Stan continued, "all single kinkers get to choose their bunkmates. Legman and me, we usually choose two of the new ballybroads, you know, the fresh ones."

"And if the girls don't want to sleep with you?" Lor asked.

Legman chuckled. "Never got rejected."

"No, I don't suppose you would," Lor replied.

A moment later, he closed his eyes. Just before he drifted off to sleep, he wondered if he would ever wake up again.

• • •

When Bringlebright reached the Boston train yard, Lor knew it was time to wake up when Legman kicked him in the back of head, leaving a lump the size of a hen's egg. He raked the sawdust out of his hair and followed the roustabouts out of the crum car.

"Time to put up the cookhouse," Fat Stan told him. "Whenever we move, the cookhouse is the first tent up and the first tent down."

The men worked zealously for two hours, pitching the tent. Then the cookhouse staff spent another hour preparing the morning meal. When they had finished they raised a red flag.

Stan spotted it and yelled: "Breakfast!"

Despite the fact that his stomach ached for sustenance, Lor couldn't eat. Apprehension had made him nauseous.

"I'll pass," he said.

Fat Stan shrugged. "Suit yourself."

After their meal, Legman and Stan rejoined Lor and walked him through the rigors of their work: unloading wagons from the flats, erecting the remainder of the tents, moving the heavy props into the big top. Late morning, the red flag went up again, but still Lor could not bring himself to eat.

By five o'clock in the afternoon, Lor's back was so stiff he could hardly bend over. He felt weak as a newborn. All he wanted to do was settle back onto that squalid floor for more shut-eye. But when the flag went up for the third and final time, he knew he had to fill his belly.

Lor had been anticipating little more than large kettles simmering over open firepits. But the cookhouse far exceeded his expectations. He let out a low whistle when he entered.

Everywhere he saw red-and-white gingham tablecloths. They provided a zesty and festive touch to the otherwise plain setting, where dozens of folding tables and benches stood in perfect alignment. Lor was about to take a seat when Stan stopped him.

"That's not your place," Stan warned, quick to point out that seating in the cookhouse was divided by rank.

Lor's place, it turned out, was on the other side of the cookhouse and beyond a long, dark curtain that ran the length of the interior and divided the "long side" from the "short side"—or as Fat Stan pointed out, the yokels from the moneybags. The long side seated the workingmen and their bosses. But everyone of prominence—management, ticket sellers, candy butchers, front door men, ushers, performers, and sideshow personnel—ate on the short side. With its smaller, more intimate tables, the short side was far more inviting. Lor felt the same pangs of jealousy as he had when he had seen Barnacle's watch—and the same determination to prove himself.

"Do they get the better food too?" Lor grumbled, as he and Stan took seats with the rest of the roustabouts.

"Nah," Stan responded. "We all get the same thing—and as much of it as we want. There's a saying: 'A circus moves on its stomach!' And I tell you, friend, a truer thing ain't never been said." Fat Stan rubbed his considerable belly.

Lor still didn't have much of an appetite, but when a green-eyed man set a huge plate of food before him, he felt his juices start to run. Tonight was Southern food night. His plate was heaped high with buttermilk biscuits, skillet-fried cornbread, dumplings, fried chicken, grits, creamed corn, collard greens, and enough red-eye gravy to drown all of Alabama. There was even a thick wedge of pecan pie, should Lor have room for desert. Fat Stan watched him pound down his food.

"See, it ain't so bad on this side," he said. "If you ask me, I'd rather stay here. Over there's all rank and file." Stan waving a drumstick in one hand

and a fork in the other. "You got the equestrians at one table, the aerialists at another. Everybody in their own little world."

"How does the ranking work?" Lor asked, staring at the curtain and imagining the scene beyond.

"The bosses are at the top," Stan explained. "Then come the people who handle money: ticket sellers, front door men. After that, the more skill, the higher the status. Ranju—the chief animal trainer—he's at the top." Stan pointed to a wild-looking man who walked about the cookhouse, seemingly without destination.

"Acrobats and tumblers next," Stan continued. "Clowns and jugglers are the low men on the totem pole. But outside of them, you got a whole new chain of command: the outside talkers, the little top performers, the skilled second-class acts like the magician and ventriloquist. The showgirls are low too. 'Cept for the boss's new lollipop. She gets to sit with the head-honchos. Not near Mrs. Barnacle though."

Lor chewed a bite of his pecan pie. Delicious, he thought. Stan, despite all his jabbering, was already on his second piece.

"Then there's the freaks," Fat Stan observed. "They don't really fit any bill. They keep separate, just like everyone else. They sleep together, eat together, even hump together. Boy, that must be a sight!"

Without warning, Legman Jack reached over the table and stabbed the last chunk of Lor's pie.

"Hey now, get your own damn dessert," Fat Stan grumbled. Lor, who still feared Legman, didn't say a word.

"I'd of taken *your* pie if you hadn't eaten it already," Legman snapped.

Undeterred by Legman's retort, Stan carried on. "Folks 'round Bringlebright have respect for the freaks. But you put 'em with the gillies and trouble's sure to brew. The freaks—they got their own sleeping quarters too. Same as most folks: three or six to a station. And like everyone else, they're separated by sex. 'Cept it's not always easy to determine who's who. You take Wonder Boy with Half a Torso, for instance. He's only half male. Then there's Choalla the Bearded Lady. No one's ever seen what's under her skirts."

Out of nowhere, the same green-eyed man who had brought their plates interrupted Fat Stan. He tapped Lor on the shoulder. When he had Lor's attention, he announced that the ringmaster wished to meet with him in his private car.

"Mr. Barnacle recommends that you come in suitable attire," the man continued, with reference to Lor's shabby ensemble. "At seven o'clock—prompt."

When he left, Legman Jack, who had overheard every word, exhaled sharply. "What kinda voodoo you put over Barnacle, pigpen? You're only an eight-ball, yet somehow you've managed to grab that bastard by the nuts."

But Lor only shrugged, as shocked as the rest of them at the twists his life had taken in the last twenty-four hours.

"It's a good thing we don't have a new stand tomorrow," Fat Stan muttered, "or we'd already be dropping the cookhouse. As it is, you got exactly an hour and a half to wash off all them layers of grime."

• • •

Fat Stan showed Lor where to fill a bucket full with water. Handing Lor a bar of glycerin, he admitted he'd never seen the ringmaster personally summon a roustabout. Not ever.

"Legman's jaw dropped so far, I thought it would fall off!" Stan laughed. "I was pretty shocked myself."

Turning into a gentleman required much speed and diligence on Lor's part. After scrubbing down from head to toe and rinsing with unmercifully cold water, Lor began to dress. But he hesitated. The filthy fabric of his clothing felt foul against his skin. He thought about asking Fat Stan if he could borrow a fresher wardrobe, but no belt would have held up so much extra fabric. He didn't have a choice. He'd have to borrow from the other roustabouts.

Surprisingly, Rusty was the first to offer him a pair of trousers, a shirt, even a pair of woolen socks—free of holes, no less. He gave Lor shoes too, even though his feet were two sizes smaller. Lor took the shoes anyway. He'd been walking around all day with bare feet.

When he had finished dressing, the roustabouts gathered around him.

"You look good, kid. Real good," Fat Stan observed.

"Not bad for a rat turd," Legman Jack added.

At seven o'clock sharp, Lor knocked on the door to the ringmaster's private car. He was happy with his appearance. Sharp and polished, not unlike the stones on Barnacle's timepiece. He'd shaved with Fat Stan's straight blade. He'd borrowed Bar None's hair dressing, which made his hair slick and shiny as patent leather. He had even gargled with a mouthwash Fat Stan kept around for what he called "lucky nights." Altogether, Lor cut a handsome picture.

The ringmaster opened the door. Gone was his absurd striped suit. In its place: a full-length velvet robe tied around the middle with a satin sash. The color of the robe, ivory, matched the brocade walls of Barnacle's parlor. It was an opulent place. Everything was thickly lacquered, glossy, and impressive: the floors, the furniture, even the huge mahogany desk that crouched in the middle of the car like a guard dog.

The ringmaster motioned for Lor to take a seat in one of the two chairs that flanked his desk.

"You clean up well, Lars," the ringmaster commented.

"Lor."

"Oh yes. Lor."

Lor watched from his seat as the ringmaster bent down and opened a hidden compartment under the desk. After a few moments, he emerged with a silver decanter.

"My wife doesn't like me to keep drink around. She's joined the Woman's Christian Temperance Union—can you believe it? Sends letters of support to the Anti-Saloon League too. Those drys are ruining this country. They're against everything America stands for: freedom to do what we want—and drink what we want."

Lor nodded, noticing for the first time that the ringmaster was wearing fuzzy bedroom slippers.

Fetching two crystal glasses from a desk drawer, the ringmaster poured brandy from the decanter. He handed one of the glasses to Lor, then settled into the matching mahogany chair behind his desk.

"You like to drink, son?"

"No, sir. But I appreciate a taste now and again."

"That's good. I don't encourage my workers to drink. But I always say, 'a bit o' liquor can boost the spirits on a cloudy day.' It's horrible, this Prohibition nonsense," Barnacle continued. "It's already sweeping the country faster than a famine. But there are ways to fight it. I got a cousin in Toledo who's making a bundle as a bootlegger—but you never heard it from me. He smuggles the liquor over the Canadian border. Those Canadian boys manufacture so much, they like to share. My cousin's group—the Purple Gang, you heard of 'em?—they run the merchandise across the Detroit River, drag it underneath the boats or store it in coves if they have to. They're modern-day pirates."

Barnacle poured himself another glass of brandy.

"You know much about bootlegging, son?" he asked Lor.

Lor shook his head.

"Everyone's doing it. I've invested some money with another relative of mine who manufactures liquor hideaways."

"'Liquor hideaways?'"

"That's right, Lor. Places where people can store their joy-juice without getting harassed by pigs or Christian Temperance fanatics. False floorboards in automobiles, second gas tanks, hidden compartments like the one in my desk, false-bottomed shopping baskets and suitcases, camouflaged flasks and hot water bottles—that sort of thing. There's real money to be made in the business. But mum's the word, okay?"

Barnacle brought his finger to his lips in a mock "hush."

"As for the whiskey itself, we can always import it—or make it ourselves. I got a great recipe for White Mule, and it's not that cheap bathtub gin, either. You interested?"

"No thank you, sir," Lor replied, beginning to wonder if Barnacle had any reason at all for calling him here. The ringmaster refilled Lor's glass.

"I got a friend in Jersey who's got a half-acre warehouse full of every goody you can imagine: rum, bourbon, brandy, good Russian vodka, even better German lager. Over the years, I've helped him out a time or two. He tells me, 'Barnacle, you'll never have to worry about your glass running dry. Not as long as I'm around.' And I believe him. Lor, anyone who knows me will say that I'm good for one thing. And that's planning. I like to look ahead, to anticipate. That's why I called you here."

At last, Lor thought. He straightened his back and leaned attentively toward the ringmaster. As he shifted, however, he started to feel dizzy. It had been a long time since he had last touched alcohol.

Better slow down, Lor thought.

"Lor, the folks we got on the wire-walk, the Weitzmans—ever seen 'em?—are favorites among our fan base. But a successful show's got to have a new sensation each season, not the same thing served up again and again. The Weitzmans, they're real flashy, see? Lots of glittery costumes, good-looking girls in short skirts, that sort of thing. But not much substance, you understand?"

The ringmaster put down his drink long enough to twiddle his mustache.

"I understand, sir," Lor replied.

"Son, I see real potential in you—yes I do. And the reason I see potential is because you're willing to take risks. It takes either a genius or a madman to stand atop a moving train. And frankly, I don't care which you are—so long as you keep an audience on its toes.

"My point is that I'm willing to take you in, so long as you continue to shake things up. Just between you and me, Sebastian Weitzman's become a little smug with age. He's not trying anything new. In fact, I don't think he or that blond family of his has come up with a single unique routine in over three years. I see what other shows are offering and I wonder how we're gonna compete."

Barnacle once again filled his cup and tried to fill Lor's too, but Lor politely declined.

"Now, due to respect for Weitzman, I can't stick you in the spotlight right off. I'd be stepping on some toes, see? So what I want is for you to work with Weitzman slowly. Let him adjust to the fact that he's got a new performer aboard. He'll probably resent you at first. But I'll make sure he doesn't brush you off."

"What do you want me to do, exactly?" Lor asked, his head beginning to clear.

"Well, son, as I said, we're falling behind the competition—the Ringling Brothers have got us beat bad. I'm hoping you can breathe a little fresh air into the routines, see? Maybe think of some new moves, new props, new formations on the wire, anything that will keep the audience coming back for more. We've got to get new fans into the big top—and make sure the old ones return too. You get my drift?"

Lor nodded.

The ringmaster winked at him. "Good," he replied. His raucous voice softened. "I wish I didn't have to stick you with them roustabouts. Some of them are real bastards, I know. But I don't have a choice. You got two strikes against you, son. First, you're the new kid. And second, you're colored. Personally, I got nothing against colored folks, which is why I'm giving you this opportunity. But other people aren't so charitable. For now, 'roustabout' had better be your official title. It's got to look like you're working your way up the food chain. The white folks would go bananas if they knew I'd cut you a break."

Quite suddenly, Barnacle appeared tired. The bolts of excitement in his eyes began to fade, and he leaned back in his chair as if ready to fall asleep. Lor, who had been taking everything in without so much as blinking, cast cautious eyes upon him. He wasn't sure what to think of the ringmaster's offer. At face value, it appeared too good to be true. Which was why he didn't buy it. No one except Augusta had ever given him things. When it came to charity, you could trust only your mama. Everyone else expected something in return. The question was—what would Barnacle lay claim to?

"This life," the ringmaster muttered, "it can make a man tired, I tell you. So much to keep an eye on, so much juggling. And it never stops. Not for a heartbeat."

"That's the God honest truth, sir," Lor replied, gazing upon his weary host. He noticed among the knickknacks on Barnacle's desk a framed picture of a thin-lipped and serious-looking woman, her slender hands wrapped around a book.

"Nice-looking lady," Lor remarked, for lack of anything better to say.

"My wife," Barnacle replied, without much enthusiasm.

"She travels with the circus?"

Barnacle smiled wryly. "Oh yes."

"Any little ones?"

"No, no kids." He waved his hand casually. "I like to think of Bringlebright as my family. And you—as well as all the employees—as my children."

Gathering his courage, Lor sized up his slung-back, sleepy host. "I'd like to ask you a question, sir."

"Shoot."

"Why me?"

"Pardon?"

"Why me?" Lor repeated. "There's got to be a dozen fellows around here with a knack for balance. Why not choose one of them to 'shake things up?'"

Some of the flint in Barnacle's eyes sparked again. He laughed and his laugh came from deep below, like water sprung from a geyser.

"I like you, Lor. You're no fool. There's definitely something between those ears."

Abruptly, Barnacle sat up in his chair, no longer enfeebled. "I got a little girl on the side," he revealed. "Mrs. Barnacle doesn't know about her. Hooey! If she ever found out, that book she's carrying would give me a concussion—three times over. Truth is, my girl noticed you first. She says to me, 'Honey, have a look out the window. There's a phenomenon going on right under your nose.' She's the one who discovered you, all right. I wasn't sold on you. Not right off. But my girl says, 'Sugar, he's got the technique—and the looks.' I wanted to know how she could see your looks, when you were so far away. And she says to me, 'I just know. I'm a woman, and I just know.' Dames—they're mysteries. All of 'em."

"But you really like this one?" Lor asked, digging for information.

"You bet your britches! Normally I don't listen to women—they don't know what they're saying half the time. But this one—she's got me wrapped around her little finger. It's unfortunate, given this here ring." The ringmaster paused to reflect on his wedding band, and perhaps, on his challenged marriage to Mrs. Barnacle.

"She's a redhead. They're marvelous, if you can handle 'em," Barnacle continued. Lor jerked his neck so suddenly it cracked.

"I hired her as a fire-eater. She's not very good, frankly. I'm always afraid she's going to hurt herself. But no man can resist a woman who's willing to put sticks of fire in her mouth, least of all a softie like me.

"She wanted to be introduced to you," the ringmaster continued. "I was against it at first. I don't introduce my girls to other men. They're the competition, see? But you're all right, Lor. I trust you." He hesitated. "You wanna meet her?"

That all depends, Lor thought. "Of course," he said aloud, downing another drink despite his better judgment.

"Just a minute, then. She's in the adjacent room—waiting for me, I'm afraid. I'll see if she's still awake."

When the ringmaster disappeared to find the girl, Lor closed his eyes and held his breath.

Wearing a velvet robe similar to the ringmaster's, the girl sauntered into the room. Licks of fire curled around her face, the burnish of flame alighted her cheeks. Her smile was rich, red, and wet. Lor stood to greet her.

"Nice to meet you," the girl said softly.

Lor stared her in the eye, amused. "The pleasure is mine."

"My name is Cirella."

"Isn't that queer? I knew a girl in New York with the same name."

"Really?"

"Cirella," the ringmaster interjected, "has been to New York. But she's originally from a little farm town way up north—where it is, dear?"

"Maine."

"Oh yes, Maine. Said her family made a living raising hogs. Imagine that! A girl as pretty as this playing with pigs." The ringmaster snickered and slapped Cirella on her bottom. "I'll never get over the fact that you're really a small-town girl!"

"What part of Maine are you from?" Lor asked.

"Oh, just a little part. A no-name place."

"Every town's got a name."

But Cirella turned her attention away from Lor. "Darling," she cooed to the ringmaster, "I'm so tired I could faint! Can't we go to bed now?"

"You know I can't stay all night," he told her in a confidential tone.

Lor turned away politely. "I better be going. Tomorrow's only my second day—I need to rest up for it."

"So soon?" Barnacle asked. "Well, I suppose it's best we all turn in. But Lor, don't forget what I told you."

"I won't, sir."

Lor shook the ringmaster's hand goodbye. He thought about taking Cirella's too, but decided against it. If he got too close, who knew what else she would filch?

• CHAPTER EIGHT •

The ringmaster had first decided Cirella would be an ideal fire-eater when he'd experienced her under the covers. Her relationship to fire was direct. The flickers of her hair resembled a three-alarm blaze. Roman candles one moment, cooling embers the next, her eyes were every bit as unpredictable as a match in the hands of a child.

Yet it was Cirella's actions rather than her attributes that truly stirred Barnacle. He'd been with many women, many more than Mrs. Barnacle cared to acknowledge. Yet never had he felt so vulnerable as he did with Cirella. A brushfire waiting to happen was what he was. And she: a searing, scalding, scorching skyrocket sent straight to his heart.

The intensity of his ardor was matched only by his fear. For if Cirella could shoot a flare down his spine, what stopped her from detonating him completely? It was this question Barnacle posed to her once Lor had left and the two lovers retired to a makeshift bed in the adjacent compartment.

Cirella laughed and ran a finger from the base of Barnacle's throat down to his bellybutton. She had learned it was best to answer his questions with questions of her own.

"What did you think of that new boy—what's his name? Lor?" she asked him.

The ringmaster directed her hand still lower.

"He's a good kid."

"But do you think he'll make it—that he has what it takes?"

"I don't see that it matters," the ringmaster retorted, then laughed at his recollection of the meeting. "I told him to be as daring as possible. That means he'll probably fall to his death inside a month. If he lasts out the season, I'll be happy."

"So he's expendable then?"

"A darkie like him? Of course!"

As Cirella's hands worked harder, a subtle blaze in the ringmaster's netherparts gave way to an inferno. He could concentrate on little else—least of all Cirella's questions, which he was eager to dismiss.

"Darling, I've been thinking," she said.

"About what?"

"About myself," she sighed deeply. "I don't think people notice me."

"Are you crazy? Every boy over the age of twelve gets whiplash when you walk by."

"No, that's not what I mean. I mean, I don't think people notice me—professionally."

"Sure they do, darling."

"No, they don't."

Cirella halted her work under the sheets, right at the moment when the ringmaster's stick of dynamite was about to explode.

"They don't respect me as a performer," she continued, to Barnacle's chagrin. "They don't know I've got potential. But you do, don't you?"

Firmly, the ringmaster repositioned her hand. "Of course I do," he groaned in discomfort.

"If you believe in me, then why not give me a special place in the show—make me a Center Ring attraction?"

"I'll think about that," he pleaded, his voice cracking.

"Think, think, think . . . this is a time for action."

"I couldn't agree more!"

"Well, right here and now, why not agree? I'll work on my performances, and you guarantee me star billing."

Her hands crept back into place. But this time she did not electrify a heated, throbbing pleasure. Her touch was scalding—nearly intense enough to melt his manhood.

"We could try that," he agreed, fearful.

Immediately, her hands began to cool. She finished the job and a relieved ringmaster sighed a breath of relief. Finally, he could return to a state of autonomy, where his mind and body were not ruled by ravishing, unpredictable women.

A drowsy Cirella lounged by his side. He stroked her hair thoughtfully.

"Darling, I know we agreed on something just now. But to be a first-rate fire-eater, you've got to develop a superb sense of control. This isn't child's play."

"I understand that. Maybe I'll get someone to help me—someone who can lead me on the right path. Maybe I'll get Lor."

"Why him?" Barnacle asked suspiciously.

"Why not?"

"That boy probably doesn't know a thing about fire-eating."

"Maybe not," Cirella agreed, "but he knows how to win an audience."

The ringmaster didn't reveal his jealousy. It wasn't to his advantage, and besides, he was too tired to argue. In another few minutes he would return to Mrs. Barnacle and fabricate an excuse for his tardiness. He'd better be creative. This was his third late night this week.

"Fine," he replied. "Do as you please. But don't count on Lor. My hunch is he won't be around for long."

• • •

Alone and grateful for that fact, Cirella washed herself with a soapy rag and a basin of water. She washed the parts of her body where Barnacle's unruly fingers had run an uneven course, where his tongue had probed without result, where his weepy genitalia had dripped shallowly into her being. Among girls like herself, girls who had experienced his less than awesome sexual power, the ringmaster was a joke. Cirella liked to gossip with these fellow mistresses. Her favorite was Lucinda Rae, an Asian hair-hanger who had engaged in a month-long affair with Barnacle, and who referred to him as "Wilting Wally." It wasn't that Barnacle wasn't in full control of his faculties, Lucinda Rae explained. It was only that by the time he remembered anything but his own pleasure, those faculties were exhausted—and the unlucky girl beside him unsatisfied.

When Cirella had sufficiently scrubbed away all signs of the ringmaster, she lay back in bed. She liked to meditate on her life during these lazy moments, just before the haze of sleep overtook her. She never had time to think during the day, for life was a song, and she was always thinking ahead to the next verse.

She thought back to The House of Delight and all the smarmy specimens she had met there: fishermen with catfish scales under their fingernails, lawyers stinking of twofers, men of the law insisting she kiss their badges, flabby-bellied businessmen with more hair on their backs than on their heads. It seemed to her that all were the same—everyone from judges to dock-wallopers, exactly the same in her lair, dismal in their nakedness, irredeemable no matter which position they assumed.

Cirella wouldn't have bothered with men at all if they weren't financially useful. She considered them necessary, if not distasteful, instruments of change: a means of moving to her next location, of buying a new pair of shoes, of maneuvering herself into more favorable circumstances. She would never have found Bringlebright if Barnacle hadn't found her. And right now, at this very moment, she wouldn't be on her way to becoming a star.

Given her ambivalence toward men, it was strange that one had captivated her. But somehow, Lor had. At first she thought it must be his beauty. She dismissed this theory, however, when she counted how many pretty boys had gone unnoticed in the past.

And then she realized, in one of those late-night bursts of insight, that fate had nudged her toward him. Imagine, she thought, meeting at a brothel, separating, then finding each other a short time later in another state—aboard a circus train, no less! It was as if she and Lor were spirits borne of the same windblown seed.

Cirella might not have finished school, she might not have ever read a newspaper, but she knew men. She knew the sort who crept through a woman's heart without knowing it, who looked at the world through a haze of their own ambition, who couldn't be tricked into romance. Lor was one. The worst sort to fall in love with.

She thought back to her conversation with Barnacle, to the idea of propositioning Lor for his help. He was an impressive performer and, she suspected, an equally competent teacher. He'd be able to help her, for while she knew how to beguile an audience, as she had done adeptly in her last profession, her talent did not approach that of the more seasoned performers.

Lor would take her under his wing—fate dictated that he must. But what after? Cirella knew men, but she didn't know love. Her worst fear was that in its throes, Lor would soar while she would sink faster than a steel ball on the surface of the sea.

She sighed deeply and shut her eyes. She'd suspected this would happen eventually—full-blown, dead-on infatuation. There were only so many Fritzes and Mr. Tristan Thompsons she could dupe before the tables turned. Right then, Cirella wished she were Mrs. Barnacle, who found excitement not in the perils of romance, but in the safe haven of books.

• • •

After his meeting with the ringmaster and reintroduction to Cirella, Lor found himself unable to settle in for the night. Heady with anticipation, he walked the circus grounds. With every step he imagined the possibilities.

"This is it—my chance to be more than Woodrow, Opal, or even Mother could have imagined," he said aloud.

At length he stopped before the big top, whose massive candy cane stripes seemed to connect earth and sky. The more he stared, the less he could conceive of its presence. It seemed to rise like a miracle, like the very embodiment of his larger-than-life fantasies.

Lor pushed open the flap and stepped inside. Darkened by night, the tent reminded him of the inside of a cave. The sweep of black seemed like an endless corridor. The sound of wings overhead could well be bats on the hunt. An animal odor saturated the air.

At first Lor thought he was alone. But moments after he entered, he noticed another. The stranger stood at Center Ring. He had an untamed look: eyes sparked, pokes of hair bolting upright from his head. His long limbs seemed somehow separate from his body. They wheeled around disjointedly like wind toys.

Lor remembered when Fat Stan had pointed him out in the cookhouse. "Ranju: he's got the animals charmed—the gillies too. We don't know how he does it. It could be trickery—or maybe it's luck. No one knows for sure. Ranju don't tell anyone his secrets. The only person he talks to is his baby daughter."

Not sure if Ranju could see him, Lor stood very still. He hoped to catch the animal trainer in rehearsal. Perhaps he'd learn a secret or two.

Ranju waved his arms—seemingly without purpose. Out of the shadows, another creature emerged—a tiger. The enormous cat darted forward, heading for the animal charmer. Startled, Lor sprung forward, ready to help if need be. But Ranju needed no assistance. Just as the bounding tiger reached its keeper, it halted in its tracks. Meekly, it hunkered down, then bent its head.

In reverence, Lor wondered?

The Bringlebright newcomer took a deep breath, knowing he must introduce himself now that he'd made himself known. Yet Ranju was the first to respond. He turned to Lor and curled back his lips, revealing a row of jagged teeth. His hand rested on the tiger's back, fingers curled around a tuft of fur.

Lor nodded, but Ranju remained still. The air between them grew heavy with mistrust. Lor stepped back, realizing that this cave, this sacred space, could have only one master. He turned to leave, but Ranju vanished first. He slipped away quiet as a whisper, the tiger trailing at his feet.

• • •

Even walking away from the big top, Ranju could smell Lor—the same scent a mouse sniffs on a fox. Bristling danger. Ranju wondered if it were danger passed or danger yet to come.

Although he wished he could stay outside for the night, he returned to his sleep compartment. Here, his little daughter, Sara, lay curled in a basket on the floor. She slept soundly, as she always did. Unlike Ranju, she was not ruffled by the sights and smells of the human world.

He lay a hand on her brow, which was warm with dreams. Watching her, he realized she was the only real thing in the room. Everything else was unnatural: the cramped interior; the bunk, hardly long enough for his sprawling frame; the shiny gold nametag on the door. Peering at those symbols carved in fool's metal, Ranju frowned. He'd never wanted the nametag, just as he'd never wanted a private sleep compartment. But the ringmaster had insisted. Early on, dazzled by his skill, Barnacle had tried to give him everything—and to get things back too.

"Where do you come from, Ranju?"

Ranju had merely smiled.

"What's your last name?"

But Ranju hadn't known that either. Hastily, he'd adopted the name of a man from his travels—a medicine man. Omishumba.

"Spelling?" the ringmaster had urged.

Ranju shook his head.

"Fine, we'll write it like it sounds."

For a time the kinkers had tried to call him Mr. Omishumba, in deference to his ranking. But he'd resisted with such force that they soon resorted to "Ranju," or even more simply, "the animal trainer."

Pulling away from this memory, Ranju paced, impatient and limber. His considerable stride and the confines of the room allowed only three steps before he had to turn and march the other way. He longed to be outdoors, where he could walk forever in the same direction if he cared to. But he had his daughter to mind—his first priority. His only priority.

The more Ranju paced, the hotter he became. He peeled off his trousers so that his body could breathe. Clothes still felt alien against his skin even though he'd had seasons to adjust to them. Growing up, he hadn't worried about covering himself, for there had been no humans to reproach him. But now that he was around them everyday, clothing was a necessity: first, because humans were startled by nakedness, and second, because they were terrified of anything they didn't understand.

He would never choose to coexist with them if not for Sara. Ranju looked again at his daughter, at her body, delicate but resolute, at the shock of hair atop her head—soft as a cub's pelt.

His love for her became overwhelming. Eyes wet with astonishment, he looped back across time. Here, in the most precious coil of his past, he found solace.

• • •

The story always began the same way, in the canyons. Ranju couldn't have remembered this period, for he had been but a bundled baby. But his mother, Ne Ahs Jah, had passed the tale to him, and he remembered every word.

Ne Ahs Jah had been young when she'd borne him—little more than fifteen and still possessing the supple face of a child. But her eyes brimmed with the wisdom of an older soul. For this reason, she was named after the owl.

Her tribesmen embraced Ne Ahs Jah despite her oddness. Because they lived at the base of stark, merciless cliffs, they had forgiveness flowing through their veins. They never reprimanded the girl when she disappeared for weeks on end, leaving no explanation either before her departure or after. Some day, they knew, the girl would not return at all. She had a wandering spirit, one not easily sated, not even by the gorgeous blue-green waterfalls of nearby Havasu Canyon.

It was in these waters that her people suspected Ne Ahs Jah had found her husband. The plunging falls culminated in a deep gorge that whirled with dark green tentacles. Any girl who dared swim where raining water met churning basin would be swept into an underworld, the water spirit's lair. There was no way to resist him: his ice-tipped stare, his beaded skin, the plush reach of his fingers.

No one knew for sure if this seduction had been Ne Ahs Jah's fate. But one journey, she left a girl and came back a woman: her womb swollen and her eyes even more worldly. She named her child "Ranju," a name the tribesmen had never heard, a magical name that gave them more reason to believe the father was a spirit.

Ne Ahs Jah left the tribe mere days after Ranju was born. For many moons after, mother and child stayed in the desert, making their home among the stratified rock and sand. As Ranju grew into boyhood, Ne Ahs Jah showed him the animals that inhabited their barren landscape: the green toad, the jewel wasp, the sandfish, the scorpion. Much could be learned from these animals. Like the king snake, Ranju learned how to store food in his body over long periods of time so he would never go hungry. Like the tortoise, he moved very slowly, never exerting too much energy, for energy was the most precious commodity in the desert—more precious than even water. He grew the hard skin of a desert locust, which repelled the sun. He rested during the day and hunted at night, when cold currents rippled through the air.

Ne Ahs Jah and her son ate whatever they could. Among the dunes, they found ground beetles and mice. Ranju watched Ne Ahs Jah sink her fingernails into the waxy skin of the cactus to extract water, which they stored in a bag sewn of snakeskin. Ranju never remembered being thirsty. In fact, he never remembered wanting for anything at all. But his mother said they must leave: the humans had found a permanent watercourse and now they were encroaching.

They fled not to another part of the desert, but to a place Ranju had never seen before: the prairies. In the mixed grasses, some of which climbed well above Ranju's head, he saw animals quite unlike desert life: swift animals called elk, cunning animals called wolves, long-eared animals called hares.

When Ranju had grown nearly as tall as Ne Ahs Jah, she taught him a secret. Imitating the animals was not all he was capable of. He had a gift, his mother told him, a gift no human had. He understood the animals as no human could. And he could live in their world, as one of them, if he chose.

At this utterance Ne Ahs Jah seemed to vanish, not all at once, but part by part, her body changing to dust, then fluttering to the ground. In the grasses where she had been standing sat a grasshopper. The insect appeared unafraid of him and Ranju knelt down for a closer look. In its yellow eyes, in the angle of its haunches, Ranju saw his mother, not as a single creature, but as something more vast. He was curious, not afraid, and he stroked the grasshopper with a tremulous touch.

In an instant Ranju became charm-bound, entranced, and in authority of something he had always had, but didn't know about until now. He closed his eyes, watched as rain pelted the earth of his mind, and when he looked again at the world, everything had changed.

Ne Ahs Jah returned to human form and she taught him her trick: how to concentrate outward until the body becomes a sheath: transparent and insubstantial. As Ranju followed her instructions, he learned that his gift wasn't as strong as his mother's. While Ne Ahs Jah's power came as naturally to her as breathing, Ranju had to fight for command. His gift was diluted, thinned by the confluence of his parents' bloodstreams.

"Your father isn't a trickster," his mother said, in explanation of her son's difficulty. "I should never have taken him, but I couldn't resist."

Ranju struggled to achieve his mother's mastery. But he was never as fluid as she, and never as pure.

Fortunately, just at the time when youthful idealism converts into resentment, Ne Ahs Jah announced they must move again. The humans were encroaching as before. This time, they were seizing the prairies: turning over the grasses with their plows, releasing in vast numbers the voracious animals called cattle, pitching stakes as claim to the land.

Ne Ahs Jah and her son traveled to the swamps, where the earth was as sodden as the desert was dry. The intense sunlight Ranju had grown accustomed to was blotted out by a thick overgrowth: trees and creepers that crawled over both the sky and each other.

After the expanse of the desert and the still of the prairie, Ranju fought to adjust to this gloomy, macabre world, where the air continually buzzed with the sounds of dragonflies, mosquitoes, gnats, and katydids. He felt nervous among the cyprus trees, which rose from the earth like mossy ghosts. The animals that roamed this place were different as well: shiny-skinned frogs and salamanders, snakes that slithered beneath the water, turtles with snapping teeth and spiny shells, alligators that were nothing short of dragons, masked raccoons, and opossums that stowed their babies in pouched bellies. Ne Ahs Jah showed her son how to catch jackfish, but the creatures always slipped out of his hands, leaving an oily trace. Ranju was amazed by the way they leapt out of the water, almost as if to mock him, then slid quietly back through the surface.

Of all the swamp's creatures, though, none was so astounding to Ranju as the bear. He became so enamored of this lumbering being with its thick, wooly coat that he followed it for days as it hunted for grubs along the pine-covered islands that dotted the swamp. Ne Ahs Jah let her son roam freely, for she saw in his eyes what had once gleamed in her own: a thirst for independence at any cost.

Maternal sympathy wasn't the only reason for her disregard, however. The swamp inspired trepidation in Ranju, but in Ne Ahs Jah it inspired nostalgia. Its lakes and pools, the moisture that clung to the vegetation, the droplets slick along the feathers of the anhingas—all reminded her of her husband. She missed the water spirit's touch, the rush of the falls around her body. And even though she thought she could leave the desert forever, she suddenly found herself longing for Havasu Canyon, where he was waiting for her to come home again.

When Ranju found the human girl, huddled between two bear cubs, in a swamp nest that served as the brown bear's den, Ne Ahs Jah believed it was a sign. The feral child, no older than three years, would be Ranju's companion. She would fill the void that Ne Ahs Jah herself would leave when she returned to her husband.

"But won't it behave like a human?" Ranju asked. As he stared at the girl, he remembered the many times he and his mother had moved for the express purpose of avoiding such creatures.

Ne Ahs Jah wondered about this too. She changed herself into a warbler so that she could perch above the clan of bears and observe them without their knowing. What she saw quelled her worry. The human girl mimicked her mother's ways. She was strong, self-sufficient, short-tempered, volatile. But had she evaded her true nature? Ne Ahs Jah did not know, nor would she be able to know for many years to come.

"Will she stay with me when she's grown?" Ranju asked.

Ne Ahs Jah did not know this either. Desperate to tell her son something certain, something indisputable, she told him about her decision to leave. The words tumbled out, but Ranju was not startled, only resigned. He had been waiting for this day, knowing that their paths were not the same. He believed they would meet again, although where, and in what form, was for the spirits to decide.

For many nights after Ne Ahs Jah had left him, Ranju felt a chilly presence wrap around his skin. He ground his teeth, tucked away in the shell of a fallen tree. Sleep eluded him, but when he could seize it, his dreams were dark, frightening, and above all, lonely.

Ne Ahs Jah had told him not to approach the human child until she was grown and beyond the care of her mother. He heeded her admonishment, but continued to follow the clan of bears in secret. Always out of view, in one form or another, Ranju watched the girl.

She was a true child of the swamp: calm brown waters one moment, a snapping of alligator's jaws the next. Placid, then a splash in the water, an unexpected snarl. She grew quickly, like everything else in the swamp, where life was a constant struggle to stay above the dense horizon of vegetation, to claim a patch of sunlight, and thus, a chance at survival. She seemed all arms and legs, gangly, but tough too, the soles of her feet like reptile skin. She had long scars on her torso, where she had sliced herself running through razor-rough grasses. Alligators had claimed two of her toes, but she remained steely. The creatures, in turn, were fearful of her, for she was fast, unpredictable, and above all, unfamiliar.

Seasons passed. Ranju watched his own reflection in the swamp water. This revealed a different person: thick-browed and angular, all shreds of youthfulness gone. From a distance, he could see that the human had changed too. For many years she had stayed with her mother, even when the other cubs had fled. The two had shared a curious symbiosis until the day the mother abruptly cut her loose, swatting a paw when the girl came within range of her hunting grounds.

On her own, the human was nervous. She slept in fits and starts, screeching occasionally through the early morning din of bird song. She killed more than she could eat, burying the remains where they could be retrieved again. But her memory was poor and she never dug up the same plot twice. When she foraged for food, she moved on all fours. But when she ate, she stood erect, the better to see approaching enemies. Her skin was a mass of colors: crimson and violet from the juice stain of berries, white scars, black where she had rubbed mud to keep the insects at bay, indigo eyes like the prairie sky at dusk.

She spoke to herself in a language that was foreign, if not gibberish, and Ranju knew not what she was saying. When she laughed, her large, crooked teeth transformed her whole face. Her hair, long to her hips, was snarled, matted. The individual strands, clustered into clumps, resembled patches of fur, almost a bear's hide. Her long fingernails almost a bear's claws. She hunted like a bear too, mastering a certain radius but never straying beyond. Ranju stayed outside her periphery, watching, waiting, wondering when to make himself known.

He knew it was time when her body took on the luminous shape of a woman.

He hadn't meant for the taking to be rough. But that's what happened. That day he transformed himself into a male bear: enormous and powerful. Then he crept up close, closer than he'd ever been before. When she caught sight of him, she roared in distress, charged him on all fours. Undaunted, he scooped her up with his paws and carried her away. The girl clawed at him, tore him with her teeth. He did not try to stop her. He just ran, ran until his body quivered, then he set her down upon a patch of dried twigs and horsetails.

In his haste he hadn't noticed he had harmed her. One of his claws had scraped her arm, creating a crescent-shaped wound that was bloodless, but nonetheless deep. The human, distraught not by the gash but by the abduction, cried out in her mystical tongue. For whom, Ranju couldn't know.

He tried to quiet her by patting her head, but she would not be subdued. Hours later she was still screaming. It was only when evening's darkness squelched the swamp's already thin light that she, exhausted by her own cries, fell into a deep sleep. As she dreamed, Ranju transformed into a human again and applied the pulverized bark of the swamp willow to her wound. Ne Ahs Jah had taught him that this would sooth torn flesh, and Ranju hoped, the hard heart too.

All night long he watched her, increasingly fascinated by her breathing, quick and ragged, the mad whorls of her hair, the many shades of her skin. By sunrise, he knew two things: that he loved her and that she was too wild to live.

The girl awoke more puzzled than angry. Ranju appeared no longer as a bear, and thus, was a brand new creature to her. Seeing her own kind for the first time, she took a savage turn, boring her teeth into his shoulder. Then she fell on top of him, a furor of flying hair and bare energy. Ranju grew hard beneath her. He coiled his arms around her, felt the brush of her breasts. She bit his lower lip, drawing blood. There was a pause, then she turned tender. She kissed his face with a curious mouth, tasted him with a darting tongue. When Ranju finally entered her, he was reminded of the jackfish, that wily creature he could never hold onto, and indeed, was lucky simply to see.

• • •

Once they had become lovers, it didn't take long for her belly to grow with the makings of a child. Anxiously, Ranju set about building a nest. He cleared away a circle of brush until there was nothing but dirt, then gathered pine needles and twigs, bits of leaves, feathers, rounded pebbles, pats of moss, the bric-a-brac of the swamp.

The rounder her belly swelled, the more sluggish she became. Quite soon, she was too tired to fetch her own food. Ranju hunted for the both of them. Worriedly, he stayed near the nest, for he knew the girl, in her dull state, was vulnerable to predators.

They grew closer. They learned to talk to each other in a language comprised of signals: the flickering of eyes, clapping of hands, sucking of teeth. Ranju knew that he wouldn't have stood a chance with her if not for their child. Surely by now her interest would have faded. Her wild ways would have beckoned her toward other things. But the child had soaked up her blood, paling her face. It had siphoned off her energy too.

Listless, she came to depend on Ranju, and this dependency, he believed, resembled affection.

When the day came for their child to emerge, the human's native passion returned with a vengeance. Her screams could be heard from the farthest reaches of the swamp. The hole between her legs had burst open, releasing blood, so much Ranju couldn't believe. Dark, briny old blood and new blood too: radiant as a robin's breast. He spoke to her gently, hands on her hipbones to keep her body still, but she writhed in pain. Ranju kept waiting for the baby to find its way through the tunnel of her body. But night fell, and then morning shone again, and still, the blood flowed.

Her screaming had subsided, replaced by grim moans. Ranju had tried to clean the blood as best he could, wiping it away with grass and leaves. But the smell remained, and it was pungent enough to draw the panthers. Several times Ranju transformed himself into a bear to ward them away. When the second day had passed, the stench mingled with traces of death. She hadn't opened her eye since dawn. Her breathing was haggard, frightening. Ranju had no idea what to do except sit by her side in the center of the nest. Sometimes he brought her water to drink in the long stalks of pitcher plants, sometimes he poured it on her hot brow. But she did not come to, and Ranju understood that this ring he had built around them could not ward away the spirits' wishes.

On the third day, the baby arrived: a girl, tiny and sickly. At the same moment that her soul found its way into the world, her mother's found its way out. This collision of life and death was met by a scream so penetrating that the swamp went still. Ranju couldn't be sure who had uttered it: mother or child. He knew only that he wanted to flee, to mourn alone, but the baby would not allow such vanities.

She'll never make it here, Ranju realized. She shares none of her parents' magic: my gift of shape-shifting or her mother's force. Sooner or later, she would need to return to her own kind.

This fact burdened Ranju, who could have lived his remaining days in the swamp. He had spent so much time fleeing the humans—first leaving the desert, then the prairies—that following them seemed unthinkable.

His frustration ran high, but his concern for the child, the only living reminder of her mother, overrode it somehow. He made the decision to leave. They would go at once, for if they delayed, he would never again conjure the will. Just one task remained before father and daughter departed.

He carried his baby's mother to a place where the swamp water ran deepest. Cautiously, he lowered her onto the surface. There she remained, floating for several moments. When finally she dipped, Ranju closed his eyes. In his mind's eye, he saw the jackfish encircle her, leading her in a spinning silver spiral from one realm to the next.

• CHAPTER NINE •

The morning after his encounter with Ranju, Lor joined Stan in cleaning the elephant cars. Lor couldn't believe how messy these obese gray animals were. Their stench was overwhelming, so much so that he tied a handkerchief around his face, bandit-style, to keep from inhaling the fumes. And then there was the matter of their excrement. Pieces as large as bricks. Lor and Fat Stan swept them up with brooms and specially designed scooper tools. By the time they were done, Lor felt nauseous.

"Why can't the bullmen handle this?" he complained.

"You remember what I said about rank?" Stan asked.

"Yeah."

"Well, the bull handlers are higher than we are. They get to do the fun work: feeding the elephants, bathing them, grooming them. We—you and I—get to pick up their shit."

"Wonderful."

"Hey now, it wasn't so long ago that you were unemployed," Stan reminded him.

Lor was busy thinking up a retort when the same emerald-eyed man who had summoned him in the cookhouse the night before appeared again. Lor was beginning to realize that the fellow held several different jobs, the primary one being Mr. Barnacle's henchman.

"Lor," he announced.

"That's right," Lor responded.

"Mr. Barnacle requests that you stop your regular duties at noon today and report to the big top, where the Weitzmans are rehearsing."

Fat Stan's eyes bulged in wonder.

"Just like that?" Lor asked.

"Just like that," the man responded, then turned on his heels and walked away.

"How do *you* know the Weitzmans?" Stan wondered aloud.

"I haven't even met the Weitzmans."

"Then why would they invite you to rehearsal?"

"I don't know," Lor lied.

He had taken his meeting with Mr. Barnacle to heart. As requested, he would lie low. He wouldn't arouse the suspicion of the roustabouts. No use giving them reason to think he was privileged. Legman Jack didn't need another excuse to hate him.

Stan let the matter drop and the two men resumed their work. Lor marveled at how much needed to be done. Before joining the circus, he'd taken Bringlebright's preparations for granted. Now he saw the time and muscle that went into building a canvas city.

Lor learned that the Boss Canvasman organized the layout of each lot weeks in advance. This was no easy task. In addition to the big top, there were two dozen other tents of various shape, size, and purpose to consider. Each one had to comply with varying codes and ordinances.

Here in Boston, Lor had helped erect the souvenir and concession tents, the tents for the freaks' Pit Show, the little top and sideshow, the menagerie with its exotic animals, and finally, the big top itself. And there was more. Beyond the big top, in the back yard, Lor and the roustabouts raised tents reserved for the cast and crew: the cookhouse, a dressing room for the regular performers, private wardrobe tents for the center attraction stars, a baggage-stock tent for the working horses, a ring-stock tent for the performing horses. Finally, they erected the clown tent, Clown Alley, where the joeys spent hours applying their faces.

The work was never-ending, for even when the tops were erected, the roustabouts needed to sort out the provisions. They strung bannerlines, hauled ticket boxes and bally platforms, drove seat wagons in place, installed wires, steel bars, platforms, and other trapeze equipment. By noon, Lor was exhausted. As he trudged toward the big top, he wondered grimly if Sebastian Weitzman would ask him to rig a wire. He wasn't sure he had the strength.

Once inside, he recognized Sebastian Weitzman's entourage, and by default, Sebastian Weitzman, immediately. They were hard to miss. The men were blond and husky and spoke a bristly, broken English. The women—save for one—were lean, long-legged, and yellow-tressed. The exception was a heavyset girl who served as the "bottom man": catapulting her smaller sisters onto the wire.

"Zat you, Mr. Cole?" came a voice from the assembly.

"It is," Lor replied, straining his neck to see the commentator.

An older man with a jaw so square it seemed made by a cookie-cutter stepped into view. "Et es I," the man revealed, "za great Sebastian Weitzman."

Lor bowed slightly, trying to hide a smirk.

"You not zat dirty, not like za ringmaster say," Weitzman continued, stepping away from his family and closer to the young roustabout. He swiped Lor's arm with his finger, as someone might test for dust on a table. "Es very important—cleanliness. The audience like glamour, sophistication, no lice."

Weitzman snickered, evidently aware of his strange brand of humor. "Zis es my lovely wife, Fifi," he continued.

A more wrinkled version of the blond girls stepped into view. Despite her severe haircut and the heavy liner around her eyes, Lor thought her attractive.

"And siz es za rest of my family. Too many to name!" Weitzman laughed again. "Za ringmaster say you a viz on za rope, zat I never see anything like you. I no believe him. I need to see myself."

"I appreciate that, sir."

"Good, zen less go!"

Lor's eyes opened in delighted surprise.

The world Sebastian Weitzman introduced him to was a wondrous, airborne one, for underneath the panorama of the big top, little took place on the ground. Here, members of the Weitzman family—sisters, brothers, daughters, sons, aunts, uncles, second cousins, and in-laws—pirouetted through the sky, their feet barely touching the wire, as if gliding on secret wings.

Lor quickly noticed how beautifully the Weitzmans functioned together. Like parts of a well-oiled machine, each person had his or her role—and stuck to it. Inga, the catapulter, sprung her sinewy peers onto the practice-wire with meticulous gusto. The men performed two functions. They executed the trickier routines, those that required on-wire somersaults, blindfolds, and multi-person formations. They also served as pure muscle-power: throwing, catching, and twirling the girls, who could balance with well-practiced ease on a shoulder, a head, even a fingertip.

The Weitzmans resembled each other to a degree that astonished Lor. It was as if each had been cast from the same mold, then painted from identical pots of paint: honey-gold, ivory, peach-pink. That the Weitzmans wore matching costumes only added to their singular identity. And it was a long time before Lor could tell Gretchen apart from Hanna and Bärbel apart from Elsa.

Was it his talent or his newness, Lor wondered, that aided his popularity among these pale statuettes? Lor didn't know, but before long he became a family favorite. The girls flirted. The boys caroused. Even Sebastian Weitzman embraced Lor with a special fondness.

In the weeks that followed, Lor learned much about the family's history. He learned that the Weitzman troupe was not static. Members changed over the years. Children grew up, got married, and left the clan. Older members retired early—usually around age thirty. But the head of the Weitzman family, Sebastian, always remained.

Sebastian prided himself on showmanship. He carefully coordinated each performance, utilizing sketches and diagrams for the more complicated routines. He also liked to talk, especially about the mechanics of wire-walking. The first thing Lor learned was that tight ropes didn't exist—at least not at Bringlebright.

"'Tight rope'—es old term," Sebastian informed him. "We no use rope for many years now. Use cable. Steel vire, steel rigging, everyzing steel."

The second thing Lor learned was that there were many different types of wire acts, each requiring different abilities and equipment. There was the low-wire, with the cable set six feet above the arena floor and strung between pieces of triangular framework. There was the slack-wire, similar to the low-wire, but loose rather than tight, allowing for comical sway. Finally, there was Lor's childhood specialty: balancing treacherous distances in the outdoors. This was called sky-walking. But the Weitzmans' domain, the high-wire, was by far the most sublime of the wire acts. Thirty feet in length, forty feet above the ground, the high-wire also had the reputation of being the most terrifying.

The more Lor learned about Sebastian Weitzman and the history of his show, the more intrigued he became. Through Sebastian's tendency to wax nostalgic, Lor understood that he and Fifi had first made their start as sky-walkers. They had mastered ballparks, stadiums, gorges, and canyons. Then they started having children and decided that more people crossing shorter distances was just as thrilling as fewer people crossing longer ones.

Gradually, Sebastian allowed Lor to display his own agility on the wire. He seemed genuinely happy with Lor's progress, responding to Lor the way a teacher does to his most promising pupil. Yet he was slow to show Lor his new routines. And when he did, Lor had to hide his disappointment. Sebastian's designs were mostly elaborations on old ideas.

Lor began to see why Barnacle had cooled toward Weitzman, why he feared Bringlebright would soon cease to be a viable player in the circus world. Weitzman was a man of repetition, not innovation. He would rather perform the simplest act perfectly than the hardest act imperfectly. Instinctively, Lor knew Sebastian's approach to be flawed. Having seen Bringlebright shows as a child, Lor had himself been a part of audience response. He remembered how the crowd had cheered most wildly for the dangerous routines. Fans cared little if a routine was completed, as long as it was grand. Indeed, Lor remembered standing ovations not for the performer who had achieved greatness, but for the one who had fallen in the attempt.

Of course, Weitzman placed a high premium on safety for a reason. Lor had heard the story many times now. It was whispered among the golden boys, murmured among the blushing girls. They called it only *the accident*. But of the many accidents that marred the trail of the Weitzman family's success, there was only one on everybody's mind, only one that stuck in their throats.

It had happened years ago, during the first public performance of "the human skyscraper." The Weitzmans had rehearsed the routine a thousand times. Still, when the roar of the audience dulled to a hush and Mr. Barnacle announced the act, disaster was already imminent. Audience members who were there swore they sensed danger in the air—like the smell of an approaching storm.

On the wire, two Weitzman girls, Lavinia and Edda, stood on a pole supported by the shoulder-harnesses of two men, Bruno and Waldo, who also stood on a pole held by a bottom layer of men, Eloy and Andreas. All six people carried balancing poles in their hands.

Three layers high, two persons to a layer, the skyscraper formation held stable for several moments. Then Eloy wobbled.

He struggled to regain his balance, but eventually slipped. As the pole he and Andreas supported gave way, Bruno and Waldo also tumbled. Miraculously, Eloy and Andreas managed to catch Waldo between their legs as they clutched the wire with their bare hands. They waited for the ground crew to create an improvised net below, then dropped him to safety.

Lavinia was also able to grab hold of the wire. Her hands cut and bloody from the catch, she screamed as her husband, Bruno, plummeted to the hard, earthen ground.

Bruno didn't live. Nor did Edda, who broke her spine. While the others recovered quickly and stayed with the circus, Lavinia fled and ceased corresponding with her family. Some say she took her life years later, but no one knows for sure.

Ever since *the accident*, Sebastian had become fanatical about using safety nets. Lor couldn't blame his boss for wanting security. But audiences delighted in thrills, not caution. Keeping this in mind, Lor designed a high-risk routine free of nets. Gathering his courage, he presented it to Mr. Weitzman. But the old man recoiled.

"Now not ze time for crazy ideas. Now time for performing what ve know. Vait till vinter. Vait till Sarasoda."

But Lor couldn't wait for the slow winter months in Sarasota, Florida, when Bringlebright jumped off the traveling circuit and prepared for the next year's show. By now the young wire-walker had entirely dismissed Stan's warnings of abiding by the hierarchy. In fact, Lor believed he was the perfect person to slip-slide around the rules. Hadn't he already done so for months, practicing under the big top while the rest of the roustabouts collected bull dung and dismantled tents? Lor felt proud that his schedule now revolved around the high-wire. He performed typical roustabout duties only during arrival to large cities, when the vast amount of preparation called for every hand on deck. The roustabouts, especially Legman, snarled at this arrangement. But the higher authorities didn't mind it, which was all that mattered to Lor.

In response to Sebastian's rejection, he decided to seek out Barnacle personally. Lor met him in the cookhouse.

"Pardon me, sir," Lor whispered. "I'm sorry to bother you at dinner."

"Sit down, son," Mr. Barnacle responded, motioning for Mrs. Barnacle to move over and make room for their guest.

Lor looked around briefly before he seated himself. He seldom saw the action on this side of the curtain. He noted with fleeting interest that Cirella sat at a nearby table. She met his gaze playfully, before turning her attention back to the gentlemen who flanked her on all sides.

"It's just that," Lor began, "I've tried to introduce new ideas—exciting ideas—to Mr. Weitzman, as you suggested. But he hasn't taken to them. I can't improve the high-wire routines if he won't hear me out."

With well-manicured hands and sterling silver utensils, Barnacle cut a small piece of fish. He chewed thoughtfully, silently, for several moments.

"Son," he began, "I see your point. I surely do. But these things take time, and dare I say, a touch of subtlety. Subtlety, Lor, is something every man must learn. For women, it comes naturally. Take my wife, for example."

The ringmaster glanced at Mrs. Barnacle, who seemed unaware of anything but the pages of the novel she was reading. "She's the pure, crystalline definition of tact. That's why I married her. She knows how to finesse and finagle. Her touch is delicate, never pushy. You hear what I'm saying?"

"Not exactly, sir."

"What I'm saying, Lor, is that the circus is full of headstrong men. And when one headstrong man demands something from another headstrong man, trouble is sure to follow. One of these men must bend. It is the better man, I don't mind saying, who uses subtlety, not force, to get what he wants. The power of suggestion, boy, is the strongest force of all." At this, Mr. Barnacle lowered his voice dramatically, "outside of feminine wiles!"

"I'm beginning to see your point, sir."

"Now, all this doesn't mean I'm unwilling to help you. I agree that Sebastian may need a bit of motivation—maybe even a kick in the rear. And I haven't forgotten that you're the man to give his tired program a bit of life. However," Barnacle emphasized, "if I do this favor for you, you must do one for me."

"What's that, Mr. Barnacle?"

"Stay away from the Weitzman girls," the ringmaster declared matter-of-factly, as he stabbed an asparagus spear with his fork. Quietly, from her station, Mrs. Barnacle coughed in dismay.

Lor swallowed hard.

"Pardon?"

"You heard me, son. I see the way they congregate around you. I haven't seen such a flurry of female frenzy since I was a young man."

Mrs. Barnacle coughed again, a little louder.

"Don't think Sebastian hasn't noticed too," the ringmaster continued. "He has a keen eye, even if he is getting on in years. Tell me, would *you* listen to a man who's trying to bang your daughters?"

Lor was impressed by Barnacle's powers of observation. In truth, his cavorting with the Weitzman girls hadn't led to anything more than quick kisses in the big top after dark. That enormous tent, with its secret spaces and echoes and ghost audience, could inspire passion in even the fainthearted.

"No, I suppose not," he admitted.

"That's right, son. Now, Lor, there's one more thing I need to speak with you about—and that's permission. There are some things you ask permission for, but stardom isn't one of them. Stardom is something you take, you understand?"

Lor nodded. He had no further questions.

• • •

Each week, on Sunday afternoons, the Weitzmans held a meeting in the big top. The purpose was three-fold: Sebastian wanted his clan to offer suggestions for improving the routines, to air grievances, and most importantly, to bond as a family.

The Sunday following his talk with Barnacle, Lor came to the meeting equipped with zeal, diplomacy, and the most essential ingredient, tact. He had vowed to himself that he wouldn't demand a thing. If he wanted something, he would ask for it, politely and gently. And if nothing came of his request, he would do what he needed to do.

Stardom is something you take, you understand?

First on the agenda, Sebastian asked—as he always did—if anybody knew of ways to improve the routines.

Lor immediately suggested that they lengthen the high-wire to fifty feet. It would, he suggested, shock the audience and bolster ticket sales.

"No," dismissed Weitzman harshly. "Zat es impossible. Too dangerous. Much too dangerous."

But Lor would not be so easily rebuffed.

"I'll be the first to test it," he prodded. "That way, if anybody gets hurt, it'll be me. Think about it, Mr. Weitzman. Think how excited the audience will be seeing someone from *your* troupe setting a new record on the wire! Think how much respect and admiration you'll receive, for we all know, you're the mastermind behind every routine."

For a moment it seemed as if Sebastian would again squash Lor's idea. Then he reconsidered.

"You can make ze extra practice?"

"Yes, sir. I most certainly can."

"All right. Ve see."

Several family members, including Fifi, exchanged shocked glances.

After Sebastian granted his consent to the fifty-foot walk—and noticed a marked spike in fan support—he became decidedly more lax, even allowing Lor to take the floor regularly at the weekly meetings.

"What if I rode a bicycle on the wire?" Lor asked on another Sunday.

"Are you crazy?" Sebastian responded.

"A little—but let's try it anyway."

The Weitzmans weren't without apparatus on the wire—balloons, trays of glasses, chairs, even a flaming torch. But Lor upped the ante, requesting props of such absurd proportion and peril that the audience gasped. Bicycles, wheelbarrows, fifteen-foot ladders, even a hollow piano—nothing was too outrageous.

Sebastian wasn't thrilled about relinquishing his power to the young outsider. But he couldn't deny audience reaction either. Once partly empty, the big top now brimmed over with Weitzman fans, each eager to witness the next daredevil routine. With this wave of admiration, Sebastian's strict doctrine began to change. His ban on new routines during the work season melted away. Day by day, Sebastian turned his trust over to the one member of his troupe who had no claim to his blood. He came to depend on Lor, not just for his clever proposals, but also for his business sense. Lor seemed always to have his finger on the pulse of the fans, something Weitzman himself had never taken accurately.

But there was another reason Sebastian trusted Lor's judgment: the new performer was improving. Having decided to follow Barnacle's counsel, he had ceased socializing with Weitzman's bevy of beauties. This left more room in his schedule. Now that his nights were free, Lor took advantage of the empty big top for a wholly different purpose: rehearsal.

He had been working on something new—something tremendous. Lor ached to tell someone of his brainchild, which he was convinced would forever bolster Bringlebright's reputation, or at least his own. But disclosure was dangerous, so he channeled his mounting excitement into practice.

Each night, before attempting the new routine, Lor completed two hour's worth of sit-ups, push-ups, and stretching exercises. Then he climbed onto the wire. Alone, Lor seldom faltered. However, his grand idea called for him to haul weight—the weight of a small person. He began to balance with an enormous 80-pound bag of flour flung over his shoulder. The sack had mysteriously disappeared from the train's foodstuffs car weeks before, but the cookhouse manager had attributed the theft to hungry gillies.

As he rehearsed, Lor pondered whom he should choose to accompany him on the wire. The girl would have to be compact, but this fact did little to limit his selection. Most of the Weitzmans barely tipped the scales. In the end, Lor decided that he would use Katarina, one of Sebastian's many nieces. The girl was only eleven, and therefore undeveloped in ways womanly and tempting. With a child, Lor wouldn't have to worry about his attention wandering.

May 3, 1923, was a date he hoped he would always remember.

He was to perform in the afternoon show. Since the inception of the lengthened wire, many of the Weitzmans had grown accustomed to its difficulty, and indeed, accepted the change as an improvement. That Lor, Katarina, and another Weitzman fellow would all perform on the fifty-foot wire was not unusual. The trio had already rehearsed the routine dozens of times. What was remarkable was that Lor had convinced Sebastian to remove the safety net.

"*Nein*!" Weitzman had declared at first. But gradually he'd conceded, unable to argue against Lor's flawless track record.

"Be careful," he'd said finally. "Because Katarina—za girl es young."

Sebastian had dressed Katarina in a white leotard and white bloomers. He was anxious for the audience to notice her youth. And indeed, they did. A deep, panicked silence fell when the slip of a girl stepped onto the wire. Gracefully, she tiptoed toward the men, who stood together at the center of the wire, back to back, holding above their heads a pole where she was meant to perch.

Katarina moved carefully, her mouth pursed in concentration. Upon reaching her partners, she stepped onto the back of Lor's muscled calf, in an attempt to leverage herself onto his shoulders, then onto the pole. But she never made it that far.

Ever so slightly, almost undetectably, Lor had shifted his weight, corrupting the frail balance the trio had created. Lor's feet were still curved around the wire, as they should be. His grip on the pole overhead remained steady. But his movement had been enough to send the little girl sprawling. Her feet slid. Her arms waved wildly, searching for a grip, any grip. At the last possible moment, one of her hands made contact with Lor's ankle, which she clung to with all her might. The dangling doll let out a piercing cry.

Audience members climbed to their feet. From below, Sebastian Weitzman began to wheeze. His face went ashen. The grim scene reminded him too much of *the accident*. It had the same quality of suspended animation, a black moment captured in time, a photograph better left undeveloped. He averted his eyes, waiting for the inevitable screams of terror when Katarina could hold on no longer.

The lad working alongside Lor froze. But Lor knew exactly what to do. With the brave, sweeping gestures he had rehearsed, he regained his balance. Then he rocked back and forth, knowing that it would invoke more anxiety from the audience. Finally, he held steady, signaling to his partner that he was letting go of the pole overhead. In response, the man blinked, pupils dilated like black stars.

Ever so cautiously Lor crouched down and grabbed Katarina by her wrists. She cried out again, this time in relief. By now the audience dared to uncover their eyes. Even Sebastian peeked cautiously through a triangle of space between his fingers.

Lor lifted Katarina with ease, as he had so often lifted that sack of flour. She was slug-nutty from the trauma. He couldn't put her on the wire, so he carried her—her body flung cavalierly over his shoulder—back to the cable perch.

When Lor set Katarina down, the audience erupted: stamping their feet, whistling, screaming like banshees. Lor smiled proudly, waving with one hand and patting the little girl's head with the other. Weitzman smiled so wide, no one had to struggle to see the fillings in his teeth.

The dark, valiant man alongside the wisp of a girl created an indelible impression on Bringlebright's conscience, especially the ringmaster's. In that instant, Lor's value changed in his mind. Lor suddenly looked as gorgeous as a pile of money, a mountain of fresh green bills.

After the show, he hugged the performer tightly to his chest, whispered in his ear: "Son, I believe your time has arrived."

• • •

Barnacle was very happy. Ticket sales had gone up, way up, as much as thirty percent in some cities. The improvement could be attributed to any number of factors: a cleaner show, the addition of the Spanish Web act, Ranju, the ever-popular animal trainer. But if audience reaction were any indication of why Bringlebright was headed for the moon, Barnacle had only one man to thank: Lor Cole.

The gillies adored him. When Lor sauntered onto the wire, hips gyrating, pelvis a little too prominent in those tight, spangled leotards, the girls began to hyperventilate. The boys noticed the girls' reaction and stared at Lor a little longer, cheered a little louder, studied him harder than they'd ever studied their schoolbooks. The children, too, loved Lor, because he was a living, breathing, flesh-and-blood hero—reincarnated straight out of their storybooks.

But Barnacle, he loved Lor best. When he thought back to the day when that tattered soul had almost killed himself atop the train, he could feel his eyes well up. It was as if the Lord had dropped a money press straight into his lap.

Yes siree, the ringmaster knew a good thing when he saw it, which was why he ordered Katarina's near-fall be repeated every performance. Only now, old man Weitzman harnessed her to the wire with invisible cord and made her rehearse her screams.

At night, in the throes of success, the ringmaster liked to spend quality time with the official ledger of sales figures. He was jolly, alcohol always nearby and sometimes the redhead too. But more and more, he'd been keeping the company of men. It was safer: Mrs. Barnacle couldn't thrash him afterwards. Lor had joined the list of Barnacle's preferred comrades, although the young performer remained guarded, leery of the ringmaster's power and boisterous talk.

"We're standing at a crossroads, son," Barnacle told him one night, as the two lounged in his car and drank brandy. "And not just in terms of the circus. The world is changing before our very eyes—sometimes I wonder if I'm the only one who sees it."

"Are you talking about President Coolidge, sir?"

Lor was dressed formally in a new suit, but he relaxed his legs and tapped his feet to a popular new tune, "He May Be Your Man, But He Comes to See Me Sometimes," which played on the phonograph. Lor recognized the style: he'd heard it pouring from the clubs in Harlem.

"No, not that darn Republican. I'm talking about our way of life. My brother-in-law in Washington—I told you about him?—he works for the United States Patent Office, see? That's how my sister met him. She designed something called the 'Sour Twister.' A kitchen item for squeezing lemons. My family's full of inventors, I'm not ashamed to say. Anyhow, she took her Sour Twister to the Patent Office and the Sour Twister took her to the altar. She and an employee there—Herbert's his name—fell in love straight away. Care for more brandy?"

Lor lifted his empty glass to the neck of the flask.

"Anyhow, where was I?" the ringmaster asked, playing with his mustache.

"Love and the Sour Twister," Lor replied.

"Ah. Well, the point is, this Herbert fellow keeps me informed of all the new inventions coming out of the Patent Office. I'm fascinated, boy, when I think of the progress this country's made in the last thirty years. Why, we've had motion pictures, aspirin, plastic, airplanes, military tanks, even the radio. Not to mention the little stuff—the pop-up toaster, windshield wipers, crayons. The brassiere for heaven's sake. This is a fertile time for the minds of the American people, Lor. Don't you doubt it for a moment."

"I don't, sir."

"And no slowdown's in sight! Herbert says the patent applications keep rolling in—better and better inventions too. Things that are going to affect the way we sleep, breathe, walk. Heck, the way we chew our food! Herbert has to sign off on these applications. I've said to him, 'If you come across a sure thing, tell me first.' People have been known to invent the same thing at the same time. Then it's up to the patent office to determine the rightful owner. You understand my meaning, Lor?"

"Mr. Barnacle," Lor dared, "is that shrewd?"

The ringmaster shrugged. "Mark my words," he continued, "we'll see a lot of change in our lifetimes. You know what's next—what's going to get hot as blue blazes?"

"I don't, sir."

"Playing the stock market. Men are going to buys stocks, son, as if they were hotcakes. And not just big-time investors either. I'm talking about little men, fellas like you and me."

Lor had no idea what a stock was, but he nodded anyway and sipped his drink.

"The wealthiest men—Rockefeller, Carnegie, Vanderbilt—made their money the old-fashioned way, through hard work and grit and tangible resources: oil, iron, steel. But the new wealth, well, that's going to be a different story. Men will simply trade pieces of paper, buy and sell at the right time, to make a *fortune*."

Lor watched the ringmaster closely, gauging how much of his zeal was based on drink and how much was pure excitement. Lately, he'd been scrutinizing the ringmaster and selected others with almost maniacal dedication. He needed to know the precise chain of command at Bringlebright, not just the roustabouts' version. He needed to know who held the power and who craved it, who was feared and who could be made to fear. It was the only way to rise. His star was climbing, but he wouldn't be satisfied until it shone the brightest.

"How's about another drink, Lor? And what about a look at some of my pictures? My friend's a casting agent. He sends me proofs of up-and-coming starlets. Gorgeous girls—not much clothing on either."

"I'd like to, sir, but I think I'd better turn in."

Apologetically, Lor shook Barnacle's hand, then exited. The ringmaster let his light-hearted smile slip from his face. Alone, without company to distract him, he appeared like someone else: an old man. There were always moments like this one: moments between engagements when sadness drifted through him, brought on by nothing in particular, or maybe by everything. Everything that he thought about once the room had gone quiet.

Meticulously, he organized the items on his desk: cap on the ink bottle, ledger in the drawer, papers reshuffled and sorted into neat piles, brandy stowed into one of his many clandestine hide-aways. He looked at last at the desk's surface, a pressed leather plain. It was smooth, not at all like the sharp little teeth that chewed up his thoughts, reminding him that his chatter was but a slapdash attempt to keep out the fear. He hadn't done enough. Wasn't good enough. Was exactly what he'd always feared he'd become: a charlatan.

Deeply he sighed, glad that he had drunk enough to numb himself. In a moment, he would paste his smile back on and return to his wife. She would be cross, as usual. But he preferred her face, the stern predictable lines, the glowering gaze, to this desperation.

• CHAPTER TEN •

Lor had moved up in the world. He no longer shared a crum car with Legman and Stan. Instead, he occupied a private compartment, with its own set of shelves and even a rug for the floor. He no longer shared in the roustabouts' work, for at long last, he was an official member of the Weitzman troupe. He was, according to the pitchmen, Lor the Fabulous Wire-Walker.

Although Lor worked exclusively with the Weitzmans, he was also considered a solo performer. A Center Ring attraction. As such, he commanded star perks: his own wardrobe tent, expensive costumes, meals on the *other* side of the curtain. Of all the privileges, though, Lor liked his train compartment the most. He'd never had his own room. He and Woodrow had shared the same corner, and even the same cot, growing up. This small space, humble as it was and nothing like the decadently furnished quarters of the ringmaster, brought him great pride.

Having one's own space, Lor soon realized, also guaranteed freedom. Here, blessedly free of crass bunkmates, Lor could do whatever he pleased. Just now, he turned in circles until the room spun. Dizzy, he threw himself onto the bed. He smiled, waiting for the ceiling to still, realizing how proud Augusta would have been. He was on his way.

Without warning, someone rapped on the door.

"It's me," a voice announced.

"Me who?"

"Cirella."

Lor stood up, chuckled, then slid open the heavy metal door. He hadn't had much contact with the redhead, although he thought frequently of the role she'd played in getting him here. She was the ringmaster's dame and strictly off-limits—a shame since she was easily the best-looking girl around. The fact that she'd made off with his money no longer aroused his anger. Maybe he should have clung to his grudge, but these months of success had dulled its edge. Instead, when he remembered that incident in New York, he admired her grift.

"You know you shouldn't be here," Lor warned, voice stern but gaze soft.

"That's not so. Mr. Barnacle gave me permission."

"He gave you *permission*?"

"To work on my act," she clarified. She stood in the doorframe, Lor's arm blocking her way. "You gonna invite me in?"

"I suppose," he said, backing off.

Stepping inside, she ogled his room, consuming its details with that burning stare of hers. Before Lor could say anything, she had seated herself on his bunk. She kicked off her shoes, little embroidered Chinese slippers—the same kind the acrobats wore. Red lacquer dabs dotted each of her toenails.

"I heard about your promotion. It's the talk of the town."

"Really?" Lor asked, trying to hide his delight.

"Oh yes."

"Nice to know."

"It must be," Cirella replied, tilting back her head. Her neck stretched elegantly. "I've been promoted too," she announced. "I'm not as big a star as you, of course. But the ringmaster says I'm a good enough for the Center Ring. What do you make of that?"

"I saw it coming. Bringlebright couldn't ignore you for long."

Lor expected her to blush. Instead, her eyes met his with determination. The heat of her gaze—white-hot and volatile—irritated his skin, caused droplets of sweat to form on his forehead.

"You really told the ringmaster you were seeing me?" he prodded. "I don't believe he'd let you come."

"Mr. Barnacle doesn't control me."

"Mr. Barnacle controls everybody," Lor corrected.

Cirella smiled, swinging her long legs like a little girl. "You act like he's a god. He's just a man. An ordinary man, at that."

"Whatever he is, I count him as my friend."

"He might be a friend now, but he wasn't on your side before. When you pulled that stupid stunt on top the train, *I* was the one who insisted we stop. The ringmaster said it didn't matter if the ride killed you. Said it wouldn't matter, in times like these, if there was one less Negro around."

Lor licked his bottom lip. She was trouble, no question about it. "Why should I believe you? Don't you remember New York?"

"Oh that," she said, shrugging off the accusation. "You would've had to pay double what was in that pouch—if you'd stuck around for my services."

Lor had had enough. Cirella had ruined his mood. Moreover, she had made him doubt himself. He took her arm and hauled her off his bed, steering her toward the door.

She struggled against his grip. "Please, I'm not here to argue. I came for help with my act."

"Why should I help you?" he demanded, releasing his hold.

"Look, I may put up a good front, but I know my weaknesses. I don't have your kind of talent. I've got the ringmaster—for now. And I've got *this*." At the mention, she tugged a red ringlet, pulling it straight. "Don't you see? I need more."

Lor eyed her thoughtfully. She had more than she let on. Her luminosity, light-fingered touch, easy manipulations—these were assets at Bringlebright, for it was not always the most talented performer, but the most cunning, who succeeded. She knew what she was doing. And Lor knew to keep his distance. The trouble was, the longer he watched her, the less he cared about the warning signs.

"I wouldn't know what to do for you," he muttered.

"Sure you would. I just need some pointers. Someone to tell me right from left."

"I don't know."

"I wouldn't take much of your time."

"That's not what I'm worried about."

When she took a step closer, Lor had to turn away. So close, staring at her was like staring at the sun.

"What worries you?"

But Lor ignored her question. His only choice was to refuse her. Trouble was, his words tumbled out all wrong.

"If I help you, you have to understand it's as a favor—a favor to Barnacle," he replied. "I don't owe you a thing and I don't care what role you played in getting me here."

"Whatever you say."

He could feel his feet beginning to burn. He was standing on a pile of smoldering tanbark. And there was nothing to do except fan the flames.

"Don't expect me to be soft either. I'll tell it like it is, even if you don't want to hear it."

"Okay—I accept."

"You what?"

"I accept," she said, laughing.

Lor could scarcely believe what had just transpired, not even when Cirella rose on her tiptoes and planted a soft kiss on his lips.

"You and me, sweetheart," she told him. "We're gold dust twins, both of us wanting the same things. Goddamn, I just hope we get them."

• • •

"Watch and be amazed!" Lor shouted to an invisible audience. "Watch and be mystified! Ladies and gentleman, you've never seen anyone like her: Bringlebright's very own fire-eater. The only woman on earth who eats fire for breakfast. Red-hot pokers for lunch. The only woman who breathes smoke, not air. I introduce to you: Cirella the Fire Enchantress!"

Delighted, Cirella watched him speak into an imaginary megaphone. She clapped until her fingers tingled. The noise filled the empty space of the big top, climbing its deserted stands. A single spotlight broke the black interior. It plucked Cirella from the darkness.

Although there was no one around, Cirella rehearsed in full costume. She needed to see if any parts of her wardrobe—the drape of a neckline or the dangle of moonstone earrings—would interfere with her routine. Her hair posed the biggest liability. She wore it back, lest a stray flame ignite its Medusan masses.

Tonight, Cirella sported a simple black catsuit, snug and unadorned. Nevertheless, she wasn't safe. She couldn't be—not when she swigged kerosene and sucked on hot coals.

"Do I need to drink this stuff? It smells awful," she remarked, referring to a fire-resistant lotion concocted by Bringlebright's resident doctor, Lucy Loon. It was so promising that Mr. Barnacle joked, half-seriously, he wanted to market it to fire departments.

"Yes," Lor replied, "but gargle it first. Smear some on your lips too."

Lor was no expert in fire-eating. He had distilled all his knowledge from the ringmaster and the roustabouts. Although Cirella was the only fire-eater on the official roster, virtually all the performers knew something about the subject. As Fat Stan had remarked, "When you get a job here and you don't know nothing, they teach you fire. I'm not sure why. Maybe 'cause anybody can do it, but nobody *wants* to."

In truth, Cirella knew more about the craft than anyone. Like Lor, she'd been listening to the kinkers. She'd also been practicing. She knew she was lucky to have a Center Ring timeslot. Fire-eaters were normally bally performers, second-tier acts stuck in the sideshow, sometimes with the freaks. The true reason for her premiere billing had less to do with her affair with Barnacle and more to do with a simple, seedy fact she'd learned back in New York: People loved to watch beautiful women put things in their mouths.

"Should I lean like this?" she asked, bending so far back her long braid of hair touched the floor. She wobbled on high heels.

"Yes, but take your shoes off."

Barefooted, Cirella regained her balance. "Is this better?"

Lor nodded.

She picked up her torch: a metal rod with a thick wooden handle and two inches of cotton wicking around its tip. She'd spent weeks designing it. Before happening across a suitable model, she'd experimented with a dozen that had done her wrong. A rod without a handle burned her hand. Wool rags burned too sluggishly. Waxed thread around the batting dribbled off and seared her face. Copper wire scorched her mouth.

Fortunately, this torch was perfect. Cirella dipped the cotton batting into a vat of gasoline that Lor had siphoned off from a nearby circus vehicle. She waved the wand, shaking off the extra fluid. Then she took a match to the tip. A sunburst exploded.

"You ready?" Cirella teased.

"If you are," Lor replied.

Again, she bent back, until her head was level with the ground. Painstakingly, she held the torch at an angle perpendicular with the floor. She opened her mouth wide. The heat of the burning fuel singed her lashes. Quickly she inserted the torch tip, then closed her lips around the stem, but not too tightly. She had already learned the hard way that her lips could sizzle on the hot metal. The flame consumed the oxygen in her mouth. A moment later, it expired—snap!—like a cap from a bottle of pop. Cirella extracted the torch. She grinned, though her lungs ached.

"Attagirl!" Lor cheered, slipping his arm around her waist. "Remember not to take out the torch before the flame's finished," he reminded her. "Fat Stan told me that new air will revive the fire."

"I'm not a dumb Dora, Lor."

"No, you're not. But don't get smug. Your act is riskier than most."

"I'll be fine."

And she believed that. The interior of her mouth sported a mass of welts and oozing sores, yet she did not fear the torch. Nor did she think the fire would betray her. A certain alliance existed between them, girl and element, for both were wonders of nature: unpredictable, damaging, and glorious in their misconduct.

As Lor watched her swallow more flames, then a mouthful of boiling water colored gold to resemble oil, he deliberated on how the performance could be improved. It was astonishing to watch a woman like Cirella risk her life to entertain the audience. But every circus had a fire-eater.

The gillies would want more, something new. And Lor wanted to accommodate them.

"Are you good at balancing?" he asked.

"I . . . I suppose so. Never thought about it really."

"Here," Lor said, dragging the heel of his shoe through the dirt of the big top floor. "Walk on this line—but don't look down. Walk with your eyes straight."

She cocked her eyebrows, but followed orders.

"Good!" he congratulated. "Now do it again, but this time shut your eyes. Think—instinctively—where the line is under your feet."

Again, Cirella obliged her tutor.

"How was I?" she asked him.

"I've seen worse."

"That good? Gosh! What are you getting at with this balancing business?"

"I think," Lor said slowly, "I've found a way to make you a big name."

"Yeah?" she asked skeptically.

"How do you feel about heights?"

"Oh, I see what you're up to! You want to put me up there on the wire! No way. I've seen the way old man Weitzman operates. I get hot under the collar just thinking about it!"

Lor put his hands on her shoulders, which he was surprised to find trembling. "Listen to me. Hear me out."

"What about the low-wire? Why couldn't I walk the low-wire?"

"It wouldn't have the same effect—and you know it. The audience likes to see us defy death. Why do you think the ringmaster makes me repeat that episode with Katarina? By bringing your act to the high-wire, you'd be a double-threat: eating fire *and* defying gravity. The audience would go mad!"

"But I don't have any training."

"A few months ago, you didn't have any training in fire-eating either."

Cirella looked at him tentatively. The weight of his hands on her shoulders remained, a steadying force.

"Maybe. Maybe I'll try."

"You'll try?"

Cirella watched a smile find its way onto Lor's lips. It was a real smile, not the wide, forced one he used for the audience. It clarified his whole face. And in that moment he appeared so fresh, so vital, Cirella wished his reassuring touch were a full-fledged embrace.

A few weeks later she got her wish. She and Lor had just finished another rehearsal. He swiped a cotton candy from the stand, though the candy butchers would've given it to him free. It looked like a bouquet, white cone vase and pink sugar petals.

"For you, madam," he said, getting down on bended knee.

She giggled and sank her nose into its syrupy fragrance. When she came up for air, the sugar webs had tangled in her eyelashes. Lor tried to pluck them out. But they remained, so he kissed them away, tongue darting over her eyelids.

She grabbed his hand and they crept between two prop wagons. This shadowed crevice was a poor shield. But Cirella hardly noticed. Her back settled against the scratchy wood. She quivered as slivers pricked her skin. Her hand dropped. The remaining cotton candy fell, tumbling into the dirt. Lor tried to pick it up, but she stopped him. She moved his fingers to her lips, then down the fine slope of her chin. Lor's fingers kept moving, settling at the tiny well at the base of her throat.

She pulled him toward her, resting her ear to his chest. She believed his thumping heart had quickened for her.

Somebody hobbled by. It was Gus the train conductor, clutching a bottle and too drunk to notice anything. Lor and Cirella nevertheless huddled deeper in the blue-black of the wagons' cast. Although daylight would shine for several hours more, Cirella swore they'd stepped into dusk. She tried to catch her senses. But they arrowed up, lost in space. There was nothing she could do. The harder Lor's heart pounded, the more she wanted to see it: a brilliant red bird, feathers tufted, rare in this everyday jungle.

"I'd better go," Lor whispered, his hand slipping away.

She grabbed it back.

"Stay," she urged.

Inspired, he began to kiss the inside of her wrist. At the House of Delight Cirella's patrons had often complemented her on her arms. Long, lithe, and graceful as a dancer's. The white bows of a young birch. But lately she'd been wearing long sleeves, even at the edge of summer. The veins in her forearms had bobbed to the surface—bruised and clotted. Pushing back the cloth, Lor exposed them. She drew back, embarrassed.

"What's wrong?" he asked.

"Nothing."

But he knew. He'd watched her undress one day and seen the marks, like smashed plums.

"It's the toxins—from fire-eating."

"No," she replied.

"What then?"

"I don't know."

"It *is* the fire-eating," he insisted. "The smoke, the ash, the gasoline—you might as well be drinking poison."

"I don't know what you're talking about."

Cirella took a step back and found herself out of the shadow. Sunlight dappled her skin. It shone so nakedly. She shuddered, for she felt naked too. Then she realized it was only her arm, the ugly smudges apparent for all to see.

• • •

"You're a genius, Lor," Barnacle roared.

The two clinked glasses of aged Jamaican rum. Several months of work with Cirella had indeed paid off. Audiences were piling in to watch the routine. Lor had to admit, he was surprised. He had always acknowledged Cirella's allure, but he had doubted her deftness as a performer. It wasn't just her failing health. Her muscle tone and flexibility could never match those of the girls who had started training as children. Yet on the wire, she'd worked magic.

"I wasn't sure about it at first," the ringmaster continued. "Fire-eating on the wire? It sounded like something the devil himself would dream up. Weitzman didn't like it either."

"I know," Lor agreed. "It took some persuading. I'm learning German so I can better argue with him."

The ringmaster howled. "In the beginning, I wouldn't have paid a thin dime to see some broad play with fire forty feet up. But I gotta tell you, it's addictive. I cheer like I'm leather-lunged. And you—you my boy—are the mastermind behind her success."

"She's good. But I worry about her," Lor confessed.

"How's that?"

"She's hurting herself."

Tentatively, Lor revealed all he'd seen: the angry lesions, the bloody noses, the way she bit back the pain. Once, he told the ringmaster, she'd run to the edge of the big top and retched blood. Lor had carried her back to her train compartment. He'd forbidden her to work, but she'd returned to practice the very next morning.

"The rigors of her routine exhaust her," Lor continued.

"She's been avoiding me," the ringmaster admitted. "Now it makes sense."

Lor stiffened. Barnacle obviously didn't know she'd ended one affair only to start another. "It's not your fault, sir. The physical hardships—they're keeping her from a normal life."

"Ah, but who has a normal life here? It's the circus, for Christ's sake. It's a shame," Barnacle continued. "Cirella was a good girl. But I'm probably better off. Never in my thirty years of marriage has Mrs. Barnacle been so disgusted with my hanky-panky. She's taken to going on midnight strolls. If I didn't know better, I'd say she's philandering—to get back at me."

Thinking about Mrs. Barnacle's prudish demeanor, Lor nearly smiled. "I'm sure there's no need to worry."

"Let's hope so. With women, you never know."

"Getting back to Cirella," Lor ventured, "I believe she should take a break. Just for a few weeks, until she recovers."

Barnacle had been tossing peanuts into the air, catching them in his mouth. This last one, however, bopped off his nose. "Are you kidding? The girl's hotter than a Mexican tamale! Taking her off the wire would stop the momentum. It would ruin everything."

"But . . ."

"No if, ands, or buts!" Barnacle insisted.

Lor reached into the sack of peanuts on his boss's desk. He could argue no further. Already, he was treading on dangerous ground. Resignedly, he cracked a shell in half, thumbing the nuts from their mirror cavities. He told himself that all stars must wink out, no matter how bright they'd once shone. It was the way of circus life. But the sentiment didn't ease his mind.

• • •

Lor rolled off Cirella's bunk, yawning, eyelids rubbed open. Sleepily, he pulled on his trousers. He stretched his sinewy arms above his head, enjoying the faint pull of awakening muscles. He'd need to hurry. His rumbling belly told him breakfast in the cookhouse would soon be over.

Under a sheet, Cirella stirred. She opened her eyes, pretending that she was seeing morning for the first time. In truth, she'd been up for hours. She'd watched Lor steadily through the night, imagining herself in his dreams. She liked to watch him as he slept; he seemed so boyish, so malleable. She could almost convince herself that he was hers.

"Can't you stay a bit longer?" she asked drowsily.

"Gotta rehearse. It's late already."

"Please?" she prodded.

"Can't do it."

Seconds later, Lor scurried from her sleep compartment, shirt unbuttoned, his half-off socks flopping on the floor. Watching him, Cirella felt anxiety mount. He'd done it again. Left her bumpy-browed, empty.

During her life, Cirella had been in many binds. Somehow, she'd always wriggled out. But with Lor, she was stuck. She knew of no way to grab hold of his heart. Try as she might, she couldn't make him feel the love that tunnels vision, that salts fresh-licked wounds. She understood that he'd been cheating on her all along—not with a woman, but with the airy span of wire. And she understood that it would always be this way.

With a sigh, Cirella stood up. She dressed, eyes closed, trying to ignore the changes. Her skin lay limp, sagging at the hinges of her elbows and knees. The blotches that mottled her stomach reminded her of a spoiled banana. She brushed her hair, marveling at the number of strands twisted around the bristles. Had she always lost so many? She wasn't sure if love or fire-eating had made her this way. She felt both manic and drowsy. At a moment's notice, her gaze would blur. Three times a day, she picked at her meals. Not even the desserts, the thick custards and her favorite raspberry-cream pie, tempted her anymore.

There were other changes too, changes that she'd seen in her mother before her siblings were born. Changes that she herself had felt years earlier, before paying the neighborhood woman two bits to remove the problem. But this time was different. This time she'd thought it through and arrived at a realization. If she couldn't have Lor, she'd at least have his baby.

• • •

She didn't plan on telling him—not right away. She'd learned on the streets that a baby forced decision. With a kid, a man either stayed or left. The dilly-dallying and shilly-shallying of love vanished. And a woman, nipples swollen and sore, either had one child to nurse—or two.

Until the baby was born and he made up his mind, Cirella would shield herself. She would tell Lor that she no longer needed him as a teacher. And she would tell him that he was no longer welcome in her bed.

Cutting him loose proved difficult at first. The nights stretched long. As she lay in her bunk, nostalgia took hold. She remembered staring at Lor's softly trembling eyelids. She remembered trying to force herself into his dreams. When finally she slept, her body curled like a wounded animal's. And when she woke, the salty residue of tears encrusted her eyes.

Yet as days pressed into weeks, and weeks into months, a change occurred. The love she had wanted to give to Lor, she gave to the baby. All her emotions tunneled in, feeding a private joy. Finally, here was someone to tell her secrets, her songs, her secret musings. Here was an audience who would never turn away.

Her belly grew in sync with her rapture. It rang high on her body, just as her breasts dipped low. She hunted the costume tents for ways to conceal herself. She traded her sleek bodysuits for billowing gowns with strategically placed ruffles. She waited for the kinkers to take notice. Yet none did. Perhaps they had yet to look past the other changes: white lines zipping across her fingernails, skin scaling like a snake's. They called her a crumpled rose, a blaze put out too fast. But Cirella knew better.

She could feel her baby kicking from within. On wire's edge it drummed: her blood ally, her secret talisman, the one love that would be hers forever.

"I'll give you anything," she promised. "The whole world in the palm of your hand."

Cirella told her secret to only one other person: Lucy Loon. The circus doctor had instructed her to come once a week, for the fire-eater's pregnancy boiled with danger.

Waiting her turn one afternoon inside the medical tent, she watched as Lucy realigned the elbow of an equestrian rider. The man swore in agony as the doctor popped his dislocated joint into place.

"That's the thanks I get?" Lucy teased. "A curse word?"

"Nasty old hag," the rider muttered on his way out.

"Should have left him the way he was," Lucy told Cirella. She offered the redhead a seat on the cot where the rider had flailed.

"That's one thing I've noticed," Lucy continued. "The women endure pain, the men whine and grumble. And I ask you—who is the weaker sex?"

Lucy took Cirella's wrist and felt her pulse. Then she slung a stethoscope around her neck and listened to her patient's heart.

"Open your mouth and stick out your tongue. That's right."

Lucy probed Cirella's lymph nodes. With her fingers, she stretched the skin around Cirella's eyes. Excess fluid strained under her lids. Lucy bumped the young woman's knees with a mallet. Not even a twitch.

"Lay back," Lucy instructed. She felt Cirella's stomach, pressing gently against the growing baby. "You're not gaining enough weight," she observed.

"I'm not hungry lately. Food doesn't taste right."

"Gasoline has a way of dulling one's appetite," Lucy sniffed.

"There's another thing," Cirella hesitated. "I vomit all the time. Sometimes there's blood." She tilted her head, her eyes penetrative. "I worry about the baby."

Lucy put down her instruments and fixed Cirella in her gaze. "I've held back—it's not my job to interfere with circus matters. But I can't bite my tongue any longer. Your job is killing you—and your baby too. Do you hear me? No human's meant to ingest what you have."

Instinctively, Cirella wrapped her arms around her belly.

"You must find something else to do," Lucy continued. "You're chummy with the ringmaster. He'll give you what you want. I've seen the both of you canoeing."

"It's not like that anymore."

"Mr. Barnacle has a long memory. Ask him. I'm sure he'll accommodate you."

"It's not that simple," Cirella argued. "I love what I do—and I'm good at it. The fire—it boosts me higher than I've ever been."

"You like that you're always tired? You like the peeling skin, the joint pains? Right now you're at the threshold. A few more weeks of this, if you're lucky—a few more months—and you'll have permanent damage. Body convulsions, kidney failure, it could be anything. You'll black out and it's possible you'll never wake up."

"What about the baby?"

"Everything you're going through, your baby's going through too."

With effort Cirella sat up. Her mind spun, this time from Lucy's admonitions rather than from her health.

"My baby is the most important thing," she stated. "Isn't it possible that everything will be all right?"

"Anything's *possible*. But you've already assaulted your child with so many different substances. I can't predict what its problems might be."

Cirella tasted metal in her mouth, coins rolling on her tongue.

"I can't make you quit," Lucy continued. "And I'm not going to go to the ringmaster, if that's what you're worried about. He'd have my head if he knew I was telling someone not to perform."

"Please, you mustn't say anything. I'll tell him myself."

"It's his, I assume. Sure is a ladies' man, that Mr. Barnacle. Over the years, I've had half a dozen girls in trouble by him."

Cirella shuddered. "What did they do?"

"They opted for removal, got sick for a few of days, then went on with their lives. The same thing I would recommend for you, frankly."

"Well, my baby's not Barnacle's—and I'm not getting rid of it."

"If it's not Barnacle's, whose is it?"

Cirella had prepared herself for this question. Her belly bounced beneath her voluminous clothing like a bobbin on water. The kinkers would see what she'd caught soon enough.

"It's mine," she asserted.

• • •

Months had passed since she'd turned him away. At first, Lor had immersed himself in work. On the wire, her words stung less. But slowly, the bitterness tainted even the air in the sky.

As usual, he returned to the earth fragile, bones stripped to the marrow. He stole back to his train compartment and locked the door behind him. He tore off his clothes, flopped down on the narrow bunk, and stared keenly at the water spots on the ceiling. How long he lay there, he wasn't sure. But it must have been hours. Old man Weitzman would be angry with him for skipping another rehearsal.

He heard Gus blow the whistle four times in a row: Bringlebright's call to board. Belching smoke, the engine moved from the departure yard onto the main line. Dust sifted through the ventilators. Outside, the ash cat barked orders. Lor buried his face in a feather pillow.

Earlier that day, he'd seen her in the cookhouse, plate piled high, her little teeth gnashing buttered bread. Only one thing could make a woman so ravenous. Right along he'd squelched his suspicions. But now he had little doubt: Cirella had left him for someone else.

When the train started rolling, so too did his thoughts. He imagined what the man must look like. In tantalizing detail, he imagined what they'd done together wrapped in night's silken layers. And although he hadn't considered Cirella his girl—not truly—jealousy wound tight around his chest.

He knew he should let go. He knew he should find Mr. Weitzman and climb back on the wire. Instead, he went to Mr. Barnacle. He wanted a peek at those photographs of up-and-coming starlets. Perhaps the enticement of other girls would once and for all extinguish Cirella's specter.

He'd expected supple curves, pin curls, leggy stretches ending in high-heeled shoes. But opening the door to Barnacle's parlor, he'd never counted on seeing himself.

The poster leaned against the front of Barnacle's desk. It was larger than life—larger than even his dreams. Lor the Fabulous Wire-Walker, it shouted. A drawing of his own face, juxtaposed with a silhouette of a wire-walker, made Lor stop in his tracks.

"Not a bad picture, son," Barnacle remarked, appearing suddenly. He'd been there all along, but Lor's eyes hadn't roved from the poster. "With me, the artist has to tighten the jaw and take some padding off the chin. With you, he took the exact likeness. One thousand copies I've printed—to start. The advance men are already hanging them up. I'm hoping the ladies don't pluck them from store windows and building fronts. They used to do that with me! Months after the circus had left town, husbands would find my pictures stashed in their sheds, barns, cellars. Some of them were covered in lipstick kisses. I tell you—I had my share of worshipful fans."

Lor sank down in a chair, half-stunned.

"I don't think I need to say," the ringmaster continued, "what an honor it is to have your own poster. You're playing with the big boys now. There's no going back. From here on in, it's forward, march!"

Lor remembered the Bringlebright posters from his youth. Two weeks before the circus came to New Haven, those posters wallpapered the city. There was no avoiding them. Go to the bakery, and clowns scampered by. Go to the barbershop, and aerialists swung past. By the time Bringlebright finally came 'round, folks were already intoxicated. They couldn't wait to take off an afternoon, or maybe a whole Saturday, and let the magic of the circus saturate their souls.

Since joining Bringlebright, Lor had seen many more posters. But these weren't like the ones from long ago. They focused almost exclusively on Ranju. The flash of animal incisors, wild hair ablow. Walking by those posters, Lor felt the push of jealousy from behind. Often after he'd seen a poster of Ranju, he'd train all night. The need to outdo the animal trainer was an effective motivator. He'd exercise until his muscles ached, walk the wire so many times it seemed his whole life dangled from that line. And all the while, he'd pray for the day when Barnacle valued him as much as he did the animal trainer. Now that Lor's face anointed the posters, that day seemed closer than ever.

"How do you feel, Lor?"

"Like a hundred bucks, sir."

"Good, good. Would you like a drink?"

"Yes, please. A big one."

Barnacle smiled and poured brandy into a tumbler. It appeared to Lor like a butterscotch-colored oasis.

"Now, son, what's cooking? You dashed in here like you had a hound dog on your ass."

Lor took a sip of alcohol, a slow burn down the throat. His eyes fused to the poster. He realized how much he wanted to stay at Bringlebright—Cirella and her new beau be damned.

"I've had a lot on my mind. And I just wanted to . . ."

"I know, I know," Barnacle interrupted, waving him off. "You just wanted to tell me you're eternally grateful. I'm like a father to you. You don't know how to thank me properly, right?"

"Everything you say is true, sir, but . . . "

"Your talent was raw at first," the ringmaster interjected. "But so is a diamond, before it's polished. I saw that in you—a faint gleam from beneath. I saw that and took a chance. Thank God I did."

Lor sighed. "Yes, Mr. Barnacle, thank God you did."

At the exact moment that Lor knew he would never again be offered the opportunity to look at those pin-ups, the door slid open. In stepped the very person he sought to forget.

"My dear!" the ringmaster exclaimed. "What an honor!"

Sheepishly, Lor hunkered down in his chair. He tried to maintain an aura of nonchalance. He wondered if Cirella could see the pleading behind his mask. He hoped for a look, just one, short-fused and brimming with all the longing he'd been denied. But when she glanced at him, her eyes skipped like stones on water. He wondered about those nights when he'd awakened from a deep sleep. He'd rolled over to find her staring, eyes wistful.

Her gown flapped so long Lor couldn't see her feet when she strolled into the center of the parlor. He watched her as she whispered something to Barnacle, something hushed and tremulous.

The ringmaster smiled blandly. Lor couldn't read his reaction, but it became apparent seconds later.

"Lor, I hate to push you out, but the lady needs privacy."

The wire-walker rose, hesitant. Yet the ringmaster quickly took his arm and shuttled him to the door.

"Tomorrow, son, check in with my assistant tomorrow. We can talk then. He has my schedule."

Lor stole another look at the redhead, but she pretended not to notice. The next thing he knew he was on the wrong side of the door, Cirella's secrets locked behind a steel barrier.

• • •

Within five minutes, she confessed everything: how she'd taken another lover, found herself pregnant, and kept her condition secret through countless shows and rehearsals. She assured the ringmaster that the child couldn't be his—the time frame wasn't right. But he seemed not to care. Nor did he question her on the identity of the baby's father.

Cirella had prepared herself for anything: threats, beat-downs, the mad jealousy of a cuckold. But never had she expected this: sheer apathy. Mr. Barnacle was silent for a long time. Then he asked her a single question. How would the baby affect her act?

"I've talked to Lucy Loon," Cirella conceded. "She told me that the routine—the gasoline and fire and all—are hurting me and the baby. If it's all right with you, sir, I'd like to try something new, maybe the low-wire. I know my looks have suffered. But I would be content doing just about anything."

Behind his desk, Mr. Barnacle's knees jiggled. He pretended to read the weekly Bringlebright fan mail. As Cirella spoke, he found himself unable to look at her—such a beautiful girl gone to spoil. No wonder he hadn't noticed her condition earlier. He could scarcely look past her face. Her skin resembled an overripe tomato's peel: all puckers and loose folds.

"Well, dear, I'm not sure that's possible."

"Mr. Barnacle," she argued. "Now that I'm going to be a mother, I can't be as reckless as I once was."

"Your health is very important to us all, of course. But you're exaggerating the danger. I've known fire-eaters who have performed for thirty years, with nary a sign of decline. It's all how you handle yourself."

The metallic taste in Cirella's mouth became overwhelming. She swallowed hard, remembering the many vulgar moments she'd taken Barnacle's member into her mouth. Without warning the baby kicked, reminding her that she'd like to do the same to the ringmaster.

"I'll leave if you ask me to continue. I have to do what's best for my child."

Mr. Barnacle glanced up then. His gaze was cautious, measured. He didn't want to give anything away, not the pity he felt for the girl's crumpled looks, not the anger over her decision to dismiss him, and above all, not the disappointment. To him, her pregnancy was the ultimate jab, a pointed poke at his manhood. He might have been unable to contain his rage if not for the fact that he felt sorry for her. He could almost see the black blood running like nightshade through her veins.

"I'll accept this as a necessary—although not welcome—leave of absence," he responded. "But it can't be prolonged. Not if you expect to stay on payroll. When you return, you can take whatever position is open and suitable."

"Thank you, sir."

"And Cirella, one more thing."

"Yes?"

"You will need to do a final show."

"Yes, sir. I expected as much."

"When an act ends," Barnacle ventured, "it must go out with fanfare."

"With fanfare," she echoed.

Cirella waited. Certainly he'd have more to say. Certainly he'd offer a final, thoughtful word on their ill-fated romance. She smiled encouragingly. But lips once winsomely sweet twisted corkscrew tight. In the mirror of his eyes, she saw herself as he did: cheeks sunk, hair combed around her face like a shield.

"You may go now, Cirella," Barnacle declared finally. He stared at her a moment longer before his eyes fell flat.

• • •

The Lovely Lady in Red. The Enchantress Above. Blazing Beauty. Mistress of the Flame.

She wore a hundred different monikers in the circus bibles. But on this performance, the last before her leave, the ringmaster called her simply Fire Lady. It was just as well. The audience already knew who she was. Word of her traveled faster than the Bringlebright train. Lips in a tizzy as they described how her hair was brighter than any flame, how her skin could withstand the most scorching heat, how she was the most exquisite woman on earth.

The spotlight zoomed through the hazy air, halting when it found her. She stood ready on the cable perch. The gillies hooted. They tried to imprint her image on their brains so they could talk about her after Bringlebright had departed. She was stunning, all right. A tad heavy in the midriff. But legs long enough to pass for stilts. And that hair: a snaky red braid down her back.

Lor watched from the sidelines as Barnacle introduced her. The audience fell silent. Lor knew their hush masked a silent frenzy. Against the tent's rise, the wire seemed thin as thread.

"Tonight, ladies and gentlemen, Fire Lady will be attempting something never done before—something never done *successfully*. Watch and be amazed, watch and be astounded! But whatever you do, don't say a word. This routine requires the utmost concentration. We can have no distractions!"

Somewhere in the audience, a baby yowled.

"On the wire—high above the perilous ground—Bringlebright's very own Fire Lady will swallow a flaming stick *as she stands on her head*!"

Lor licked his lips, which were dry as talcum. He looked at the ringmaster, who had done himself proud in a top hat, riding boots, jodhpurs, swallowtail coat, and red bow tie. Then he watched as Cirella stepped onto the wire.

High above, the redhead felt the baby pummel her from inside. She tried to comfort it with a lullaby, something about a cradle rocking and a bow breaking. Yet the child would not be stilled. Quivering, she wondered—did her baby know something she did not? She looked around, but detected no sign of danger. She took another step, then realized she had forgotten to put on her safety harness.

She could have stepped back onto the platform to take this precaution—Lor and Sebastian Weitzman would have demanded it. But her act had already begun. This being her last, she didn't want to demystify her peril before the gillies.

Instead, Cirella directed her attention toward the torch. It burned steadily in her hands. She allowed herself to stare, although the flame would hypnotize her if she looked long enough. Funny thing about fire: its edges sway like the hips of a woman, but its center remains steady. It was at the center that Cirella noticed something she had never seen before. Herself—safe in the fire's care as warm, soft ripples massaged her body. She saw herself as she had been long ago, pulse blinking as she ran with Mattie along the docks and through the shipyards. She watched herself leaving The Prison, letting Fritz hold her hand as she plotted a way to take leave of him.

Beautiful she had been then, but unsatisfied. Even at the House of Delight, where she'd had more money than she could possibly spend, she'd sought something better—a place where comfort, notoriety, and adventure collided. Here with her baby, nestled in the fire's cradle, she thought maybe she'd found it.

Cirella felt neither shock nor pain when the torch licked the bottom of her braid, beginning its fateful climb up the red rope of her hair. Pretty soon electric quivers flew in all directions. An inferno enveloped her face. Cirella let go the torch, then let herself go too.

As she fell, no one made a sound. Perhaps they were too awestruck by her beauty. For never—not even in health—had Cirella appeared so enchanting. Her body floated down to the earth weightlessly, gown fluttering about her with ceremonial solemnity. She offered no resistance, no spare motion against the flames that leapt from her head.

When at last she struck ground, the gillies burst from their silent cocoon. They stood up and wailed like sirens. To distract them, the clowns flew to the edges of the ring. Yet their gags could not keep panic from rising in the big top.

Terrified, Lor sprinted to Cirella's side. But the ringmaster was already there. He found the girl on her back, her legs crumpled beneath her. He patted out her burning hair with his own hands, saw that the fire had burned her scalp and the edges of her already piteous face. He whispered to her, "My dear, hold on just a little longer." But she gave no sign of response. He dared not move her, not even when the audience broke all rules of decorum and rushed the ring.

"Get back!" the ringmaster roared savagely. "All of you!"

Lor turned toward the gillies, prepared to fight. Meanwhile, Lucy Loon lurched through the crowd, shoving away onlookers eager for a peek. She put her ear to Cirella's mouth and nose, listening for a breath.

"She's alive?" the ringmaster asked. Lucy moved her ear to Cirella's chest, where deep within, a muted heartbeat thumped.

"Barely. We need to get her out of here."

"Hey Rube!" the ringmaster bellowed, so loud the roustabouts outside the big top immediately put down their playing cards and stood erect.

In a matter of seconds, all the circus—from the clowns and riders through to the acrobats and showgirls—mobilized. They stood before Cirella, Barnacle, Lor, and Lucy as a single wall. Barnacle nodded to them, like a general to well-trained cavalrymen. And they knew from that gesture, so small and indiscernible to untrained eyes, that they must force these intruders from their space no matter what the cost.

• CHAPTER ELEVEN •

The circus band played "The Stars and Stripes Forever"—the song kinkers know as a call to arms. The circus as their shield, Barnacle and Lucy hoisted Cirella onto a stretcher. Then they sped her to the relative safety of the medical tent. Meanwhile, more gillies stole over the low rail dividing the stands from the rings. Many were kids, tugging at their parents' hands. The little ones didn't worry Legman Jack. He was more concerned with the adults. Something about the circus sent them back in time. They became the bullies they'd once feared. They squatted in reserved seats, threw peanuts at complete strangers, yelled the ripe cusswords from their youth, and right then, crossed the boundary between spectator and show.

"If they want to be in the circus, let them be in the circus!" Legman declared. With Fat Stan on his left and Bar None on his right, he advanced toward the unfurling ruckus. He appraised his adversaries as he rolled up his sleeves. Intrepid women revealed themselves.

In his head, Legman heard the sound he always heard during a fight: voices tingling together like angry music—a calliope playing too fast. A gillie challenged him, but the roustabout was ready. He dodged the first punch gracefully, as if he were in a different sort of ring. Then he struck the gillie in the chin with a right-hook. The man fell like dead weight.

Legman relished the tenderness of his bruised hand. The pain caused the music to heighten. It reached a deafening pitch. As he curled his fist tighter—thumb on the outside so it wouldn't get smashed—he smiled in joy. He was a kid again, the best fighter on the block, the most revered of all the boys, the one no one could touch. He threw a punch into the jaw of a second man, knocking him flat. And the world was again startling.

Legman twirled around lustily, shouted to anyone who would listen: "I'll take you! I'll take every last goddamn one of you!"

• • •

Back in the medical tent, Lucy Loon set about the difficult task of stabilizing Cirella. Having seen so many disasters, Lucy was by now hardened to them. She didn't shoulder the responsibility of a life when it was put in her hands. Nor did she condemn herself when a patient died. She was a maintenance professional, not a miracle worker. She'd repair what she could, stitch together what was stitchable, and monitor the vital signs of life. The rest, she reasoned, was in God's hands.

Cirella, the doctor decided quickly, would likely end up not only in God's hands, but also in his house. Both her legs were broken, as were her hipbones, and several bones in each of her feet. Because the patient lay immobile on the stretcher, it was difficult to tell if she had suffered spinal injuries. Nevertheless, Lucy pronounced the possibility of paralysis likely. She tended to the burns on Cirella's head and neck, but she worried more about the problems she couldn't see.

"What can be done?" the ringmaster bellowed from behind the busy doctor. She sighed. Under normal circumstances, she didn't permit visitors inside her tent.

"I don't know," Lucy told him. "I can't very well crawl inside her and have a look."

"I mean about *that*!" he responded, pointing to Cirella's stomach.

"So you do know about the baby. Wouldn't have guessed by the way you let her go up on the wire."

Normally, Barnacle would not have allowed anyone, particularly a woman, to speak to him so tersely. But here in the medical tent, a domain clearly beyond his control, he found himself smarting from Lucy's words.

"Is the baby all right or not?" he persisted.

"We lost it the second she hit the ground."

For the first time, Lucy noticed Barnacle's blistered digits. Carefully, she took his hands and wrapped them in clean, cotton gauze.

"Do you know for certain it's dead?"

"If you threw a baby off a cliff, would it survive?"

"Even so," the ringmaster commanded, "I insist you check."

"It will have to be removed," Lucy sighed, securing the last of the cloth around Barnacle's left thumb. "I'm surprised her body hasn't aborted it already."

She cut off Cirella's costume with scissors and removed the girl's underthings, temporarily losing her composure when she saw the state of her patient's pubis. All the hair had fallen out.

"Look away, please," she instructed Barnacle, "even if you have seen this before."

Lucy moved the head of the stethoscope around Cirella's naked belly, listening for a telltale sign. Immediately, a heartbeat made itself heard.

"Amazing. I think it *is* alive," Lucy breathed.

Quickly, she took her tools, made an incision across the bottom of the fire-eater's abdomen, broke the bag of water, disengaged the baby from the pelvis, and, finally, plucked it into a world it was not yet ready for.

"A boy," she declared.

Barnacle stood agape, astounded that the process of birth could happen so quickly.

Lucy clamped and cut the cord. Then she removed the webby yellow membrane of the amnion, which had twisted about the baby's head. It fell carelessly to the ground in translucent streamers, expelling a salty, rank stench.

"What is that?" Barnacle asked.

"The caul—some swear it's a sign of luck. I knew a seaman who wore one in an amulet bag. Thought it would keep him from drowning."

"Do you believe in such hocus-pocus?" he asked her.

"Of course not," Lucy chided.

Next, she tilted the baby downward so that his mucus drained. Finally, she thrust his slimy, wrinkly body into the ringmaster's hands, proclaiming: "You take it! I need to fix the mother."

Lucy removed the afterbirth and repaired Cirella's uterus. Meanwhile, Barnacle hovered nearby, shaking with nervousness. Although the ringmaster had no prior knowledge of infants, he sensed immediately that there was something amiss about this one. It wasn't just the surreal birth. Even through a layer of blood and debris, he could see something strange, something *bumpy*.

When Lucy at last finished her work on Cirella, she reclaimed the baby. Gently, she washed him with moistened rags. But at the third swipe, she flinched.

She couldn't believe she hadn't noticed them earlier. Warts. All over his body they sprang like hills, like round ripe clusters of grapes. A startled Lucy stretched out her arms, gasping. The bumps were clumped together in the most unfortunate of places—rising from the crags of his knees, in the tiny webs between his fingers and toes, surrounding his knobby penis. Mercifully, the baby's face was clear. But his most afflicted regions—the legs and arms—were a terrible sight to behold.

Tentatively, the doctor investigated the baby for other problems. Yet aside from the bumps, he appeared well. Normal, even, with hair the color of his mother's and skin a shade darker.

Generally, Lucy prided herself on being a fact-finder, a follower of scientific truth. Occasionally, she indulged in a well-founded hunch. But staunchly did she avoid anything esoteric: black art, voodoo, witchwork. In the case of the baby, she concluded that the deformity was a direct result of Cirella's miasmal ingestions. But buried deep below her logical conscience, Lucy's superstitious spirit suspected that the baby's caul, its bumps, and its ability to live through a magnificent plunge meant something else entirely.

She had delivered many babies in her time. She had seen swollen, blue, suffocated babies; hare lipped babies; babies with dropsical heads; even bits of babies that had never grown whole. But never in all her years had she seen a newborn like this. Strange, of course. Ugly, certainly. Unique—there was no question. But most distinctly, Cirella's baby was miraculous.

At the moment of Lucy's realization, the tike began to cry. He seemed so pathetic, so distressed, she cradled him against her. Accordingly, her superstitious spirit sent warning tremors down her spine, the same way it did when she happened across black cats and broken mirrors.

"Do you want to hold him again?" she pleaded with the ringmaster. But Barnacle had backed away to the edge of the tent.

"No, no. I must go," he sputtered, twirling his mustache. "Lord knows what havoc the gillies are wreaking. Despicable people, really. It's too bad our business depends on them."

And with that, he fled.

• • •

In the hours following the baby's birth, Lucy tended to the injuries the kinkers had sustained while fighting back the gillies: a sprained ankle, a black eye, two fat lips, and seven broken fingers. She was haggard, bushed by the long day and the prospect of looking after a newborn. She stared at the babe and mentally flipped through the list of female circus performers who were currently nursing. The baby needed milk, the security of a motherly bosom. Pensive, Lucy sat down. Her round chin sat squarely on her shoulders, for her neck had long ago become lost in the doughy roll surrounding her face.

Lucy watched Cirella, hoping against the odds that she would survive. The fire-eater jerked one direction, then another. Her brow knitted together in unsightly pain. Her teeth rattled as if she were chewing on gravel. When finally she awakened, she opened her eyes to Lucy Loon's appraising stare. She remembered a dream in which the bottom half of her body had up and walked away from the top. Crawl as she might with her hands, she had been unable to catch her lissome legs. Slowly, coming to, Cirella felt her belly and head throb, but felt her lower body not at all.

"Lucy?" she murmured weakly.

"Be still, dear," the doctor answered.

"What's happened?"

"You've had a spill."

"From the wire?"

"Shhhh—rest now."

Distraught and perturbed by the cow-faced maid's vagueness, Cirella struggled to sit up. Again and again she tried, but her legs lay dead as driftwood. Lucy watched her somberly, knowing that Cirella would never walk again.

"Lucy!" she scolded impatiently. "Help me!"

Anxious to avoid the truth, Lucy stood up, picked up the baby, and brought him to Cirella.

"Look here, you've given birth to a son."

Cirella's eyes widened at the sight. Her tongue felt strange, textured like a whetstone. It took her several long seconds to understand that this toadlike creature belonged to her. How had such a homely thing emerged from her body—the once-glorious shrine of red and white? *Her* baby should have sparkled. *Her* baby should have emerged in a triumphant choke of stardust. She worried that there had been a mix-up. Perhaps Lucy had stolen her child, who was surely beautiful, and replaced it with one of the freaks'. But then she observed the color of the newborn's skin. Milky coffee. No one else would notice, she thought, because those terrible tuberosities absorbed all attention. But Cirella could see, plain as day. The baby was Lor's—and her own.

"I had to remove him from your womb," Lucy explained. "There was no way to induce labor when you were unconscious."

Cirella stared at her baby intently. Her fear had fled, and although she didn't have the strength to pick him up, she managed to twist to her side and study him with her eyes and fingertips.

"The ringmaster helped me to carry you here. He was extremely worried about you," Lucy continued.

"What happened to the rest of my act?" Cirella asked cautiously.

"Well, dear, it had the most dramatic ending I've ever seen."

It came back to her then—in terrifying snips and cuts—the way the fire had seduced her. Unnerved, she tried to cuddle closer to her son, so warm and vulnerable beside her. But her body resisted all movement. She wondered how she would care for herself. She wondered how she would safeguard her child.

"Leave us for awhile, Lucy, will you? I want to be alone with him."

"I'm not sure that's a good idea—you're still very weak," the doctor retorted. But Cirella continued to plead.

"Ten minutes," Lucy conceded. "I'll be back in ten minutes."

Alone with her baby, Cirella talked to him about many things. How he was lucky to be a boy, for girls were apt to wither. Boys could always rely on strength, or cunning, or at least, brute force. She stroked his cheek, then fell silent. Who would love such a bumpy creature, she wondered? Who would endure the torture of looking at him—even if he did have sort of lovely eyes? Who would prepare meals for him, touch him when he cried, wipe his tears and snotty nose? No one else but she, yet she did not have the resilience a mother needed.

I must teach him to endure, Cirella thought. She wouldn't be able to protect him forever—if for very long at all. Circus life was fierce—life on the Outside even more grueling. She must toughen his hide, make him buck the torrent of spit and vinegar that would surely roll his way. How to do it? As the boy's only protector, she would also be his first enemy. Cirella felt an ill-conceived loyalty start to kindle.

Using the remainder of her strength, she used one hand to keep her son from squirming. She tried not to touch the whelks and wheals that bubbled from his flesh, but she couldn't help it. What was strangest about her son was not his disease, but his immunity to it. Indeed, the boy was oddly serene, unmistakably healthy. He possessed none of the sickly lavender tint she had seen in other babies. He breathed heartily. Stoic seemed his expression.

She hated to corrupt his good nature, but it had to be done.

Cirella clasped her free hand over the baby's mouth. He didn't react at first. So placid, he seemed to doubt that any harm could come to him. Yet the longer Cirella's hand remained pressed to his lips, the more his pacified eyes cried out. His body turned bright, then pale. His tiny hands, fingers still curled, began to flail. He writhed. He tried to cry, but could not open his mouth. Grim determination spread over the crippled fire-eater.

"One, two, three," she counted to herself, "four, five, six, seven, eight, nine . . ."

The baby's thrashing calmed to a dull sputter. His eyes, now glazed over, began to roll back.

"fourteen, fifteen, sixteen . . ."

At twenty, fire reentered the baby's countenance. A fury overtook him. He had been christened with the will to live. His dainty fingers grabbed her hand, pulling, fighting, already resenting.

"Ah, but you will make it," a delighted Cirella cooed. She removed her hand from his mouth. The baby breathed in greedy gulps.

Cirella embraced motherhood at the exact same moment that she thought of a name: Stalwart.

• • •

When Lucy reentered the tent she found Cirella sleeping and the baby beside her animated. At the sight of the plump doctor, the little thing seemed to squirm in welcome.

"Such a good little boy! Yes, you are!" Lucy said, for like most people, she could no more resist an appreciative baby than she could a good dessert. She picked him up, rocked him, inhaled his buttery-sweet baby smell, and thought once again that he needed to feed. She had remembered two newly lactating mothers: Choalla, the Bearded Woman of the freak show, and Wendy Veltwester, a carpet clown. Wendy was Lucy's first choice for obvious reasons. Yet the doctor was unsure how to approach her. Should she suggest the woman take the baby as a civic duty to Bringlebright, a worthy charitable cause, a favor to Cirella, a righteous Christian deed?

As she wavered between these possibilities, there came a purling underbreath: "The blaze—it comes again!"

The quack turned to find Cirella awake, but fading quickly. There was nothing more difficult to describe or easier to detect than death on its approach. Lucy didn't know what was enabling Cirella's demise—any of a hundred injuries might be the culprit—but she wasn't surprised. In fact, Lucy had never expected the fire-eater to wake up in the first place.

Lucy had seen death enough times, in this very tent and on that very cot, to recognize it when it called. At precisely such times, the doctor wished a man of the cloth traveled with Bringlebright. Someone to perform the last rites. Someone to lead the deceased on the rightful course toward salvation. Someone to organize a burial, contact relatives, sort through the this-and-that which death always leaves in its negligent wake. Lucy sighed. These cumbersome tasks would fall into her hands, she knew.

"My son—his name is Stalwart. Don't forget," Cirella said in a dulcet whisper.

"I won't, dear."

"He's a special child. Watch out for him."

Lucy took her hand.

"I sense his gift," Cirella continued. "I felt it inside me. But I'm not sure where it will lead."

The girl's voice went still. Death rolled in on a silent tide, tugging her body and soul into a deep sea as it receded from the shores of the living.

• • •

Under the big top, the ringmaster stood on a podium and announced the news: how Cirella had passed, but left a special gift in her wake. Before him, faces flinched quickly, then settled back into calm. Shock value had a short life span at the circus, where trains had to roll and tickets had to be collected no matter what the crisis.

"We have not yet decided where to place the baby," Barnacle announced. "But rest assured, little Stalwart will be in good hands."

Sitting on the straw-covered ground, stretching fingers to toes, Lor felt his throat twist shut. He gagged softly. Liquid dripped from his eyes—not tears, but his life force being squeezed like juice from a lemon.

"Where is the baby now?" spoke up Lucinda Rae, the hair-hanger who had been chummy with Cirella. The very same question had caught in Lor's mouth.

"For now the baby resides with Lucy Loon. She's monitoring him closely. As you know, Cirella's tumble was a bad one." The ringmaster's voice cracked slightly, leading to the gossip Lor knew would ensue.

"Do you think it's Barnacle's?" one showgirl whispered to a second. Both ladies were baton twirlers. Earlier, Lor had watched their silver tinseled wands flick in circles.

"Maybe," conceded the other. "It could be anyone's. I didn't really know Cirella. But I could tell, just by looking, she was an opportunist."

"Have you seen the kid?"

"I don't think anyone has."

"I hear it's deformed."

"You don't say!"

"Yes, bumps everywhere. Pimples upon pimples."

"How horrid."

"Indeed!"

"You think the father is one of the freaks?"

At this, Lor stood up and brushed off the flaxen blades that clung to his pants. He blinked fast, discombobulated. Those girls were talking about his child, his son. And yet they would never know unless he announced it. Here and now, his pride on the line, he must say something. He opened his mouth, but his jaw locked. He tried to reason with himself. Instead, Augusta's vitriolic warnings trundled through his head.

Dare you speak? Have you forgotten so quickly all I've told you? It's the purity of the white woman they're trying to protect. What a bunch of hooey! Trouble would have followed if you looked at her the wrong way. But you—you've gone and rolled in the mire.

Hear me now! Don't say a word or they'll come after you. They'll tie you to the trees, chop off your fingers one at a time. Distribute them like pieces of toffee. They'll lop off your ears, and just when you think you can stand it no more, they'll throw cold water at you. Knock you back into reality. This ain't no fish story, boy. I've seen it myself. In the end, you'll burn or hang. If you're lucky, they'll put you out with a pistol.

The ringmaster had finished and his audience was breaking up. People resumed their practice at various stations under the big top. Lor felt as if he'd stepped on a merry-go-round, endlessly revolving as the rest of the world flew past in a moiled blur of color. The circus band began to rehearse. He was grateful for the bleating of trumpets and rat-a-tat-tat of drums: they drowned out the last of Augusta's reproof. They also kept him from speaking out. But by then, Lor wasn't so sure he had anything to say.

• • •

Wendy Veltwester, her clown make-up half-removed, tugged back the towel from around Stalwart's body, then flicked her fingers.

"Absolutely not," she declared with nose wrinkled.

"He's a lovely boy, despite his condition," Lucy reassured her.

"I said, 'no.' I'm busy enough with one baby and a four-year-old besides."

Lucy, who had wrapped Stalwart tenderly and carried him in a basket all the way to Clown Alley, took this opportunity to sling back her shoulders.

"Any good Christian would see this poor, meek child as an obligation," she declared.

"I'm not a God-fearing woman, Lucy Loon. Don't try to threaten me with that religious mumbo-jumbo."

"If you don't care for religion, maybe you'll listen to the ringmaster," the quack barked, undeterred. "He insists, as a civic duty to this circus, that you care for this baby. He orders you to take the child and allow him to feed freely of your milk."

As a matter of fact, Lucy had yet to consult with Barnacle on this point. After Cirella's death, they had discussed only what to do with her remains. For all the razzle-dazzle of his train car, the ringmaster was a frugal man, especially when it came to death, which he regarded as an irritating expenditure. Death was all cost, no return. With famous performers—those who would get press—he had no choice but to do the proper thing: send the body to the family in the best casket available, or pay for the funeral service out of Bringlebright's own budget. But with minor performers, the ringmaster was more slippery. He'd been known to deposit corpses on the stoops of local funeral parlors, order the roustabouts to dig holes for self-service burials, even toss cadavers into nearby waters in sacks weighted with stones.

These cheap tricks, however, would not suffice for Cirella, who was beloved of the gillies. The ringmaster would not be able to minimize costs even if he wanted to, which he didn't, since the redhead's death filled him with guilt.

Of course, none of this did Lucy divulge to Wendy Veltwester. Only that Cirella's son needed a caregiver.

"If Mr. Barnacle feels so keenly about the brat," Wendy retorted, "he can let it suckle from his own teat!"

This exchange thus settled where Stalwart would spend the next several years of his life. In the care of a mother likewise different and homely: Choalla.

• • •

In all the world, there were two types of freaks: natural and self-made. The ringmaster had hired a few of the latter, people who willingly sacrificed their normal physical appearance to tour with the circus: Helga the Human Pin Cushion, The Tattooed Turk, Magical Margaret the Magnet. Yet Barnacle much preferred the congenitally different. He considered them more precious for two reasons. First, their terminal oddness made them safer bets. Even if they wanted to return to the Outside, the Outside would never have them. And second, if they procreated—and they often did—Barnacle doubled, sometimes tripled, the return on his investment.

Choalla perfectly exemplified Barnacle's thinking. Born herself with long, soft hair on her cheeks, forehead, and neck, Choalla had recently given birth to a daughter with the same abnormality. The ringmaster didn't doubt that this child, Jojo, would stay on at Bringlebright when she grew up. After all, where else could a girl like that go?

The freaks stayed together—this was another thing the ringmaster had learned. They were much like any other community: individuals and families knitted together because of common needs—the most important being protection. Protection was in fact behind Choalla's acceptance of

Stalwart. She didn't like the idea of nursing a baby seeded by an unknown man. But she would do it because if she didn't, the boy would suffer the gillies' interminable revulsion.

Well fed, clothed, and cared for, Stalwart flourished, learning to crawl, walk, and even speak before Jojo, who was two months older. Pretty soon, the tot became a favorite of his peers, the cherished member of an extended family. Lucas the Alligator Head tucked gingersnaps into his pockets; the Oriental Giant and his wife, the Living Skeleton, showed him their collection of seashells; Cleo the Camel Girl let him practice her harmonica; The Midget Triplets, Mo, Lo, and Bo, played tag with him on the circus lot; Wonder Boy with Half a Torso lent him his prized possession: a ten-gallon cowboy hat; and Baby Jane, the Fat Woman, fed him sick on saltwater taffy.

Others also paid visits. The ringmaster kept shamefaced tabs on him. He hoped he could rescue Stalwart, as he had not rescued Cirella, and therefore escape the culpability that haunted him. Barnacle resolved to remove the boy from the freak show eventually, to put him somewhere decent. But where? Stalwart was too young for physical work, too strange for the spotlight. At a loss, Barnacle juggled many ideas, but held fast to none.

Lucy, too, kept an eye on the boy. She told herself that seeing Stalwart regularly was a medical necessity. As he grew older, though, his bumps receded, making his appearance quite tolerable. He had improved so much that had he been another patient, Lucy would have dismissed him. Too bad memory kept him close to her heart. His impossible survival, miraculous birth—she had to believe that more marvels were in store. She watched the boy with a careful eye. She watched for his gift. She even bought him a journal. When Stalwart grew old enough, she would present it to him. Then, maybe, pages would tell the story that her eyes couldn't explain.

In time, Ranju also noticed Stalwart—and his impression was lasting. When the little boy turned three, he found a mouse that the roustabouts had engaged in a cruel game of kickball. At the end, they'd neglected to put the poor creature out of its misery. Unable to move, bloody fur matted, the mouse stared with cowering eyes as Stalwart approached. Gently, the child scooped it up and placed it in the pocket of his coveralls. Then he brought it to the one person who knew everything about animals—even how to heal them. Ranju was impressed with the young boy's caring, but not surprised. He had sniffed it on the child long ago: displacement. Stalwart smelled like wild mint in a sea of skunk cabbage.

Of all Stalwart's visitors, though, one came most often—two or three times a day. Something lured Lor. Maybe it was the care he held back. Maybe it was protectiveness. Maybe pride and guilt drove him to spy, to crouch low behind barrels of water, to pass the freaks' table in the cookhouse, to trail the boy through the big top. Whatever the catalyst, Lor couldn't wrench free. He wanted to clutch the boy in his arms. He wanted to claim him. Instead, he watched the days flip past until they were too numerous to count.

Stalwart, of course, was too young to remember Lor's snooping. He was too young to remember many things, even the reason why he was not destined to spend the remainder of his childhood, or any of his adult life, with the freaks.

Few at Bringlebright recalled exactly when it happened. Maybe because everyone had tried to forget. But Cleo the Camel Girl remembered it. So did Wonder Boy. He still shuddered each evening, when the nightmares wracked his body.

During a show in Little Rock, Arkansas, two gillies bought General Admission tickets. They were boys, brothers, at the cusp of adolescence. Like everyone who visited the freak show, they first noticed the bold advertisements painted on the outside of the tent: *Novelties! Oddities! Physical Phenomena's Peerless Prodigies! Corporeal Curiosities! Bodily Bloopers!* The boys entered the tent with eyes wide. They saw what they expected to see: creatures who violated all laws of normalcy.

"They're no better than animals!" shuddered the younger boy, staring at Choalla. "See there—they've locked *her* in a cage!"

Choalla jumped and howled, as the ringmaster had instructed her to do. He wanted the audience to think her dangerous. He called the bars her gimmick. Choalla didn't mind the clatter of loose steel. She kept a key to the cage in her shoe. Twisting her arm around the bars and fishing for the lock took time, but she was patient.

"They're worse than animals," replied the older boy. "At least animals have a place in this world."

They talked it over that night. How people like that weren't people at all. Both lads had received new rifles for Christmas. They'd shot sparrows, morning doves, ducks—one had even killed a jackrabbit. But the freaks were a different sort of game.

"Are you scared," asked the younger, "that Pop will get mad?"

"I reckon he'd do it himself if he could."

The next day, the boys paid for a second show with the rest of the money they'd earned from chores. They tucked their guns inside downy coats, although summer still sweltered. In front of the freak show tent, they listened to the pitchman. Voice rumbling, sweat pouring off his forehead, the talker offered a free preview of the curiosities inside—Mo, Lo, and Bo juggling balls and Lucas the Alligator Head snapping his giant jaws. The smaller boy cowered. He decided he wouldn't set foot inside after all.

"C'mon! Don't be a 'fraidy cat," his brother coaxed. "You've already seen what's there."

"You go alone—or else I'll tell everyone you're the coward."

"Fine. But you'll regret it when Pop congratulates *me*."

Nervously, the older boy stepped inside. He looked past the other grotesque characters to the Bearded Lady. She stared back, recognizing the boy from yesterday. Choalla felt tired. Her feet ached from standing for hours. She looked forward to evening, when she would prop up her heels and finish the fat novel she'd borrowed from Mrs. Barnacle's library.

A few more customers, she sighed. *Then I'll rest.*

The boy peered through the bars expectantly. She put on her scariest face and shook her arms. She waited for his mouth to open, revealing a tunnel of dark fear, the scarlet bell of his uvula. Instead, a smirk smudged his lips.

What's he thinking, Choalla wondered?

The boy ruffled through his coat. Choalla saw the butt of a rifle and took a step back. But her realization came too late. A shot sounded. Some of the freaks screamed. Others were caught in the inertia of panic compounded by terror.

Choalla experienced a few moments of explosive pain before a second shot, to her head, made her feel nothing at all. She slumped down. Blood flowed heavy and final. A burgeoning slick surrounded her body. Lucas the Alligator Head and Mo, Lo, and Bo ran to her cage. They tried to shake open the door. They looked anxiously for a key. But the prison bars held fast.

The boy watched the chaos around him with unflinching satisfaction. Seconds passed before he noticed the splatter of blood on his hand. He was surprised—it was red and warm as his own.

• • •

The boy managed to kill Choalla, and to maim two others, including Jojo, before the roustabouts piled into the tent and pounced on him.

The incident received a lot of press. What was more tantalizing, after all, than a boy-hero battling God's miscreations? The ringmaster had his assistant buy all the papers. He tracked the story carefully. But the national presses never picked it up. The publicity ended on the outskirts of Arkansas.

What was left, then, but to clean up the boy's mess? Barnacle buried Choalla in a plain pine coffin. He allowed the freaks to congregate for a short ceremony, where he himself said a few words. Then he called a meeting with Ranju.

"I'm putting Cirella's son, the lad with the bumps, in your care," he said simply. Ranju nodded, having known already that he would become Stalwart's ally.

PART TWO

• CHAPTER TWELVE •

March 4, 1937

Dear Journal,

Lucy Loon says when you keep a journal you should write in it as much as possible, even if you don't feel like writing. That won't be a problem—I have lots to say. I think you, Journal, will suit me fine.

My name is Stalwart—but a lot of people call me "Bump." I'm a brat of the Bringlebright Traveling Circus: thirty cars long, four elephants strong. The best little circus you'll see in these forty-eight States. It's a traveling show. Like everyone else, we roam by rail—making stops in all the major cities: Tulsa, Tucson, Boston, Charleston, Philadelphia, Springfield. The little towns too. You name the place and chances are we've passed through.

I was born at Bringlebright. My mother was known as The Lovely Lady in Red, Blazing Beauty. Her real name was Cirella. I don't remember her. She died when I was born. But people still reminisce. "A gracious lady, a fine lady," Barnacle once said. "Didn't know her personally, of course. She was my employee. But I could tell, even from afar, she was a show-stopper."

The one thing I know for sure about my mother was that she was a force of nature. Men couldn't take their eyes off her. The roustabouts smack their lips when someone says my mother's name. I can see why. The pictures I have of her show a sky-dancer: red lips, cunning smile. She was long-lined, too thin. Maybe she had to be. How else could she trick the air into holding her?

Many people want to talk about my mother. But not so my father. To start with, no one knows who he is. There are theories. He might have been a journeyman with eyes only for the road. Or maybe he was a kinker—here then, here all along. But I can't believe that. I think, by now, I would have recognized him.

My birthday is May 2nd, which means I'll turn fourteen in about two months. I work as an assistant to Ranju, Bringlebright's chief animal trainer. Ranju has a daughter, Sara. We don't have much in common, Sara and I. She's older and very beautiful. I have what's called a condition, or ailment, maybe even a deformity. It all depends on whom you're asking.

My back is covered in bumps. So are my arms, legs, hands, and feet. I was born this way and it looks like I'll be this way forever. People tell me the bumps used to be bigger, that they looked much worse. I don't remember. I think they look pretty bad now.

Lucy has tried everything to get rid of them. When I was eight she gave me a salve made of snake oil. When I rubbed it on the bumps, they swelled up. After that, I tried picking them off. I managed to scrape off seven or eight, but got so bloody I had to stop. Those bumps grew back—and bigger than before. Lucy suggested we burn them off, but when she took fire to my arm, she burned off all the hair.

Lucy is Bringlebright's irregular physician, but sometimes I think she's more irregular than anything else. Even so, I care for her and she for me. She said she went out of her mind with worry when she first saw me.

"Didn't know if your inside was as strange as your outside," she said.

That remains to be seen, Journal!

March 8, 1937

Hello Journal,

I told you we travel by rail—in a train thirty cars long, four elephants strong. We *do* have four elephants. But the rest is not quite right. The truth is, Bringlebright has two trains. A good deal of the time they travel separately. Usually, the cookhouse goes on the first train, since the roustabouts need to pitch it early. The menagerie animals, pie car, big top, wagons, and heavy props travel on the first train too. The second train holds the horses and seat wagons, and of course, the kinkers and dormitory cars.

For a small show, we have all we need. Flatcars loaded with wagons. Boxcars containing cargo. Palace stock cars for the animals. The freezer car for foodstuffs. A fancy parlor car where the managers relax. The Hi-Cube, an oversized boxcar used to transport the large props. The Gondola, a long, open flatcar for hauling the center poles. Not to mention Bringlebright's custom-made numbers: the horseboxes and elephant cars. Our train—she's a beauty—from the cowcatcher at the front to the beanshack at the rear.

March 20, 1937

Dear Journal,

It's time I introduced you to Ranju—my boss. He's a very mysterious man. If you ask him where he's from, he'll say "under the thunderous clouds, in the heart of the canyon." The truth is, it's hard to get a straight answer from Ranju. Even though I work with him every day, I don't know him well.

But I do know one thing: Ranju didn't grow up right. He never learned manners. I've never seen him eat with a fork and knife, just with his hands. When he has food, he doesn't leave a thing—not even the core of an apple or the bones of a chicken. He doesn't wear much clothing either, not even when it's chilly. Many nights when the train's stationed for a spell, Ranju will sleep outdoors. Sometimes he sleeps under the big cat cages. It's funny, but when he does that, the cats act real calm. Ranju never sleeps in his bunk, although the ringmaster gave him his own sleep quarters—something every performer wants.

No one knows exactly how old Ranju is. His face is young, but he talks about things that took place fifty years ago. Sometimes I think there's something not right about him. His eyes are light-colored, almost clear, even though the rest of him is dark. When you look into those eyes, it's like looking down a well. You can see clearly to a point, but only your imagination can see the rest. Ranju's mouth stays mostly shut when he talks—and I think I know why. Once, when he was wrestling with Maxine, our Siberian tiger, he opened his mouth to growl. That's when I saw his tongue is forked.

March 25, 1937

Greetings again, my faithful little book.

Already I like having you, Journal. Usually I have so many feelings locked inside me. But tonight I feel relaxed, like I should after a long day.

Sara and I had a strange conversation today. I asked her if she thinks her father is a regular fellow.

"What do you mean?" she demanded.

But how could I describe the serpent's tongue, his bottomless stare? Once, too, I swear I saw black claws sprout from his fingernails. But I couldn't tell her. Ranju is her father, after all.

"Nothing," I answered.

She didn't speak to me for the rest of day.

Journal, did I mention that Sara has eyelashes as long and beautiful as a giraffe's? Her eyes twinkle when she's around orangutans, which are her favorite animals. (Just for the record, Journal, mine are the elephants.) Her dark hair is thick as a horse's mane. It smells of new rain. She wears it in braids, usually half undone. Sara doesn't pay her appearance much mind. Her boots are always steeped in animal droppings. There's hay stuck in her clothes. But she's lovely even so. And brave. She's not afraid of the polar bear, even though he is the most dangerous of all our animals. She'll go right into his cage during feeding time.

Speaking of feeding time, I just saw the flag go up. I think we're having stew tonight. That's when the cook throws in a pot all the food we didn't finish yesterday. Ugh.

May 28, 1937

Mrs. Barnacle's the one who taught me how to write, Journal. She's Bringlebright's schoolmarm. She's also the ringmaster's wife—but just between us, she isn't his *only* female companion.

Mrs. Barnacle teaches everything we would learn in school if we lived on the Outside, including reading and writing. I'm a little old for lessons now. But sometimes I go anyway. I sit on the floor inside the school wagon with the children. I watch Mrs. Barnacle as she dots an "i" or crosses a "t." She works slowly because the children are of different ages. Some of them, like the Chinese acrobats, don't even speak English.

Mrs. Barnacle is methodical about everything. She becomes upset if a book is upside-down on a shelf or if one of us has applesauce stuck to our shirts. Maybe that's why she didn't take to me at first. My bumps are disorderly. But I caught on to spelling quicker than anyone. After that, she warmed up. She even gave me a dictionary. She said my nose was always stuck in it anyhow.

Lucy Loon gave me you, Journal. She says I have so many ideas floating about my head, I might as well write them down.

Lucy knows I spend a lot of time thinking—about my mother's death, and who my father is, and if Sara will ever like me, and whether I'll always be ugly, and how animals make far better friends than people do.

April 4, 1937

It's nightfall, Journal. Whenever night comes, I get the shivers. Night is a time for sleep, but also for secrets. I know what the roustabouts are doing with the showgirls. I know about the animals too. The elephants nuzzle one another. Their trunks swing to a hidden, amorous rhythm. When we're riding the rails, all four of our pachyderms travel together. Sometimes they comfort each other by poking their trunks through the air ventilators at the top of the wagons and "holding hands."

The other animals are just as affectionate. The lion cubs snuggle against their mothers. The tigers bat each other playfully. Sometimes, when the skies are starless, the cats pace their cages in solitude. Perhaps they're lost in dreams of their homelands—the lions of the wind-swept African savanna, the tigers of the mangrove forests of India. Whenever the train travels the open prairie, the cats cry into the night. They thump against the walls. Ranju says they do this because they yearn to escape.

There isn't much sound beyond the whirring of the train as it speeds along the tracks. When we're stationed for the night, you can hear the crickets trill. The crickets travel with us, burrowed deep in the animal hay to avoid detection. But when night falls the males are all bravado. They scratch their forewings together to create high-pitched sonatas. Like all music, theirs is made to attract females.

I lay awake listening and imagining what is happening in the other sleep quarters, in the animal cars, in the small towns we pass and the cities we cross. I feel lonely thinking about the warm bodies clustered together. And of course, I think about Sara. She shares a sleep car with five other girls. True stars such as Lor the Fabulous Wirewalker get their own place. But Sara doesn't mind where she sleeps. In fact, she's confessed to me that she prefers to spend the night in the orangutan car. What a daring creature!

April 7, 1937

Journal, have I told you about my friends, the roustabouts? They're like characters out of books: pirates, gangsters, and gunslingers. Of all the roustabouts, Legman Jack is my favorite—and a true chum.

During the traveling months, Bringlebright employs the roustabouts to do rough work. But most of them aren't full-time hires. They don't go to Bringlebright's winter quarters in Sarasota like the rest of us. Rather, the same guys join up in the spring, and leave when the snow starts falling.

The roustabouts are a tough lot. The ringmaster says they require "frequent disciplinary action." I don't know if that's true. But I can't deny the gossip that's always circling their heads. Affairs, brutality, lying, thieving, arson—you can say anything, but it's probably been said before. I try to filter out the talk, but some seeps in anyhow. Last week, kinkers were saying Fat Stan pushed another roustabout off the moving train. It's called red-lighting because the victim sees the red taillights disappearing up the track—if he lives to tell about it. I'm not sure if Fat Stan did it—and I'm not asking any questions.

To make the roustabouts stay on, Bringlebright's management holds back half their wages until the end of the season. All those planners don't want any trouble. It would be easier if the roustabouts didn't like their bad reputations. But they do everything possible to maintain them—from starting rumors to breaking noses. I can't blame them. What's a gunslinger without a "WANTED" poster?

April 15, 1937

Dear Journal,

The roustabouts' gambling schedule is as follows: Monday, Gin Rummy. Tuesday, Poker. Wednesday, Blackjack. Thursday, Pinochle. Friday, Hearts. Saturday, Napoleon. And Sunday—the day of rest—Patience. Because it's warm, the roustabouts play outside. They use a wooden crate as a table and sit on spare pieces of canvas.

Tonight is Pinochle night.

Legman Jack deals the cards. He and Bar None are partners, as are Fat Stan and Rusty. Spider sits out the round because he doesn't have a partner. I tell him I know how to play. But he doesn't want me. I don't have money.

I rest on top of a trunk. From this perch, I can see that Fat Stan is a king short of a run in spades. Rusty, meanwhile, has a hundred aces already in hand. Although they are partners, I know they'll outbid each other, thereby driving their own team into the ground. I've seen it a million times. Only Legman knows how to play it safe.

The fire nearby provides necessary provisions—light so the roustabouts can read their cards, smoke so the bugs don't swarm. My job is to stoke it. I oblige the roustabouts any way I can. Ours is a simple relationship. I do their bidding and they let me hang around.

"Bump, get me another cannibal burger," Legman Jack demands. He's referring to raw ground beef that many of us eat between meals in the cookhouse. We stick it between wedges of bread and smother it in mustard to hide the gaminess.

Although we travel constantly, meat is a priority for Bringlebright's crew and its animals. Legman Jack says he needs the protein to maintain his muscleman physique. The cats need it too. When fresh meat is low, someone always travels ahead of the train to buy old horses from local farmers. Sometimes I'm in charge of the slaughtering. I hate the job. I smell the blood on my clothes for weeks afterwards.

I fetch a cannibal burger for Legman and sneak another one into my pocket. Later, I'll feed it to Maxine.

We're in the sleepy train yard of New Haven, Connecticut. The roustabouts are due to start unloading the wagons off the flatcars at four in the morning. By five they'll begin pitching the tents and testing the heavy equipment. It's already late, hours past sundown. But most of the roustabouts don't sleep much. Legman Jack does, though. He gets help from the bottle.

Years ago, Legman told me he's a jailbird. He didn't mince words when he told me what he was in for. Murder. How he broke out of prison is a secret. Legman would only say, "The Lord works in mysterious ways."

I try to concentrate on the game, but the stars are unusually bright. I get distracted counting them, until I feel Legman Jack's eyes on me. And on you, Journal.

"What do you write in that thing, anyhow?" he asks.

"Words?"

"What?"

"Words!"

"Words are for saying, not for seeing," Legman declares. "If you're going to waste your time with that nonsense, there's only one thing you should be reading."

"What?" I ask.

"Girlie magazines!" he laughs, pleased with himself.

"Forget about Bump. Get back to the game," Rusty declares, perhaps eager to bid on his hundred aces.

But they never do go back to the game. Somehow, they get to talking about Lor Cole—how they met him over fifteen years ago in this very train yard. I try not to listen, since I've never felt right around Lor. He doesn't approach me often. But his eyes follow me all the time. They give me a creepy feeling. I can't understand his gaze. Sometimes it's full of wonder. Other times there's fondness and even a hint of regret. This isn't a lot of malarkey, Journal. It's true! You can tell a lot from a man's eyes. But Lor's are always changing and I can never decide once and for all what I think of him.

April 19, 1937

Tonight I got an awful scare, Journal. I was hanging about the roustabouts, as usual, when Legman suddenly threw down his cards.

"Let's wrap it up," Legman announced. "I've got a meeting at midnight."

Rusty's eyes twitched back and forth. "You gonna meet a skirt?" he giggled.

But Legman doesn't take slams, least of all from blockheads like Rusty. "You shut your trap."

"Aww . . . come on. Just wanted to know if you're dipping into the honeypot tonight. I know!" Rusty exclaimed. "It's that brown-haired piece o' jail bait who works with the animals!"

At this, my ears perked up. Was he referring to Sara—*my* Sara?

"Keep your jang in your pants," Legman replied coolly.

"You gonna muffdive? You gonna, Legman?"

"Shut up, mushhead," Bar None intervened.

When Legman left, I left too—quiet as whisper. I needed to follow him, to see if his "honeypot" was indeed Sara. As we walked in the direction of Sara's sleeping car, I thought I would vomit. But when we passed the monkey wagons, already loaded aboard a flatcar and waiting for the morning shove, my heart fell back in place.

I don't know what girl Legman was visiting, but it wasn't Sara. I know because Sara was right there in the orangutan wagon. How relieved I felt! But I couldn't get over my need to protect her, so I decided to keep watch. For hours, I observed her playing sweetly with Bringlebright's orangutans—little Suki, and her mother, Maple. For hours I observed her, but in secret.

April 28, 1937

I've been busy lately, Journal. A few days ago one of the small concession tents caught fire. All our tents are coated in paraffin, which is water-resistant, but also flammable. That's not a comforting thought during a lightning storm. Heck, I even get nervous when someone lights up.

I helped the roustabouts clean up the mess. But that was only the beginning of the trouble. That same day one of our clowns, Wendy Veltwester, ruined the afternoon performance by pulling the wrong audience member into the ring. Wendy thought she was working with a shill. But the guy turned out to be a gillie, with no idea that he was about to be made a fool of. When Wendy threw a pie in his face, the gillie turned round and punched her in the jaw. A fight broke out, but the other clowns saved the day, acting as if the whole scene had been staged.

Wednesday, we were supposed to take off for Peoria, Illinois, but no one could find Gus. The ringmaster ordered everyone to search for him. Hours later Sara found him face down under Maxine's wagon. He had an empty bottle of tequila in his hand. There was no way to wake him. We tried everything: icy water poured down his back, black coffee poured down his throat. The ringmaster was ready to operate the train himself. We were six hours late to Peoria. In circus time, Journal, that's six days.

Then came another problem: we ran out of souvenir booklets. The ringmaster ordered a new batch from a local printer. Alas! The printer botched up and introduced Mr. Barnacle as Mr. Oyster—on over one thousand copies. Mrs. Barnacle sent me to the shop to set things straight. She said, "Stalwart, you read so well. Make sure they do it right this time." But a youngster with bumpy skin doesn't always get respect, so I brought along Legman. He stood there looking fierce, flexing his muscles, and in no time at all, the shop reprinted our booklets—at no extra charge.

Bringlebright sure can be a whirligig, Journal. I wish I could nap now, but it's feeding time for the elephants. I better get there before they throw a tantrum.

April 29, 1937

Today, Sara, Ranju and I spent the better part of the day quieting the elephants. They were terrified. A stray dog kept circling their wagon, growling and baring its teeth. The dog was scarcely bigger than a housecat. Even so, the elephants huddled together in one trembling mass. Ranju coaxed them into leaving their wagon only when Sara and I shooed away the dog. I think he was hungry, so hungry he had lost sight of his size. Out of pity, I gave him some soup bones from the cookhouse.

As the chief animal trainer, Ranju supervises all the animal acts. But he works mostly with the elephants and big cats. As for the other animals, he gives the secondary trainers broad leeway—so long as they conduct themselves right.

Since I work with Ranju, I don't see the other acts much. There's Suki, Maple, and our other monkeys. The dancing polar bear. Rosie the hippo. The equestrian team, which can do just about anything: bareback riding, vaulting, saddle-standing, acrobatics, you name it. Every other season Barnacle contracts a temporary animal act too. In the past we've had doves, alligators, and sea lions. This year it's a rhinoceros named Julio.

Even though Ranju doesn't do much supervising, the other trainers respect his methods. The only thing Ranju demands is gentleness.

He condemns unnecessary force. And when he sees one of his people using it, his eyes glow with a vengeance that's every bit as scary as his forked tongue.

May 1, 1937

Dear Journal,

Today, Baby Jane the Fat Woman gave birth to roly-poly twin boys. Everyone felt glad for her and dropped by the medical tent to wish her congratulations. I picked some white and yellow daisies that were growing near the lot and brought them over. I was hesitant at first. I'm always shy around the freaks. But I dare admit why only here.

Sometimes I wonder if *I* belong in the freak show, Journal. With my bumps I'm not much different than they are. Lucy said I used to live with the freaks when I was a baby. But I was given to Ranju's care because I had a way with animals. Is it possible, Journal, that I'll be traded back some day?

I know the freaks aren't bad folks. They're good-hearted. But I don't want to live with them. I want so much to stay with Ranju and Sara. I want so much to be a regular fellow. I want so much for Sara to notice me *as a regular fellow.*

There, I've said it, Journal!

Baby Jane smiled when she saw my flowers. She gave me kisses on both cheeks. I didn't know it, but I carried her lipstick smudges on my face all day. I noticed them only when I caught Lor staring at me.

• CHAPTER THIRTEEN •

May 2, 1937

I'm in fine form today, Journal. You can probably guess why. I turn fourteen today.

Birthdays aren't a big deal at Bringlebright. I suppose we're too busy for them. Except for Mr. Barnacle. He always celebrates his birthdays in high style. He invites everyone to his parties, even the circus band and the freak show. But most of his attention goes to the showgirls. They come to Mr. Barnacle's birthdays in full regalia: sequined costumes, rouge, high-heeled shoes. They gather around him like flies to a fallen ice cream cone. I know why. Whichever girl falls into Mr. Barnacle's favor is treated like a queen. He'll give her anything: fancy clothes, candy, flowers, even special billing—until his next infatuation comes along.

It's a perfect day for a birthday, Journal. A perfect day for *my* birthday! The sun is high in the sky. My pockets are full of all the gifts people have given me. Legman, on behalf of the roustabouts, gave me a bottle of beer. Lucy gave me another salve to try on my bumps. This one's an oil made from plants with exotic names: comfrey, tea tree, wild thyme, bergamot. It was a thoughtful gift. But I don't intend to use it. I'm sick of cures that never work.

Earlier this morning, when I was working with the elephants, Mrs. Barnacle also gave me something: a beautiful silver watch. It's the nicest thing I own—my pictures of mother aside. The watch has a long chain with a piece of metal like an anchor on the end. It doesn't have numbers on it. Rather, it has little vertical lines and V's and X's. Mrs. Barnacle says these symbols are a fancy way of telling time that the Romans discovered.

My last gift, but not my least, came from Sara. It's a trinket on a string—"a necklace for boys," she said. The trinket's a little elephant made of clay. The elephant's painted blue. Sara said she picked it out because she remembered elephants are my favorite animal. Circus folks are very superstitious, Journal. That's why I asked Sara if the trinket had any secret meaning—would it bring me good luck or a long life?

"In India, elephants are a fertility symbol," she said, smirking.

My face turned very red, Journal.

May 11, 1937

Since I received my elephant necklace, my life seems plumb full of the critters!

Ranju, Sara, and I have been teaching three of Bringlebright's pachyderms—Lydia, Lavender, and Lucky—how to perform the Long Mount. I asked Ranju why we weren't using Sally, our forth elephant, but he didn't say.

The Long Mount's a tough routine, Journal. If you ask me, doing it with only three elephants is a handicap. Larger shows, like the Ringlings, do it with ten elephants or more. But Sara says we have to make do with what we have.

The routine has the elephants marching into the big top, kicking up clouds of dust as they go. They walk in a line until Ranju tells them to stop. Lavender, our oldest and largest pachyderm, stands at the front, all four feet on the ground, while Lydia places her front feet on Lavender's back. Similarly, Lucky places her front feet on Lydia's back. To watch these gigantic creatures perform the trick is testament to their agility. But not to their intelligence. They become annoyed when the gillies applaud, as if to say, "Do you think this is all we can do?"

After today's rehearsal, Lucky, Lydia, and especially Lavender were peevish, like we'd embarrassed them. It took a lot of stroking and coddling to get them to forgive us. I slipped Lavender a carrot, even though Ranju told me not to reward bad behavior. I couldn't help it. I felt sorry for the old gal.

May 27, 1937

I think it's prophetic—is that the right word?—that I've been talking so much about elephants. Suddenly, that's all everyone is talking about.

Something's wrong with Sally. She's gone mean.

Ranju says it's because she was born in the wild. He says you have to breed animals in captivity—the way Lydia, Lucky, and Lavender were. The animals that are born wild stay that way. I think Ranju feels very badly about Sally. He says he can't blame her for refusing to adjust after what we put her through: confinement when she's used to wide open spaces, blocks of hay instead of fresh grass, the top of a tent rather than spacious sky. We took her away from her family too. I understand how she must feel. There is nothing worse than missing one's parents.

June 4, 1937

Things have gotten worse with Sally.

To be honest, she's never been easy to handle. But I've always liked her *because* she's strong-minded and willful. These are admirable qualities, Journal—except, maybe, if you're an elephant in a circus. No matter what people say, I think her behavior is understandable. She was kidnapped to a place where she's had to work against her will. Wouldn't you fight back? Her story is like the slave stories Bar None tells.

The bullmen have given up trying to tame her. It's gotten to the point where no one but Ranju can predict her behavior. She'll be quiet and restful one moment, manic and angry the next. The bullmen won't go in her car because she throws tantrums, stomping her feet and thrashing her trunk. Now, they open her door only to throw in another bale of hay or to change her water. Since I last wrote, no one but Ranju's bathed her, or oiled her down, or tossed dirt onto her skin, or even led her out of confinement. She's depressed. I can see it in her eyes, which are cloudier than they used to be—drained of her usual zest and verve.

Ranju's been trying to coax Sally out of her sadness. Each day, he spends more and more time with her. I've tried to spend time with her too, but Ranju says it's better that I don't enter her car. So I stand on the side and talk to her as best I can. Sometimes Sara comes too. Together, we sing silly songs. We open the door to put in treats. Even though Sally doesn't show it, I think she appreciates our company.

I have faith, Journal. If anyone can pull Sally out of her sadness, it's Ranju. He has a magical hold on all our animals. They trust him—they think he's one of their own. And if you want to know the truth, so do I.

June 10, 1937

The ringmaster came around to see Sally today. He heard the rumors flying about how she's gone bad. As soon as he walked within ten feet of her wagon, she acted up a storm.

I suppose Mr. Barnacle got scared. He declared Sally unsuitable for public display. That really irked me, Journal, since half the showgirls throw tantrums like Sally's every day and *they* never get into trouble.

"She's too unpredictable," the ringmaster told Ranju. "What if the beast goes haywire around a small child? What if she charges into the audience during a performance? It's possible," he said ominously, "that Sally's becoming a rogue."

Ranju disagreed, of course. He told the ringmaster that Sally wasn't a rogue, but she could never be a performer. She hadn't endured the journey from India to America. Something in her had broken. She wasn't going to bounce back. Not without trouble.

"I've been trying to sell her," The ringmaster responded, "to a zoo or another circus. But no one's biting. They think the price's too high. But what am I going to do—give her away? That pachyderm eats one hundred and twenty-five pounds of hay each day. Do you have any idea how much these damn elephants cost me? Ranju, you train her so that she's useful and cooperative," Barnacle concluded. "Or I'll make a decision I don't want to make."

June 21, 1937

Ranju's been trying.

He's pushing Sally to adjust. He's put her back with the other girls. But they just ignore her—much like they did before. Elephants are like people—you can't force them to get along.

Anyhow, Sally's changed a bit. Instead of acting dangerous, she's become blue. Ranju can barely convince her to leave the car. And even when she does come out, she's sorrowful, slow, lost in whatever thoughts elephants think. If Sally were a person, Journal, I think she would try to kill herself.

We've been working with her day and night, urging her to participate in the standard routines: tail up, trunk up, balancing on the tubs. It's hard, because Ranju still won't let Sara or me near Sally. He's scared of what she'll do. As always, we support her from the sidelines and let Ranju do the real training.

The ringmaster thinks she's making progress. He likes the way she's become meek, the way she submissively stumbles through the motions of each routine, head down. Barnacle must be a dolt if he believes Sally's mindless movements are an improvement. The fact that she's lost her spirit only means we're losing her.

Tonight I went to check on Sally before I went to bed. She looked at me with her big sad eyes, as if to say, "Why do you keep me here? Why can't you let me be?"

"I'm sorry," I told her.

But she just lay down, her huge body heaving, then falling with a thud. She wouldn't look at me again, no matter how much I apologized.

June 27, 1937

It's only been a month since Sally first started harassing the bullmen and throwing fits. But the ringmaster thought she was ready for a comeback.

He was dead wrong, of course. Ranju warned him, but Mr. Barnacle overrode Ranju's suggestion anyhow. Judging from today's fiasco, I'm sure he regrets it.

The show in Charleston, West Virginia, was Sally's first in a long time. She went bananas—ramming the props, stomping her feet, standing on her back legs, charging the stands until the gillies started to scream.

I was there, Journal. I saw it all. One of Mrs. Barnacle's books on the Civil War says that the Confederate soldiers returned home with an "unholy look in their eyes." That's exactly the way Sally seemed to me.

The ringmaster ordered one of the bullmen to shoot Sally with a sedative gun. Ranju got angry because he doesn't believe in such things. He started to yell. When he opened his mouth, I caught sight of fangs: long and deadly. I thought my heart would stop, Journal.

When Sally collapsed, Mr. Barnacle put an end to the show. Sara and I led Lydia, Lavender, and Lucky back to their wagon. We petted and rubbed them for awhile, for they were as shaken as we were. Then we went to see if we could help Ranju. We found him on the ground beside Sally, opening her mouth and sticking his head inside.

I knew what he was doing—checking on her teeth. But the ringmaster got worried that Ranju was trying to hurt himself.

"What're you doing, you crazy bastard?"

"Impacted molars, cavities, infections—she might be acting this way because she's in pain," Ranju informed him.

In the end, Ranju didn't find anything. Later, when Sara and I were alone with him, he went back to his original theory—that Sally was rebelling against captivity.

"And nothing can heal that," he informed us.

When Sally awoke from the sedative, she seemed weak and troubled—like she couldn't remember what had happened. She climbed to her feet, but stood awkwardly, ready to fall again. For the first time, Ranju allowed me to approach her. She looked down at me—hazy,

bewildered, spent. This wasn't a dangerous beast, I knew, only a sick animal.

"It's all right, Sally," I whispered to her. "We'll take care of you."

But now I wonder—will I be able to keep that promise?

June 28, 1937

The townsfolk are livid about yesterday's performance. Sally's thrashing trunk is all over the front page of the *Charleston Times*.

The reporter said Sally didn't hurt anyone directly. But an older fellow suffered a coronary on account of the turmoil. All those gillies—they want retaliation. And the ringmaster—he wants an end to the problem.

He called Ranju into a meeting this morning. It was a nerve-wracking time. Sara and I kept busy working alongside Bringlebright's equestrian director, Al Fick. The trick riders were performing a dangerous new routine, and Fick wanted Sara and me to run alongside them and act as spotters. I enjoy working with the horses because they're so beautiful, especially the Clydesdales and Arabians. But they're not very smart, not like our elephants.

The riders were performing rosinback. The routine has them standing up as the horses gallop. Sara and I powdered the riders' slippers with rosin so their footing would stay firm. At one point, as Sara rubbed one rider's foot and I the other, I noticed her hands: smooth and soft and perfect. Then I looked at my own. What a mistake! The bumps seemed to glare back at me like a hundred ugly eyes.

When Ranju returned from the meeting, he told Sara and me the details. Mr. Barnacle had ordered him to restrict Sally's diet. He wanted to wear down her resistance. Ranju refused to comply with the ringmaster's orders. He said you can't punish an animal with cruelty—its suffering would only come back to haunt you.

"The only solution is to sell the elephant to a private owner," Ranju informed Barnacle. "Sally isn't right for circus life."

"The trouble with you, Ranju," Barnacle shot back, "is that you fuss over the animals like they're babies. We're running a business here—not a nursery!"

Ranju said he'd pack his bags before he'd starve an animal. But Barnacle would never fire Ranju. It's clear, from the freaks through the funambulists, that Ranju is the best performer on Bringlebright's roster.

July 5, 1937

Barnacle assigned the job of breaking Sally to Joe Skakel, a bullman.

Skakel's been Sally's keeper for seven days now. As for Ranju—he's been ordered by the ringmaster to avoid both Skakel and the pachyderm. But he visits Sally anyway. Late at night—when no one else is around. He says Sally doesn't sleep. She only cries and whips her tail fretfully.

Skakel's frightened of Sally. You can tell by the way his hands tremble. He won't look her in the eye either. That's no good, Journal. Any good trainer knows that you *must* make eye contact with the animal you're working with. If not, how will she learn to trust you?

To compensate for his fear, Skakel uses heavy-handed tactics. You could say he's a bully.

Sally's not looking well. Her eyes have gone yellow. The skin on her head's affected the worst. It's cracked and peeling because she's not taking care of herself. By the looks of things, Skakel's not taking care of her either.

• CHAPTER FOURTEEN •

July 19, 1937

The situation has gone from bad to worse, Journal. Skakel's beaten Sally to a pulp. She's a walking ghost, timid and lifeless. Most people feel sympathy when they see an animal in such poor health. Skakel—he's relieved.

He hasn't unchained her legs since he became her trainer. So I was surprised today when he let Sally out of her car. He wasn't worried she'd go buck-wild. He's licked her so good she doesn't have the energy.

As Skakel paraded Sally around the lot, it was clear that he was showing off. Sally hardly enjoyed the walk, although it was her first in so long. Her knees kept buckling. And he'd harnessed her head so tight she couldn't lift it. She let out several pathetic cries. Finally, I couldn't take it any more.

"Mr. Skakel," I said, approaching him, "you better take that harness off. It doesn't fit. You're hurting her."

"You're that boy who helps Ranju? What do they call you—Bump?"

"Yes, sir. But my real name's Stalwart."

He looked at me so long I couldn't help but feel awkward.

"Better mind your business, Stalwart. You're nothing but a monstrosity. Would've thought they'd put you out when you were a baby."

After he said that, Journal, I began to hate him. A deep-down, bubbling, boiling hatred. That Skakel, he wants me to suffer, the same way Sally is.

I've got a lot on my mind, Journal: Sally—and Ranju too. He's not doing much better than that sick pachyderm. He's lost a lot of weight. And his eyes have taken on the same sallow sheen, like he shares in Sally's pain.

Worried about his health, I went to see him last night. I went first to his car, but I should have known better—he's never indoors. I tramped around the circus lot in search of him. I finally found him in the orangutan cage with Sara. They were talking quietly and clowning around with Maple and Suki.

I didn't approach them, but I think they knew I was there. It's strange—and I don't half believe it now, in the light of day. But I swear Ranju's ears pricked up the way the big cats' do. And Sara, she started sniffing—like her nose was sensitive enough to ferret out an intruder. It was only a moment. And in the dark, I can't be sure of what I saw. But when Ranju's eyes began to glow, I cowered in spite of myself. He looked the way a bear does before it launches an assault. When a cat strikes, it swipes or claws, then backs off. But a bear—it attacks until the end.

When Ranju opened his mouth to growl, that's when I ran away. His teeth flashed, sharp and keen. A bear opens its mouth that same way. And when it clamps down, nothing can stave it off.

I didn't think I'd see any more crazy sights that night. But I did. On my way back to the train, I saw Mrs. Barnacle creeping out of Legman Jack's crumb car. Her hair was mussed and her glasses sat crookedly on her nose.

She caught my eye and gave me a look that said, "I never saw you and you never saw me." And that was that, Journal.

July 23, 1937

They say an elephant never forgets. She'll hold a grudge against a person or another animal for years, waiting for just the right opportunity to strike back.

I wonder if that's what happened to Sally. I wonder if she resented Skakel—for locking her up, for starving her, for cracking his whip against her flank, for chaining her legs, for lambasting her during training, for underestimating her intelligence, and finally, for overestimating his own.

What happened today doesn't surprise me, Journal. Skakel's caution slipped a long time ago. Today we arrived in Wilkes-Barre, Pennsylvania. It was to be Sally's first performance since the Charleston debacle. The ringmaster thought her up to the challenge. Once again, Ranju tried to dissuade him, but he didn't listen.

Skakel told the ringmaster he'd broken Sally. She was so docile, he informed Barnacle, he didn't even need his whip or elephant hook to control her.

Maybe leaving them behind was Skakel's last mistake.

Under the big top, Ranju directed the other elephants into assorted positions: Lydia and Lucky balanced on their hind legs, and Lavender stood still while a pony walked underneath her. Meanwhile, Skakel shivered with anticipation for his big moment: introducing a reformed Sally to the gillies.

I saw it before anyone else—maybe even Ranju. But I didn't say anything. I remembered the way Skakel had called me a monstrosity. I remembered how ugly he'd made me feel. And suddenly I didn't mind so much the gleam of revenge in Sally's eyes.

Skakel had Sally on a huge leash. She followed only a few feet behind him. In another moment, the ringmaster would've introduced them with words like "marvelous," "stupendous," "extraordinary," and "astounding." When Sally began to close in on the space separating her from Skakel, nobody thought twice—not even me. I thought, perhaps, in some perverse way she'd developed an affection for her new master. But when she slipped her trunk over his shoulder, I caught on. This wasn't affection, Journal. It was revenge.

All eyes were on the Center Ring, where Ranju and the trio of elephants were creating a delightful spectacle. Only mine stayed on Skakel. I watched Sally wrap her trunk around his neck—and then tighten it so Skakel couldn't breathe. In that strangle-hold, she lifted him clean into the air. A desperate cry could be heard, and that's what finally caught everybody's attention. We watched as Skakel's legs swung mid-air. Ranju rushed over. So did Barnacle and a couple of breathy showgirls. But it was too late. Sally'd choked him to death.

Still center stage, Lydia, Lavender, and Lucky stayed calm throughout the ordeal. Maybe they weren't surprised by Sally's behavior. Or maybe, like Sally, they were glad to see Skakel go.

That's how the story goes, Journal. But I don't suppose you'll like the end.

"What we have on our hands is a beast—a bloodthirsty beast. A terror that must be slain," the ringmaster announced in the cookhouse that evening. It was an unusual night. The curtain dividing the long tables from the short had been drawn. The whole place was exposed.

Before the ringmaster, all the kinkers sat rapt, forkfuls of chicken pot pie frozen in our fingers. We were on alert, Journal. But we already sensed what the ringmaster was going to say.

"Sally the elephant has already attacked the public. And now she has attacked one of our own—our beloved animal trainer, George Skakel. Unfortunately, George did not survive. Therefore, to prevent further tragedies—and indeed, to ensure our continued safety—it is imperative that the rogue elephant be executed."

A sudden undercurrent of whispers and murmurs flooded the cookhouse. Sure, everyone had heard of elephant executions, but not at Bringlebright. After all, the show was reliant on animals in general, and elephants in particular. The elephants helped the roustabouts raise the heavy center poles. They assisted the sledge gang pull the sidepole stakes out of the ground. They were indispensable for a thousand different reasons. Bringlebright folks knew this, which is why the announcement of an execution sounded as sinister as it did unwise.

"Isn't there any way to salvage the animal? If we can't use her, can't we sell her?" demanded Lucy Loon, who pounded her fist on the table.

"Sally is too vicious to rehabilitate," the ringmaster responded. "And to sell her to an unsuspecting party would be like placing a cannonball in the hands of a child. There can be no compromise. Sally *will* be executed—and she will be executed tomorrow."

Bringlebright may be a gossipy show, but we're not bloodthirsty. When the ringmaster announced Sally would be executed by hanging—to avenge Skakel's own demise—we pushed our food away.

July 23, 1937 (Evening)

Hello, Journal. I'm back again. Tonight, when I was sure everybody else had fallen asleep, I crept out of bed and went to visit Sally. I wanted to say my last goodbyes. I unlocked her door, against Ranju's wishes. But I didn't care—I just wanted to see her.

I stepped inside her world, and almost immediately, I noticed a dark figure hunched in the interior. I wasn't sure if it were animal or human, for it stood upright, but its arms and legs seemed all the same length. I could distinguish only contours, shadows and lines amid the hay. Sally's heavy musk filled the air.

"Who's there?" I called softly.

But no one answered.

Sally tickled my ear with her trunk. I pushed her away, suddenly preoccupied with our safety. Was someone from the Outside in the wagon, I wondered? Or was the intruder one of the ringmaster's minions, someone sent to do away with Sally quietly, before the first rays of dawn?

"Make yourself known," I whispered.

Again, no one answered me—at least not with words. But I heard from the figure a howl, something like the coyote calls we hear when the train passes over the plains of the Midwest.

"What's in here with you?" I asked Sally. She didn't appear to share my trepidation.

The creature stepped out of the shadows. It was not human and not animal, but an eerie cross-breed. Something like the creations I'd read about in Mrs. Barnacle's book: *Gothic Fictions*. Clawed hands, hoofed feet, tufts of wooly fur growing from the torso and stomach, black horns protruding from the crown of its head, and finally, a trunk, long and otherworldly, extending from the center of its face. The eyes—they got to me the most, because they weren't alien. They were familiar—beautiful, unknowable orbs, vast and many fathoms deep. Eyes I'd gazed into many times before.

"Ranju?" I dared.

He said nothing, but looked at me. His stare was both tender and vicious. And I knew then, as I gaped back, that I had seen something no person was meant to witness. Some sort of sacred rite performed only among animals. It was too exquisite for human comprehension. I backed away, slowly, with eyes fixed on the creature.

Sally made a noise, low and guttural. I kissed her once on the trunk, very quickly, before I bolted out of her car, locking it behind me.

July 24, 1937

It's a bleak day, Journal, cloudy and rainy and ugly. A day I wish I'd never woken up to.

The execution was even more cruel than I expected it to be. Everyone was there, all of Bringlebright, in the depressing, derelict CO&O train yard of Scranton, Pennsylvania. Dozens of gillies attended. They seemed gleeful, like they were about to watch a picture show. They might as well have brought sacks of peanuts and bottles of pop.

Sara stood next to me throughout the whole ordeal. I wanted to take her hand, not just because she's Sara, but because I needed someone to hold on to. My ears rang and my stomach felt mushy. Maybe from the dust in the train yard, my eyes kept watering. I brushed the tears away, hoping Sara wouldn't see.

She was busy telling me about Ranju. I wanted to tell her about him too—about the bizarre incident the night before—but I was too rankled to talk. So I listened. She told me how, early in the morning, Ranju had made a final plea to the ringmaster.

"'Even if you're set on this killing, let it be humane. Not a hanging.' That's what he said," Sara confided in me, replaying Ranju's conversation.

She tossed back her long braids with a jerk of her head. "Then he volunteered to put Sally away himself, if the ringmaster'd let him."

"But the ringmaster said 'no?'"

"Well, obviously, Bump!"

"Where is Ranju now?" I asked.

"I'm not sure. But I'm glad he's not here. He wouldn't be able to take this."

I'm surprised *I* took it, Journal. What a gory scene! I kept clutching the elephant necklace Sara had given me, hoping it would bring good luck to Sally, or at least a swift and painless end.

Alas, that didn't happen.

The bullmen, along with the roustabouts—who had been recruited for their brawn despite their lack of enthusiasm—walked all the elephants in a line to the CO&O train yard, trunk to tail, with Sally at the front. Just outside, they halted Lydia, Lavender, and Lucky. Legman and Stan continued on with just the one pachyderm. Sally knew what was going on, for she kept trumpeting so loud the gillies covered their ears. Yet she didn't object when the roustabouts led her to the railroad derrick, where a long chain hung from the attached crane.

Following Barnacle's orders, Legman looped the chain around Sally's neck. To keep her in place, Stan chained one of her legs to the rail. He winced when he was through, and he and Legman exchanged pitying glances. When the ringmaster announced that the execution was close at hand, the gillies began to cheer.

That's when Sara covered her eyes. I went to comfort her, but was dizzy myself. Hot dog, Journal, I almost fainted from nerves.

The bullmen hoisted Sally up, I don't know how far, maybe only a few feet. But they'd forgotten to unchain her leg from the rail. The chains grew taut, then the one attached to the crane snapped. Sally careened to the ground, causing it to quake. At that point I, too, closed my eyes. I had heard a cracking sound—no doubt Sally's hips breaking from the fall. I couldn't bear to see her, to see the pain searing her eyes.

Even as I write this entry, Journal, I admit to you that the scene seemed so botched as to be artificial. Why did the bullmen use thin chains? They know how much Sally weighs. And how could anyone be so forgetful as to fail to unchain her leg? I pray I'm wrong. But I suspect the ringmaster planned for Sally to fall. I can just imagine him bragging about the execution's "greater audience appeal."

Even though Sally had been hurt, the crowd felt no empathy. In fact, the gillies' enthusiasm only grew, even as my heart ached and Sara, beside me, sobbed.

I opened my eyes in time to see the ringmaster motion for Legman to loop another chain around Sally's neck. With downcast eyes, Legman obliged. This chain was thicker—more deadly. The bullmen once again cranked the winch. My belly couldn't handle the metallic ring of each rotation. I started to vomit. I looked up, a foul smell on my breath, but the sight was unmistakable: Sally's gigantic corpse dangled in the air.

When it was over, when the satisfied gillies found their way home, when Mr. Barnacle finished bragging to local reporters, when the roustabouts decided to drown their disgust in whiskey, when Sara followed my lead and purged her breakfast, when all was said and done, I went back to my sleep quarters—despite the fact that I had piles of work to do—and toyed with a distasteful question.

What would become of Sally's body?

A few hours later, I learned that Barnacle had sold Sally's corpse to the citizens of Scranton. He'd said they could do whatever they wanted with her remains—with one caveat: he would keep the tusks. Soon after, I overheard him telling a showgirl what he planned to do with all that ivory.

"I gotta cousin in California who'll give me a hundred dollars for these beauties."

August 1, 1937

In the days since Sally's death, Ranju has changed. Once his eyes were bottomless. Now they are entirely without boundary. They spiral like tops one moment, swing like pendulums the next. Ranju has withdrawn, but only when it comes to people. With animals he's as friendly as ever. This morning, he wrestled with Bringlebright's two pumas, Jester and Sax, for hours—letting them bat him with their paws and lick his face with their spiky pink tongues.

The most marked change in Ranju, though, is his silence. I haven't heard him speak a word since Sally's execution. What's going on deep in his head, I don't know. I believe he's thinking—meditating—the way people do when they have to make an important decision.

I mentioned Ranju's curious behavior to Sara. But I should have learned by now never to come between father and daughter.

"I think it's time you stopped playing detective, Bump," she told me. "You turn perfectly ordinary people into mysteries!"

Lately, Ranju and Sara are always together. They don't eat in the cookhouse anymore. They take their food—Sara's on a plate, Ranju's in hand—and wander off to a distant part of the circus lot. Why must they keep to themselves, I wonder? I feel so lonely every time I watch them go.

There's something else, Journal. Since Sally's death, I've changed too. I feel a kind of hunger and despair that's so deep I can't breathe. I've hit the ceiling. Lucy Loon says it's hormones. She's says everyone's got them, but they pop up worst at my age. I'm not sure if that's so, Journal, but I'm scared. The feeling's worst when I see Sara, because there's so much I want to tell her, and yet, it's all pressed down.

August 11, 1937

Barnacle's installed something new. It's called the House of Mirrors and it's an addition to the sideshow. I've never seen anything like it. It's not really a house at all, but more of a maze. And as you walk through it, you're bombarded by your own image, as reflected a million different ways by a million different mirrors. Mirrors that make you tall, mirrors that make you wavy, mirrors that stretch you out and squish you up, mirrors that turn you upside down and sideways.

I heard through the roustabouts that Barnacle didn't want the House of Mirrors at first. He was afraid the whole structure would topple. That the mirrors would break and Bringlebright would have countless years of bad luck on its hands. But Mrs. Barnacle convinced him the superstition was bologna.

"He got the set on the cheap," Legman told me. "The old dog's got a nephew in Memphis who runs a mirror manufacturing joint. Can you believe that? Seems like that bastard's got a relative in every line of business, from baking powder to booty. Anyhow, the nephew cut him a deal—half price for the whole sha-bang. Not bad when you consider the economy."

I asked Sara if she wanted to see the House of Mirrors with me, and to my surprise, she agreed. We went two days before its official opening—we didn't want to be crowded in with the gillies.

What fun we had! At one point, Sara grabbed my hand and led me to a mirror that widens your reflection. We looked as plump as Baby Jane.

"You've gained 500 pounds," I told her.

"And you look like Rosie," she squealed.

One corridor is lined with mirrors—ceiling, floor, and walls. The mirrors are ordinary, and they do nothing but capture your true appearance. I watched Sara as she strolled along, her thick braids like rope, her back straight as a tree. I marveled at her beauty because it's real, not like the showgirls', but true and wholesome and sweet. And the best part is, she doesn't even realize it.

And then, Journal, I looked at myself. Such ugliness! Lumps, and nodules, and nubs. I imagined Barnacle introducing me as his newest act.

Ladies and gentlemen, I'm delighted to extend a welcome to Bringlebright's most exciting, enthralling, and splendiferous new spectacle. In your lifetime, you have probably experienced many incredible and memorable circus super-attractions. But never before have you experienced this: a living colony of pustules, protrusions, pimples, and protuberances! Our next performer is also known as the Swami of Swelling and the Aristocrat of Abscesses. But here at Bringlebright, we know him as Bump. Here he is—on display in America for the first time evvvvvvvver!

Sara must have noticed my discomfort, for all of a sudden she abandoned her reflection and turned to me.

"What's a matter, Bump?"

"I'm all right."

She moved closer, close enough that I could see the tiny stray hairs between her eyebrows.

"It's not a big deal," she said. "Everybody has them. Look here."

She reached out her hand and I saw on her palm, smack between her lifeline and heartline, a wart.

• CHAPTER FIFTEEN •

Ranju had returned to his traincar for the first time in weeks. He slid out of his detestable shoes, which the ringmaster insisted he wear, and looked down at his bare feet, at their long length, at the dirty nails, at the tiny shoots of hair that sprouted off his toes. He concentrated, watching with cool contentment as the nails sprang out, long and sharp and curled at the ends, until at last they resembled the talons of a bird. But not just any bird. It was the vulture Ranju had on his mind.

Since Barnacle had decided Sally's fate, Ranju had thought of the vulture and of little else. Yet it wasn't until that morning, when he'd listened to Sally's last cries, painfully clear in his ears even from miles away, that he realized why. He was losing control.

Ranju lifted his sleek brown arms from his sides. One by one, his fingers metamorphosed into silver-white flight feathers. His arms sprouted the dark plumes of an underwing. When his skin was all but replaced by a tawny down, he closed his eyes, picturing the blistering sky of the desert. There, he had loved to watch the vultures circle the air in search of carrion. Beautiful, strange animals they were, with bald ruby-red heads and beaks encrusted with blood. Rocking side to side on each gust of wind, they sailed the air. They hissed when they spotted a feast: a dead animal, its body rotting pitifully on the hot sand, a swarm of flies hovering above rancid entrails. Thinking of Sally's body, of her severed tusks and broken bones, Ranju hissed too.

Humans disliked the vulture. They thought him dishonorable: feeding off the sick and helpless, always capitalizing on death. They didn't understand his value. For only in death comes rebirth. And in that sense the vulture was a noble creature: a necessary part of life's cycle.

Humans were themselves like vultures, Ranju thought, except for a crucial difference. Vultures salvaged death, returning it to a fertile ground for life. Humans, they also picked on the vulnerable—creatures like Sally, for instance. But they gave back nothing. Death was always for profit.

Wings outstretched, Ranju willed his body to transform back into that of a human. The long pinions rustled, but failed to metamorphose. He gritted his jagged teeth. These struggles had recently become more common. Ranju knew it was because he was fighting to adapt. For all the years he had lived with humans, pretended to be one of them, observing the way they slept and worked and loved and played, he had never understood them. Fickle they seemed, without clear purpose.

Before, Ranju had reacted to their ways with amusement. But over time his detachment had caved, giving way to disgust over their cruelty, which seemed so casual, so unduly careless.

Barnacle's treatment of Sally shone as a particularly gruesome example. Or course, not all humans were the same. Ranju had met several who transcended the selfishness typical of the species. Here at Bringlebright, however, there seemed to be only two: his daughter and the boy, Bump.

Ranju again concentrated on the transformation. This time, feathers dropped off his body and fluttered to the ground. Moments later, they disintegrated into dust. The giant wings receded. The razor talons retracted, sinking back into skin, waiting to be beckoned again.

Ranju had never been a true trickster—not like his mother. She'd lived separately, not allowing the humans to undermine her. All this time, Ranju had thought he could abandon her wisdom and pass in the humans' world. He had needed to, if not for his sake, then for Sara's. But now he saw that his mother's way had been the right way, the only way.

The humans' destruction of Sally tore at his thoughts like a vulture ripping into a shriveled carcass. That he hadn't stopped her murder wounded him still more. At first, he had thought silence was his only option. Freeing her would have meant revealing his true identity: that of a traitor, an adversary of Mr. Barnacle, and most spectacularly, a creature closer in relation to Sally than to the hordes of bloodthirsty onlookers who had witnessed her hanging. But now the stench of death filled the air. In reply, the circus animals—from the horses through to the big cats—released an effluvium undetectable to the human nose, but unmistakable to Ranju. The scent of mourning.

The odor pulsed through his nostrils, lodged in his throat, and Ranju gasped. He had failed not only himself, but also the creatures he cared for. They looked to him as their friend amid so many captors. Realizing this, Ranju yielded to his grief, which sprang over him quickly and completely. He had experienced this sensation before. One other time, when Sara's mother had died.

He held out his hands, marveling at the thinness of human skin. So weak humans seemed, without claws, or fangs, speed, or even strength. But still they managed to conquer, because of the guile of their actions and the poison of their words. Their treachery, he realized, he could not endure any longer. It was making him forget who he was and why he lived among them in the first place.

One last time, he beckoned Sara. She came to him quietly, the only one who knew his secret call. She stroked his hair, sensing his thoughts. She remembered all the sacrifices her father had made. How he had traveled widely, learning human culture and customs. How he had named her "Sara," a proper human name, so she would be accepted. How he had searched for work, but been turned away because of his color, his voice, his ways. Sara didn't remember whether they had found Bringlebright or Bringlebright had found them. Finally, here, in a place where the fantastic was ordinary and the ordinary fantastic, she had found a home.

But here, too, Ranju had lost himself.

"You must go," she told him in the quiet of his car. "I'm grown now. I can fend for myself."

Ranju squeezed her hand—feeling bone and tendon, the strong push of blood through his daughter's veins. Sara pulled away, the hardest thing she'd ever done. She forced herself to look in his eyes, to lie to him for the first time.

"Father," she said, "I don't need you anymore."

• • •

Both parts of the train had combined for a trip to Omaha, Nebraska. The first leg of the journey had gone smoothly. So smoothly Gus had uncorked a bottle of wine. But when he spotted a sun kink, a section of rail bent from heat expansion, he threw the bottle aside. Mind in a tangle, he applied the emergency airbrakes. The sudden halt caused the locomotive to welter into near derailment. Slumped over the controls, breath like a distillery, Gus didn't remember acting as switch-tender. But he did remember the dispatcher's orders.

"Stay where you are."

Now Gus waited for permission to continue or turn back. He relayed the news to the ringmaster, then ambled back to the cab to reclaim his discarded bottle. Meanwhile, shaken kinkers emerged from their sleep quarters. Gingerly, they stepped into the dusky air. They found themselves in a no man's land. Cornfields stretching as far as the eye could see. A claustrophobic riot of stalks.

Amid the confusion, a shadow passed along the train. It possessed thewy limbs, a noble bearing, a mane of nettles. The shadow stopped at each of the animal wagons. Its fingers fell on the locks, unbolting each. One by one the wagon doors flew open. The animals drew close to emancipation, peeking their heads into the open air. Confused, they stalled, suspicious of a trap. But when Jester and Sax finally leapt to freedom, the other cats also slipped away. The horses whinnied, then leapt to the ground, collectively trampling a trail through the stalks. Rosie plowed her own path. Bringlebright's polar bear floated from view like a white ghost.

Only the elephants remained. Perhaps they hadn't the courage for the steep jump from train to earth. Or perhaps they were too smart for liberty. After all, one of their own had already paid a terrible price.

The kinkers joined forces in the rescue. The showgirls, in their nightclothes, ran bare-footed through the cornfields. Spider and Bar None trailed Maxine with a giant net. The equestrian team rounded up the horses with lassoes. Lucy Loon collected the monkeys. Stalwart quelled a distraught Lavender, while Sara trekked after Suki and Maple. In the end, most of the animals were collected. Others were picked up later, following frantic reports from nearby towns.

One kinker did not join in the chase. He was the only one, aside from Barnacle, with keys to every cage. Ranju fled with the animals. He hadn't wanted to go—he knew Sara, despite her protestations, needed his aid. But he couldn't bend any longer, nor could he return to what he had been.

He walked naked through the stalks, listening to the animals cry out in a brief, glorious moment of deliverance. On a strangely windless evening, he breathed easily for the first time since the swamps.

• CHAPTER SIXTEEN •

September 12, 1937

Dear Journal,

Everything is different without Ranju. And everyone feels it. The cookhouse crew doesn't sing or cut up jackpots anymore. The Weitzmans are brooding. Lucy Loon is in a temper. She keeps treating people for ailments they don't have. Take Legman Jack. He went in the medical tent to get his tooth pulled and left with a bandaged arm.

Mr. Barnacle is the worst off. He walks around worried, feet dragging like anchors. He keeps whisking people away to secret meetings. They must be talking about Ranju's replacement. Don't they know that he is irreplaceable? Nobody on this earth can duplicate Ranju's way with the animals.

In the cookhouse we don't eat like we used to. We push our food around our plates, build gravy moats out of our mashed potatoes, mash our lima beans with our forks. No one talks, but I believe we're all thinking the same thing. What are we to do without Ranju? What will become of Bringlebright? Will we once and for all lose the battle to Ringling Brothers?

I don't sleep much. I keep wondering where Ranju might have gone. Certainly not to another circus. No one would hire him with a scandal looming over his head. I can't see him living among the gillies either.

They wouldn't understand one another. Maybe Ranju went to live among animals, in the woods, or the mountains, or along the sea.

Life goes on, but it's uncertain. Sara and I and the other hands do all we can to care for the animals. We keep them fed and bathed and in clean quarters. Still, the order we're used to is gone. I never realized quite how much Ranju did around here. In his quiet way, he ran the whole show.

Another reason for the somber atmosphere—the ringmaster has held back wages for the fifth week in a row. He blames the hard times. He says no one wants to put down the little money they have for a circus show. I don't mind so much—what do I need a lot of dough for? But the low-wagers, like the roustabouts, are suffering. They blow all their earnings on gambling and the pie car, and at the end of the day, have nothing to show for it.

Maybe President Roosevelt can fatten people's wallets again. People look down on him because of the wheelchair. But looking different doesn't have to be a failing. *I* know that, Journal.

September 16, 1937

A strange encounter—that's what today brought. I had just brushed Lydia with her favorite long-handled broom and washed her good. I was getting ready to rub her down with neatsfoot oil. But the gallon jug was almost empty, so I gave her a few oats and ran to the supplies car. Lor buttonholed me there. It was a queer meeting. If you ask me, Journal, everything about Lor is queer.

"You've grown up, boy," he told me. "I see you've sprouted another inch."

"Yes, sir."

"No longer a child, eh?"

"No, sir."

Somehow, Journal, Lor seemed as nervous as I. He stepped forward tentatively.

"I see you talking to those roustabouts a good deal."

"Yes, sir, we're friends."

"Friends?"

"That's right."

"They *are* interesting," Lor sniffed, shuffling his feet. "You know, Stalwart, I've got some time on my hands. If you ever need another fellow to knock about with . . ."

Talking like that Lor looked so earnest, so vulnerable, I nearly forgot that I didn't trust him. I felt, for the first time, I might understand him. Is it possible, Journal, that even famous people get lonely?

"That's a kind offer, sir."

"You don't have to call me 'sir.'"

"All right . . . Mr. Cole."

"Call me 'Lor.'"

He helped me pour the vat of oil into my jug. For a second, his hand rested next to mine. Lor's was dark and tough. Mine bumpy. But they were similar somehow. I saw a likeness in the stretch of our fingers and the scuff of our nails.

September 18, 1937

Today Lor approached me again. He told me about an oak tree growing at the edge of the circus lot—an oak tree so majestic he had never seen its equal. Although I was busy, I followed him there straight away. Journal, Lor was right. The tree was ancient, I could tell by its thick, stooped waist and scarred skin. It must have had many stories to tell, of worms sliding between its gnarled roots, of birds shaded under its wind-rustled leaves, of wild storms that had ripped through its branches. I thanked Lor for showing me such a wondrous thing. But he stared at me expectantly.

"Are you telling me, boy, that you don't mean to climb it?" he asked at last.

"Climb it?"

"Haven't you ever climbed a tree before?"

I shook my head and Lor looked as if he'd been struck dumb.

"That's a shame, boy. Because right here is a perfect climbing tree. Look at the branches—they're set apart in just the right way. I think you ought to have a go. I'll give you a boost and you have a look around. How's that?"

"All right," I ventured.

Lor clasped his fingers together, making a cradle for my foot. I stepped into it gingerly, then grabbed the nearest branch. I hauled myself up, feeling altogether different than I'd felt on the ground.

"Climb higher, if you want," Lor called. "The view gets better the higher you go."

I looked up at the crisscrossing arcs of branches, the patches of blue sky between green leaves, the dapples of sunlight that filtered through the tree's great jumbled beauty. And I indeed wanted nothing but to climb higher.

A funny thing happened then, Journal. Perched on a branch and staring into the sky, I saw that the world is different than how I thought it was. The circus lot seemed neat as a pin, not at all like the scurry of commotion it is when I'm on the ground. But more than anything else, it seemed *small*. I was astounded by this idea—that my whole world could compress so suddenly. I hardly felt it when the branch jiggled and Lor settled down beside me. He, too, seemed lost in thought.

"Lor?" I asked him.

"Yes?"

"Thanks for showing me this."

He smiled. I watched the hard edges of his handsome face soften and his eyes dance like sunlight on water. He looked almost like a boy, the boy he must have been when he'd climbed trees like this one every day.

• • •

Lor had witnessed the similarities: same long stride, same eating habits, each food pushed to its own quadrant of the plate. But never had the likeness been so distinct as when Stalwart had climbed the oak. When Lor had squinted at the sky, he had seen himself in the reach of the boy's hands, in his steadfast ascent. It was that moment, a glistening bridge between his past and the boy's present, that Lor couldn't get off his mind. He smiled suddenly, the same way he had up in the tree with the boy. It puzzled him that Stalwart could mean so much to him when their connection had gone unsaid.

Then again, lately, he'd been puzzled by a great many things. For instance, so many years after he'd left Fair Haven, he'd started to think about home again. He thought about Woodrow, whom he'd ceased corresponding with only a year after joining Bringlebright. He thought about Augusta, who still spoke to him from the grave. Most of all he thought about Opal. What would she be like now? Would she look the same, contemplative and discerning? He couldn't imagine her any other way. Yet she must be different: raising a child by herself would have made her even more steely and resolute. He wondered, too, about her child. By now it would be a young adult, about the same age Lor had been when he'd first decided to set out.

Lor shuddered, distraught over how many years had passed. He had little to account for them—only a handful of remarkable memories. And even these, the brightest pages of his history—saving Katarina from a terrible fall, listening to the ringmaster call him a star—were beginning to seem nondescript, edges fraying, ink blurring on moldy paper. He wondered why he no longer drew inspiration from his accomplishments. He wondered why he now spent his time examining the past rather than anticipating the future. Before, the sensation of steel under his feet had been all he needed. He'd taken comfort in his daily trips up the incline wire, in his hours of stretching, in the insipid, tiring exercises that were also his gateway to celebrity. He had been content to stand alone, for here—in the glowing circle of the spotlight—he had also achieved the only dream that had ever mattered: immortality.

Why, then, were regrets piling around him in a claustrophobic heap? After all this time, he suddenly wondered what lay in the shadows beyond the circle of light. He lamented forsaking Opal, Cirella, and Stalwart for his other companions: air, applause, and the wire. He couldn't be sure where these doubts were coming from. He knew only that after so many years of complacency, he no longer felt sure of himself.

Lor looked in the small mirror that hung in his sleep compartment. He looked at the dense stubble on his jaw and decided he needed a shave. A joey at Bringlebright who had been a barber on the Outside operated a make-shift barbershop inside Clown Alley. He charged twenty cents, but did a bang-up job. Lor used to delight in settling back in the padded chair, closing his eyes, and allowing steady, professional hands caress his face with warmed shave cream, a soft-bristled brush, and a steaming-hot towel. Lor had gone religiously, until the clown had nicked him—not a bad cut, but unsightly—smack above his upper lip. Nicks were sloppy, as sloppy as missing buttons. For a week, Lor waited impatiently for it to heal. After that, he didn't trust anyone to touch his face.

He continued to stare in the mirror. He wondered at the man who stared back—a little too old for Lor's taste. In youth, beauty had been a constant companion—expected if not wholly appreciated. But as the years wore one, Lor was becoming more aware of its flighty nature. He regretted having taken it for granted. He wished he'd paid more attention to its essence, for now, his profile cut a little less sharp. Both vainly and in vain, he searched his individual features for answers. Did his skin no longer stretch taut? Had his teeth lost their polish? But no, each piece appeared achingly perfect. It was the consummate reflection that had tired.

Lor unscrewed a jar of Burma Shave. He shaved slowly, wielding the blade with the care of a surgeon. When he finished, he scooped out a blob of hair dressing and rubbed it between his palms. Just as he went to slick back his hair, he noticed something: the first indisputable sign that his looks were fading. Right at the temple, sat not one, not two, but three gray hairs, clustered together like an evil triumvirate.

"Rotten devils," Lor whispered. He plucked them out with a tweezers, then wondered if he had made a mistake. He remembered the saying, "If you pluck one, two will take its place," and winced. He dreaded the day he'd wake up to an entire head of smoky wisps.

He had a long day in store—rehearsal with the Weitzmans, two performances, his exercise routine, a costume fitting, a trip to Lucy Loon's because his ankle burned, another rehearsal, and at the end, a meeting with Barnacle. He looked forward to this last appointment because he knew what he and the ringmaster would discuss. Barnacle had come to count on him for his input. Since Ranju had fled, the showmen had tried to arrange the performances accordingly, to showcase the animals without really using them, but to no avail. The gillies were unhappy. Same-day ticket sales were down. Bringlebright needed a replacement. And Barnacle needed Lor's help in choosing one.

The wire-walker was nervous. He'd spent much time worrying about how Ranju's popularity eclipsed his own. He had fussed and fretted, agonized and stewed. But now that Ranju had left, he didn't feel the triumph he'd dreamed about. Instead, he felt weighted down by responsibility. Without Ranju, he would be Bringlebright's undisputed top performer. He would be the one struggling to maintain his supremacy while those around him gossiped about dethronement. All those incremental triumphs had finally led to the summit. Lor could stand proud at the top. Instead, looking forward, he saw the inevitable descent. He realized perhaps he had been happier as the underdog, scrabbling and clawing his way up.

• • •

"Come in, come in!" the ringmaster declared. He was chewing and his words tumbled out a tiny hole at the side of his mouth. Lor sniffed the air. It smelled of something rich and savory. "The cookhouse was abominable tonight. Just abominable! Didn't you think so? My stomach growled even *before* I finished eating. You know, son, I remember the good ol' days when I let the cookhouse spend whatever they wanted on whatever menu they concocted. We ate like kings! Lobsters, steaks, Champagne, you name it! I never thought like those Ringlings: 'skimp on food and save on profits.' I always thought—we must eat well and eat right!"

Lor winced when he thought back to dinner, to the sodden rice and chicken giblets and overdone biscuits.

"Now I know what you're thinking, son. Food's not as good as it used to be? And I

agree. I couldn't agree more. I've had to slash the cookhouse's budget. The money's not there and the prices are climbing. Milk is twelve cents a quart. Bread, ten cents a loaf. Potatoes, twenty cents a peck!"

Lor looked down at Mr. Barnacle's desk, to the source of that wonderful aroma. The ringmaster's gaze followed Lor's.

"A filet steak—cut straight from the tenderloin. The steak that makes other steaks blush," Barnacle revealed. "The frenchies call it *filet mignon*. Leave it to them to complicate something simple. I told my assistant: 'Find this for me. I don't care how many men you gotta bribe, how many cows you gotta wrestle. Get it—and get it for me *tonight*.' Want to try?"

Lor's mouth watered, but he shook his head.

"Come on, lad. The grub in the cookhouse will fill you up, but it won't satisfy. It's food for a pauper. A filet steak is fit for a king. Consider it a treat—for all your hard work. You're a star—the biggest one we've got now. You deserve the best."

Lor felt his cheeks flush.

"All right. Maybe a bite."

"A bite?" Barnacle smiled jovially, then rang a brass bell on his desk, signaling his mysterious henchman. He arrived within seconds.

"Another steak, please. Medium rare."

"Well done," Lor corrected.

"Medium," the ringmaster insisted. "You'll eat like a nobleman while you're in my care." The green-eyed man nodded, then scurried away.

"Sit down," the ringmaster urged. "I've been meaning to ask your advice on something."

"Anything."

"It's Ranju that concerns me. Not the man, specifically. But the stir he's caused, and the problems he's left behind. I've lost hundreds of dollars on his prank."

"It's a pity—what he did," Lor replied.

Barnacle took a bite of his steak, chewed it thoughtfully. "Ranju *always* thought the animals were suffering. He had a chip on his shoulder bigger than a dinner plate. He probably thought he was acting righteously by setting them loose. Goddamn fool. I was correct in thinking he couldn't control Sally. His heart was too big."

Lor smiled sympathetically, surprised by the ringmaster's fervor. "It's true that he cared for animals as much as he did for men."

"Maybe more!" the ringmaster agreed. "All those complaints. 'You don't treat the animals right.' 'They need more food.' 'They need more exercise.' 'Their cages aren't big enough.' Has everyone forgotten that we work with beasts?"

"I haven't," Lor countered.

Barnacle proceeded to devour the rest of his steak with savage satisfaction. When he finished, he looked at Lor with bloody juice smeared around his mouth, a piece of parsley garnishing his teeth.

"Enough of Ranju—we need to move on. That's why I asked you here. I want your recommendation on his replacement. I've thought of some alternatives. What do you make of Barker the equestrian?"

Lor pondered the idea. "Barker's an old man," he said at last. "He tires so easily."

"Jimmy, Barker's son?"

"Too inexperienced, in my opinion."

"Lyle Whitehead, the bullman?"

Lor paused. "He's the best of the bunch. But even Lyle lacks . . . what is it . . . that spark, that flare?"

"Magnetism."

"Yes!" Lor agreed.

"No, Lyle's not a natural leader. But you've touched upon my dilemma. Lor, it's never simple to find someone with the kind of charisma you or I have. It's even harder now, in this recession. I can't afford to poach a trainer from another show. We simply don't have the green."

At this, the ringmaster leaned over conspiratorially. "At all times I used to keep ten dollars in my pocket," he whispered. "Just in case of emergencies. You know how much I keep now?"

Lor shook his head.

"A goddamn quarter! I'm clean out of money and ideas, son. Lyle, Barker, Jimmy—any of 'em would do. They'd take the promotion with a smile. But promotions come with raises. And I don't have anything to spare."

Lor looked at Barnacle's eyes. They sat tired over dark, drooping bags.

"What you need is a transition man," Lor suggested. "Someone already familiar with Bringlebright's methods. Someone who can do the job adequately until the economy swings back."

"A homegrown proxy?"

"That's the ticket."

"But who?"

"I don't know," Lor admitted.

Suddenly, hope drenched Barnacle's face. His eyebrows rose like rockets, deepening the crinkles on his forehead. "I don't know why I didn't think of it earlier!" he exclaimed.

"What?"

"Bump and Sara. They would be dynamite. They've worked side-by-side with Ranju for years—they know all the tricks. But even better, they wouldn't ask for money. I'm sure of it."

Just then, Barnacle's assistant slipped back into the car. He carried a smooth china plate, quite unlike the scratched tins of the cookhouse. Barnacle had dined on his desk. But there existed no similar surface in the car, so the assistant set the plate atop Lor's lap. The steak was still sizzling. Into Lor's upturned hand, the green-eyed man placed a silver fork and knife, wrapped with care in a lace-trimmed napkin.

"That's all for now," Barnacle instructed his assistant, who with a slight bow retreated.

Fine as the steak smelled, Lor no longer felt hungry. Barnacle's pronouncement had killed his appetite. He tried to imagine Stalwart in a position of power. He tried to imagine competing against his own son for audience attention. But in his mind's eye he could see only the tree, where he and the boy had huddled close amid the whispers of trembling leaves.

The ringmaster grew impatient as Lor stared wordlessly at the plate.

"Try it, will ya?" he asked at last.

Nervously, Lor nodded. He unfolded his napkin and collected his utensils. He sawed off a corner of the filet, momentarily daunted by the flash of crimson at the center. He placed the bite into his mouth and immediately he felt a little better. The juices exploded over his tongue. He had never tasted anything so palatable. As Lor ate he was able to push aside his newfound concerns. He watched the ringmaster pour him a glass of wine—red liquid comfort. He took another bite, then a sip of alcohol, and surrendered himself entirely to the simple pleasures of food and drink. Uncharacteristically off-guard, he didn't sense the ringmaster's eyes appraising him.

Now, as on other occasions, Barnacle noted every last detail of his popular star: how Lor chewed his food, the swell of his chest, the desperation and determination that mingled in his temperament, sometimes auspiciously, sometimes not.

The passage from scrappy young tramp to bona fide star had done little to alter Lor's character. Barnacle hadn't trusted Lor then and he didn't trust him now. In fact, his apprehension had only grown over time. He considered Lor both dangerous and brilliant. Though he feared the wire-walker, he couldn't help but adhere to the Machiavellian notion of keeping one's friends close and one's enemies closer.

Lor must always be within my field of vision, Barnacle decided as he thumbed his mustache. He could match me—maybe even outdo me—if I let him stray.

• CHAPTER SEVENTEEN •

September 20, 1937

A few years ago Sara built herself a radio. It plays pretty well, considering she built it from scraps: sawed-off boards, copper wire, thread spools, cardboard tubes, tin foil, waxed paper, cigar-box wood, screws, cork, tacks, washers, cellophane, and paperclips. She built a speaker too, so she wouldn't have to wear headphones.

Usually Sara plays her radio at night, outside the orangutan cage. Suki and Maple like the music, especially the newer melodies. Sara likes it too. She knows all the popular dances. I've seen her practicing them alone, but tonight, after a lot of prodding, she persuaded me to be her partner.

"This isn't going to be pretty," I told her.

"It doesn't matter. I just need *someone*. I'm sick of learning the girl's steps *and* the boy's."

"I'm warning you . . . "

"Even if you stand still, it's better than no one at all."

She met me at half past seven outside the orangutan cage, and boy, did she look smashing! She wore a green dress with yellow ribbons in her hair.

"Thanks, Bump," she said in response to my admiring expression. She twirled around and her dressed twirled with her.

"Where'd you get the duds?"

"I sewed them."

"Gee whiz. How long did it take you?"

"I don't know. A few weeks. I ran out of thread in Kansas and didn't buy more until we got to Oklahoma."

Sara fiddled with the radio. She found a big band station. A fast and jazzy song was on. "Perfect," she exclaimed. "I've been practicing this new thing: the jitterbug."

"Never heard of it."

"Here, I'll show you. Watch my feet."

I tried to follow what she was doing. The steps were light, gentle, smooth as cream. They suited Sara perfectly. But they didn't suit me at all. My brain filled past the brim with all the directions she gave me, and everything I tried came out wrong.

"Your feet are like bricks," she cried in dismay.

"I was thinking boulders."

"Do your shoes pinch?"

"No."

"Am I going too fast?"

"Going slower won't help. I told you: I can't dance."

She looked me squarely in the eye. "You need to relax."

She knelt down and reached under Maple and Suki's cage. Seconds later she emerged, bottle in hand. She took a sip then grimaced, the same hard look the roustabouts get when they booze.

"Try this," she instructed. "It'll make your worries melt."

"Whoa!" I said, recognizing the bottle. "Where'd you get it?"

"I swiped it from Legman Jack. It's called Sherwood Straight Rye."

"He'll kill you if he finds out."

"He won't. He has so many bottles stashed around, he can't keep track of them all."

"I wouldn't risk it."

"That's because *you*," she said, pointing her finger, "always do exactly what you're supposed to. Where's the fun in that?"

I took a sip all right, Journal. Then another. It went down like fire and I wondered if I'd cough up smoke. We didn't dance after that. I told Sara I was too tired, but really, I was having trouble walking. I couldn't wait to get to bed, but I *did* agree to meet her tomorrow for more practice. I suppose the Sherwood made me do it.

September 21, 1937

I was a little better today—at dancing, that is. I still tripped over my own feet. I still forgot to hold Sara's right hand with my left. But all my mistakes were worth the price of watching Sara. When we swung out, she concentrated so hard she didn't notice me staring. Heels clicking, head tilted back, eyes closed, she spun, slowly at first, like a figurine turning on a music box. She waited for the tempo to burst. That's when she broke out, blood hammering her cheeks. The spinning quickened and so did my dizziness. Her hair whipped back. The edges of her dress began to flutter, faster and faster, until at last they flew up and around her legs. I wondered how the lines of her back, and arms, and legs remained straight. Why didn't they buckle, as my heart did, in the face of that fury?

The moment ended, but the memory remained. I fixated on it until I couldn't think of anything else, not even the Sherwood Sara placed again in my hands. Should I have told her, Journal, about everything I feel? Or would such a confession ruin me?

"I miss my father," she said suddenly.

I had wanted to ask her about Ranju for some time. But I hadn't been able to strike up the nerve. Now, as she broached the topic, my stomach knotted.

"He hated Bringlebright, you know," Sara whispered. "You and I were the only people he liked."

I took another swig from the bottle, though my eyes watered.

"Ranju always appreciated your way with the animals, Bump," she continued. "How you befriended them."

"Thanks," I whispered.

I wanted to ask her why Ranju had left. Why he'd set the animals loose. Sara's the only one who might know. But somehow it didn't seem right. We'd settled into a peaceful sort of quiet, clean and pure, and I didn't want to ruin it."

Tired, we sat on the ground. She rested her head on my shoulder, then nodded off. I started to doze too. I had hazy dreams, what Legman Jack calls "drunkard dreams." I dreamt that Sara and I were dancing in a huge hall with a gilded ceiling. Other couples danced too. But none had our grace. Sara wore the same yellow ribbons in her hair, and these outshone the room's most lavish gold adornments. A band played one of Sara's favorite songs and she began to twirl. Her body spun so powerfully the other dancers retreated to the edges of the room. But I stood close. If she succumbed to the tornado winds of her own might, I swore I would be there to catch her.

September 24, 1937

At breakfast this morning, Mr. Barnacle's assistant met Sara and me in the cookhouse. He told us that Barnacle wanted to meet with us at three o'clock. I can't explain why, Journal, but Sara and I started to giggle. Not small giggles either, but big, explosive, embarrassing giggles. Mr. Barnacle's assistant stared at us, not knowing what to do. Seeing his serious face we became very self-conscious and fought to control ourselves. But the second he left, those giggles erupted again and we couldn't stop until we were both out of breath.

We worked hard all morning and early afternoon. So hard, in fact, that we barely thought about the meeting. By 2:45 we were filthy. Sara had been kneeling in the elephant wagon and now had dung clinging to her knees. I wasn't much better, sopping wet from bathing Lavender. We considered changing, but thought better of it. Mr. Barnacle always looks pristine, but looking good is part of his job. Our job is to take care of the animals—so what if it shows?

When we met him, the ringmaster acted as if we were a couple of ballybroads. His eyes twinkled and he fingered his mustache. He shook our hands vigorously, like we'd won first prize at a carnival booth. Then he brought out a cake, four layers high, and frosted alternately in chocolate and strawberry. I wondered what we had done to deserve such a greeting.

"Is it your birthday?" I whispered to Sara.

"No."

"Maybe it's *his*," I speculated.

"Kids, relax," Mr. Barnacle announced, voice booming. But as I was about to sit down, I saw him eye my wet clothes. "I thought it would be nice," he continued, "if we sat on a blanket on the floor. Picnic-style."

Sara and I exchanged glances.

"Children, I asked you here because I have something to tell you."

Mr. Barnacle settled on the floor, then straightened a crease in his trousers.

"Is this about my father?" Sara asked suddenly, "Because I don't know . . ."

"No, no, my dear. This has nothing to do with Ranju."

The ringmaster began to cut the cake. It smelled so good it distracted us from our discomfort. He placed each slice on a little plate, passing the first to Sara, the second to me, and keeping the third for himself.

"I forgot forks," he said apologetically. "We'll have to eat with our fingers. Oh, but I almost forgot."

His legs cracking like rickety boards, Mr. Barnacle stood up and rushed to his desk. He pulled three hats from a drawer, each one more silly than the next.

"These belong to one of the clowns. But she won't mind that I borrowed them."

Mr. Barnacle insisted we put them on. He even wore one himself—a pirate number with a stuffed parrot perched on the top. Again, our giggles returned.

"It's a party, you see," Mr. Barnacle told us. "A party to celebrate a very special event."

"Mr. Barnacle," Sara said delicately, "we don't understand . . . "

The ringmaster put down his cake long enough to pinch her cheek. "Such funny children you are!"

Sara looked at me pleadingly.

"Mr. Barnacle," I attempted. "Is it a holiday?"

"Yes, Bump. You might say it is."

We watched the ringmaster carefully, expecting him to say more. Finally, after he had finished his cake and cut himself an even larger slice, he spoke again.

"I asked myself, now that the wonderful Ranju is gone, who can lead the animals with a sure hand, a noble hand? I didn't have to think but a second before two names came to mind. The names of two of my most competent people: Stalwart and Sara."

Sara nearly dropped her wedge of cake.

"I want," he continued, "to make a spectacular act—a team act. And I can't for the life of me think of a better team than the two of you. We can get started right away, if there aren't any questions. Do you have questions? No? Good. We need to plan, then plan some more: logistics, your new training and rehearsal schedule, costumes, props, and of course, organizing your first act. But first . . . "

Mr. Barnacle once again climbed to his feet, this time spryly. Maybe his own speech had invigorated him. He dug around his huge desk, unearthing a mountain of mementos—lollipops, a corkscrew, ledgers, books, photographs, a handful of marbles, women's jewelry. Finally, he found what he was looking for.

"Contracts," he announced. "Once you sign them, everything will be set. *You* will be the new chief animal trainers."

Sara and I gaped at one another.

"You read them," she whispered to me. "Make sure they're all right."

I did read them, Journal. But I couldn't make sense of the phrases. I wanted to retrieve my dictionary, but Mr. Barnacle looked at us so eagerly. His every movement made me nervous. I didn't want to let him down, so I jotted my signature. It looked funny sitting there, not at all official, and I wondered if I had just made a monumental mistake.

"Mr. Barnacle," Sara asked. "What will happen to our old jobs?"

"Well, we're not really re-assigning your old positions. We're combining your old tasks with your new ones."

"So we'll be doing twice the work?"

Mr. Barnacle hesitated. "That's one way of looking at it. Another slice of cake?"

Sara cast me a look of disbelief, but she signed her contract too.

September 25, 1937

Sara and I spent yesterday making sense of the ringmaster's news. I still taste cake in my mouth, sweet on my tongue. I feel a little dizzy, like I'm living in a daydream. But with so much work ahead, I know I must focus.

First we have to decide on an act. I've worked alongside the animals all my life, yet I've never participated in a show before. Once or twice I helped Ranju in the ring, but that was only when the cats were being mischievous and extra hands were needed. I've never led a performance. I have no idea where to start. Sara's in the same boat. At five o'clock this morning we met to discuss our predicament.

Sara wants a combination act, something involving both the elephants and the big cats. I reminded her that Ranju always shied away from such ploys. Animals can be trained to work with one another, but not without hazard.

Barnacle has ideas too, only his are suspicious. He's already chosen Sara's costume and given sketches to Bringlebright's designer. The sketches show a flimsy piece of fabric, dipping low in front.

"You might as well perform naked," I teased her.

"That's probably what the ringmaster had in mind," she replied.

As to what *I* should wear, the ringmaster doesn't seem to care.

Another one of Mr. Barnacle's ideas: insisting that Sara place her head in Maxine's mouth.

"Like the great Mabel Stark," he explained. "The gillies love that stuff. Especially if you wrestle with the tiger, make it look confrontational."

But Sara rolled her eyes.

There is only one point Sara, I, and the ringmaster all agree on: emphasizing the big cats' awesome attack powers. Ranju was a master at organizing mock fights. He choreographed these ferocious moments for every performance. The gillies fretted. But Ranju was never in any real danger: he knew the animals too well.

In the cookhouse over scrambled eggs and grits, Sara and I talked until our lips went blue. Finally, we reached a compromise. I allowed her a combination act and she allowed me complete supervision over the elephants. We'll have to get the ringmaster's final approval, of course. But if Sara bats her eyes, I suspect he'll agree.

September 26, 1937

The shudders happened in the middle of the night. I awoke suddenly, my body an olio of nerves. A nightmare still beat against my skull. My hands felt clammy and my mouth dry. I dreamt that in Mr. Barnacle's contract Sara and I had signed our souls to the devil. But now, awake, I can't shake the notion that maybe we did. Bewildering snippets of the contract keep coming back to me, ever more bewildering because they have no context: "this Agreement witnesseth that in consideration of the premises and mutual covenants," "subsequent to completion of the probationary term of employment," "applicable statutory deductions," "the rules and regulations promulgated thereunder."

I remember the last line most clearly: "The validity, interpretation, construction and performance of this Agreement shall be governed by one party, Barnard L. Barnacle."

Maybe I recognized it then, when I signed my name with such trepidation. But only now do I fully understand what Sara and I have done. We've cuffed ourselves to a future neither of us control.

October 1, 1937

It's not the devil I fear, Journal. It's the ringmaster.

Our new schedule, the one he designed, leaves little room for breathing, even less for sleeping, and absolutely none for breaks. If the show's not on the rails, Sara and I awake every day before dawn. We feed the animals and clean their quarters in the early morning, then take fifteen minutes to wolf down breakfast. The rest of the morning is strictly for rehearsal. Mr. Barnacle is usually in attendance, there to offer guidance, but more often criticism. My posture's crooked. Maxine's fur looks tatty. Sara isn't cracking the whip enough. The elephants aren't generating excitement. The whole act is moving too slowly.

I wish we had months to rehearse—sometimes teaching an animal a new trick takes that long. But we don't have months—Sara and I learned that today, when Barnacle lit a firecracker under our feet.

"You start your new act, before a real audience, next Monday."

Sara's jaw dropped at least a foot. "The real thing?" she gasped.

"The real thing."

You'd think with such a tremendous deadline looming we'd devote every spare moment to rehearsal, but Barnacle won't have it. Every afternoon he makes us sit in the audience to watch the show—Bringlebright's show.

"Is this necessary?" I asked him. "We know how it runs."

"You've never seen it from the vantage point of the gillies," the ringmaster responded.

He wants us to study how the audience reacts to the joeys, the showgirls, the Weitzmans, each and every performer. He wants us to notice when the gillies roar and cheer, when they yawn and scowl.

"See what works," the ringmaster instructed, "and use only those tricks in your own routine."

The ringmaster's logic isn't bad. But I don't think we need to watch the show *every* afternoon. I feel awkward, sitting there with gillies on all sides. So many years I've spent avoiding them—how can I now embrace their presence? My skin feels scratchy. My underarms go wet through my clothes. The gillies, they don't stare at me like they used to. Like Lucy says, I'm not as bumpy as I once was. But still, I can't forget that they're from the Outside. We don't belong in the same place. We even smell different. Me, like sweat and animals and circus talk. The gillies, like burnt sugar—its sweetness long gone.

October 5, 1937

If Sara and I didn't sneak away from Mr. Barnacle's iron grasp every now and again, we'd surely go crazy. Today, Sara whisked me away during the afternoon performance. We couldn't be sure if the ringmaster saw us leave. But even if he did, what could he do? He was busy in the Center Ring.

Sara said she wanted to go back to her car. She had something to show me. Her roommates—two candybutchers, two showgirls, and an equestrian—would be at the show. Even so I felt worried: Bringlebright doesn't allow members of the opposite sex in the same car.

When we reached the compartment, neither of us looked back. Sara slid the door behind us, her face red. Journal, how does it feel to be alone with Sara? Really and truly alone, without the bullmen, or the ringmaster, or even the animals? Like tiny electric shocks tingling along my spine. Like breathing the briskest, cleanest, starriest night air. Like sunlight beating warmly on my eyelids. Like a delicious secret I've been holding in so tight, it's practically breaking through my skin.

"Bump, I want to show you something. Turn around."

I looked away, and the goosebumps rising from my skin told me that she was undressing. I heard a button finding its way through a buttonhole, the swish of workpants sliding down hips. Then I closed my eyes. The image of Sara dancing stuck in my brain. I remembered her legs, mesmerizing under that green dress. I remembered the way she moved, more rhythmic than the music.

"Do you like it?" Sara asked from behind.

I turned slowly, but I didn't answer right away. I couldn't. How does it feel to be alone with Sara? Like drowning in an inch of water and not even caring.

She had transformed herself into a land-locked mermaid. Aqua sequins like shimmering scales curving over the length of her body, ending in a fishtail's flair. Silver beads in her hair and on her slippers too. The whole look was breathtaking, not at all like the ringmaster's sketch. Sara must have made the costume herself, in the lean moments between our rehearsals.

"Perfect," I croaked.

Scooping up the lower half of the costume, Sara sat on a bunk. She held a scrapbook in her hands.

"I've got some ideas," she said, "for you too."

She patted the spot next to her, inviting me to sit. I expected her to smell different, like beach sand, but she didn't.

"For our act?" I asked her.

"What else?"

"Has the ringmaster seen your costume? *This* costume?"

"No, and I don't intend for him to. Not until showtime. Then he won't have a chance to chew me up."

"He'll like it," I assured her.

"I don't think so."

"He'd be crazy not to."

Grinning, Sara opened the scrapbook and placed it in my lap. Journal, I'm honest when I tell you that her drawings rival the best work of Bringlebright's costume designer.

"I had this in mind," she said, pointing to a sketch of a caped fellow with a mask over his eyes. "I know you're self-conscious," she continued. "I thought the mask, the gloves, the cloak—they would cover you up, but make you look mysterious."

I liked the idea, but knew I couldn't pull it off.

"They'd see right through me," I muttered. "I'm better off as I am."

"Don't you see, Bump? The gillies don't want to see *us*. They want to see people every bit as dazzling as the animals."

"That's impossible."

"I know that, and you know that, but the gillies don't. We could fool 'em."

I was skeptical. But taking another look at Sara's mermaid concoction, I began to see that maybe, just maybe, she was right.

• CHAPTER EIGHTEEN •

Lor noticed Stalwart's watch in the cookhouse. The boy took it from his pocket and glanced at it briefly, surreptitiously, before tucking it away. The fine timepiece clashed with the boy's patched coveralls and soiled hands. But Lor was not concerned with this incongruity. He thought instead of his own arrival to Bringlebright. Then, the ringmaster had flashed a similar watch, a jewel-studded reminder of the many trappings Lor endeavored to have. It startled the wire-walker that he, top-drawer, still lacked the very luxury that his son toted about. How had Stalwart happened upon the timepiece? He wouldn't have pinched it. The boy was too honorable—this Lor had realized long ago.

The watch must be a gift, Lor decided. Someone had deemed the boy, *his* boy, worthy of a high honor. Lor shook his head, unsure if pride or jealousy was causing his heart to race.

Though the cookhouse would close in a few minutes, Lor couldn't resist knowing the details. He sidled up to Stalwart, who had only recently begun to eat on the short side of the tent.

"Where's Sara?" Lor asked amicably. "You two are together so often I forget who's who."

"Oh—hello, Lor," Bump replied as he applied a generous helping of butter to a slice of bread. "Sara's in her train compartment. When she has a spare moment she likes to sew."

"Sew?"

She makes dresses, all sorts of things."

"A girl of many talents, isn't she?"

"That's why I spend my time with her. I'm hoping some of her talent will rub off."

"You certainly weren't gypped in that department."

Stalwart wanted to sidestep the compliment—he didn't feel right accepting it—but he couldn't think of anything to say.

"I noticed your watch. It's a beauty," Lor continued.

Stalwart stared at his plate wordlessly. The boy was shy around all but a few people, Lor observed. He must have withdrawn early in life, when so many gazes had glued to his bumpy skin.

"Mrs. Barnacle gave it to me as a birthday present," Stalwart said after a pause.

Lor nodded. He himself had never paid attention to birthdays or holidays. What were they, after all, but sentimental reminders of time's passing?

"It must be your prized possession."

"Oh, no. Other things mean much more."

"What other things?"

Bump again went silent. He didn't know whether to divulge such personal information. Then he remembered that Lor had already risked vulnerability: he had made the first precarious step toward friendship.

"My pictures of Mother."

"Wouldn't mind seeing those. She was a good woman, Cirella."

"You knew her?"

"Oh yes. We were dear friends."

Stalwart's rigid back relaxed. His reluctance crumbled away. "I'll show you them anytime—today even."

Lor had spoken of Cirella in order to appease the boy. But when he saw Bump's expression—earnest, eager, softly pleading—he realized he must follow through.

"Yes, let's use the last minutes of the meal."

Stalwart's cheeks glowed as he led Lor out of the cookhouse, across the lot, and into his train compartment. Immediately, Lor was struck by the difference between this space and his own. He hadn't forgotten the discomforts of the roustabouts' crum car. But he had forgetten the size of that room—and indeed, of all of Bringlebright's shared quarters. Stalwart's was no different from the rest: bunks and trunks fitted together like puzzle pieces, no space between the edges. No space period.

"It's nothing like your car, I bet," Stalwart remarked.

"They're not so different," Lor lied. "And you keep this place very neat—the ringmaster would be proud."

"Thanks. You want some saltwater taffy? Baby Jane gave me a box. Everyone says it rots the teeth, but I don't care."

Lor took a piece so that he would have something to concentrate on. Here with the boy, about to share mementoes from a past he'd rather push away, the wire-walker rued his decision to come. It had been a long time since he'd let his guard down.

Stalwart bent over his trunk, whose leather top was festooned with nicks and scratches. He disengaged the lock, flipped open the brass fasteners, and lifted the lid. Inside, his pile of belongings was arranged with obvious care.

"What are those?" Lor asked, pointing to two books at the top.

"This," Bump replied, reaching for the first, "is a dictionary."

"What do you have that for?"

"It's very useful and . . . well . . . I like words," Stalwart said with a shrug.

"And the other?"

"My journal."

"I've never written much myself," Lor conceded.

"I didn't enjoy it at first," Stalwart revealed. "I started writing at Lucy Loon's insistance. She said keeping a journal would be like whispering secrets to a close friend. She said it would be soothing."

"Is that true?"

Stalwart smiled shyly. "A close friend talks back."

"But you have other friends. Sara?"

"Sure. Now that Ranju is gone, Sara's my best friend—aside from the elephants."

Lor must have misheard. The boy couldn't be talking about those appalling gray monsters—the same ones he had dreaded cleaning up after.

"You consider the elephants your *friends*?"

"Oh yes. They're sensitive, perceptive, affectionate—a thousand times better than most people," Stalwart said. He glanced at Lor, alarmed to see a stupefied expression on the wire-walker's face.

"I suppose it's hard to understand. Probably I sound silly," the boy continued nervously. He lowered his eyes and dug deeper into the trunk. Seconds later he unearthed a stack of photographs, lovingly bound with a red ribbon.

"Here they are," he announced, pulling apart the bow.

Lor took the pile from Stalwart's hands. He leafed through the stack, struck—as he'd been the first time—by the fire-eater's beauty. Cirella seemed so alive in the pictures: eyes dangerous as lightning rods in the middle of a storm. She had faced the photographer for every shot and her stare still challenged.

"Some people say she was haughty," Stalwart whispered. "But I don't believe that."

"Haughty? No. Not your mother."

"What do you remember about her?" Bump asked, kneeling beside the wire-walker.

Lor wished he had another piece of taffy—any excuse to keep from speaking. He didn't know how to respond to the boy's question. What did he remember most about Cirella? How hard he had fought to forget her.

"I remember she loved you," he said at last. "I didn't realize it then, but I see it now. Everything else in her life was second to you."

"But I was a newborn when she passed."

"It doesn't matter," Lor insisted, shaking his head. "The moment she knew you were on the way, her life changed. She knew she would love you above everyone."

"I wish I could see her again," Stalwart murmured.

"That's only natural."

"What about your family, Lor? Do you ever see them?"

It was a simple question, a fair question. But Lor didn't know how to answer it.

"No, boy. Not often enough."

Stalwart reclaimed the photographs. He was about to retie the ribbon when he paused. He stared at the picture on top, the best one: Cirella at the main entrance to the big top, dress clinging, hip cocked, finger beckoning the onlooker into her tantalizingly exotic world.

"Lor, do you ever think what you'll do after the circus?"

The wire-walker grimaced at the question. "The circus isn't going anywhere."

"It will change, though. I didn't think so before. But once Ranju left, I saw that life changes as fast as it does in Mrs. Barnacle's storybooks. You never know when you will be forced to reconsider things."

"Your imagination is running too fast for its own good."

"I can't help it. I think what I would do without Sara and the animals. I think and think, but all the possibilities seem . . . empty."

Lor couldn't understand why the boy was so agitated. He himself no longer bothered to look beyond the perimeters of the circus lot. The world started and ended here. To deny that would be to deny his whole identity.

• • •

"I don't understand why you're spending time with that bastard," Legman Jack told Stalwart. Late at night, the roustabouts had just finished a game of cards and the other players had dispersed. Only the tattooed ruffian and the boy remained. By the light of a lantern they threw playing cards into the air. Occasionally one landed in Legman's upturned cap, which sat a few yards away.

"What do you have against Lor? He's all right under that cold shell."

"Sometimes I forget how young you are."

"What's that supposed to mean?"

"That you don't know squat. At age ten, I was already wise to the world. But nowadays youngsters are getting dumber by the minute."

"Hey," Stalwart protested.

"Listen, you don't know him like I know him."

"I didn't know you knew him at all."

"Lor used to be a roustabout."

"But not for long."

"No, not for long. Somehow he found his way into Barnacle's pocket. I thought he'd become a geek in the sideshow, or something like that. But next thing I knew he was in Weitzman's pocket too."

"What's wrong with that? Lor's a success."

"He's a four-flusher."

Stalwart looked Legman in the eye to see if he were speaking through the haze of inebriation. But his whites were clear, crisp as the inside of an apple.

"You want to see something, boy?" Legman continued.

"Sure."

The roustabout reached into the waistband of his trousers and pulled out a dark, bulky object. Stalwart squinted through the ashy air until that object took on a shape, an unmistakable silhouette.

"My Saturday night pistol," the roustabout boasted. "A beauty, ain't she? I snaffled her from a sucker in California. Way back when, we were working on a fishing boat together. No one knows I have it—not even Stan."

"You've used that thing?"

"Only once. How you think I landed in San Quentin?"

Legman handed the piece to a reluctant Stalwart, who ran his fingers over its parts. The boy was surprised by its bulk, its smooth, steely cool.

"It feels sinister."

"No, you got it all wrong. There ain't nothing sinister 'bout a gun. Stroke her right and she'll do anything you ask."

Stalwart handed back the weapon, biting his lip in distaste. "Why do you carry that thing, anyhow?"

"There are lots of untrustworthy people about. People like Lor."

"I don't know, Legman. I think you've got Lor all wrong."

"Listen, I've watched Lor a long time. From the beginning he's reminded me of someone from my past—a guy I used to call my friend."

Stalwart flung a ten of clubs. It sailed past the cap, lost in the darkness beyond the lantern's glow.

"Who?"

"His name was Simms. We grew up in the same neighborhood, knew the same tough people. He was a pretty boy, same as Lor. As a kid, he would come over to eat so often my ma forgot he wasn't one of her own. As we got older, things changed. I started pickpocketing, stealing from five-and-dimes, not so much for the money, but for the thrill. I liked the rush, the feeling that I was getting away with somethin'. Simms liked that feeling to, but he wasn't true to it. Inside, he was dying for a piece of action. But day to day, he was clean-cut, not a hair out of place.

"We stopped hangin' around each other as kids. If we saw each other on the streets, we looked away. But I still kept tabs on him. I knew what he was doin'. By then I was workin' with a gang and my time wasn't my own. When I got an assignment, I had to do it. A request came in. It was a two-man job, but the boss gave it to me—a test. I was nervous. I'd seen the boss roughhouse bunglers. Around that time, Simms came back into my life. He had no job and the shaky walk of a boozer. His bad side had caught up with his good and you could see a whole new look in his eyes: the hunger for trouble he'd always ignored.

"I made the mistake of feelin' sorry for him. How could I resist an old friend down on his luck? Before I knew it, I had invited him to help me. I told Simms I'd split my share—fifty-fifty. I put the idea past the boss and he agreed. The score was simple. A guy from a rival gang was movin' money. Simms and I knew exactly where he'd be and when he'd meet his contact.

"We were supposed to rough him up—scare him shitless, then take the dough. But Simms was like a junkie who'd gone too long without a fix. He took a knife to the guy's throat—slit it open like a letter. I knew we were done for, but I thought maybe there was a way out. I needed time to think, so we ran. We reached an abandoned warehouse, somewhere on the edge of town. I told Simms we'd stay there the night while I hashed out a plan.

"I was so exhausted I conked out. Not long, only an hour or two. In that time, Simms left with the goods."

"Did the boss find you?" Stalwart asked.

"He did—because Simms paid him a visit. He'd told the boss *I* was the one who stabbed the guy and stole the goods."

"And he believed Simms?"

Legman Jack smiled an angry mouthful of yellow teeth. "Yeah, that's just it. Like Lor, Simms had a way of winning people over to his way of thinking. No matter how much I argued, the boss never bought my version of the story."

Stalwart shivered in spite of himself.

"Simms was promoted," Legman continued. "Me—I got sacked, but not before the boss' thugs broke both my arms."

"Gee whiz, Legman."

"Now you see why I don't trust Lor?"

Stalwart stood up and began to collect the errant cards around the cap. "I see why you don't trust Simms. But that story has nothing to do with Lor. They're two different people who share a couple of similarities."

"You still don't know which end is up, do you, boy? I don't trust Lor because I see in his soul what I saw in Simms's too late."

"What's that?"

Legman threw a jack of spades. It paused mid-air, vacillating, before pitching toward the earth.

"A selfishness that's beyond reason."

Bump picked up Legman's card, the last of the pile. The jack, with its duplicitous double face, jarred him momentarily.

"Sorry Legman," he said, "but I'm going to give Lor a chance."

"That, boy, is exactly the problem."

• • •

Lor walked into the big top. He did so under an umbrella of curiosity. Stalwart had invited him to watch his and Sara's last rehearsal before their premiere.

"The ringmaster made Sara and me sit through dozens of shows," the boy had told him. "Every second was misery . . . until your act came on. I watched you as I used to watch Ranju. I got that old shiver up my spine. I aspire to be half the performer you are, Lor."

Stalwart had gone on to ask for Lor's guidance. But there was only so much Lor could suggest from a distance. He offered to assess the act firsthand. To this idea the boy had enthusiastically agreed.

Inside the tent Lor noticed Sara first. She wore work trousers, grimy and threadbare, and a man's button-down shirt. She'd tied back her hair in two braids, which whipped about as she waved signals to Bringlebright's Siberian tiger. She urged Maxine to jump onto small platforms set at various heights. But Maxine appeared languid, more ready for a nap than for orders.

Lor turned his attention to Stalwart, who was coordinating the elephants into a Long Mount. The boy waved "hello," then quickly resumed his work with the elephants. Each of the pachyderms stood on her back legs, front legs resting on the elephant in front, with the lead elephant balancing—amazingly—on nothing. Stalwart whistled and the lead elephant took a tentative, lumbering step forward. With equal caution her comrades followed. Soon all three were walking in sync. The sight of pachyderms traveling on two legs seemed surreal, even absurd.

The gillies would be thrilled, Lor knew.

Stalwart motioned with his arm. The ground shook as the pachyderms dismounted, one by one, settling back on all-fours. Sara turned sharply toward the rumbling, a smile sunning her lips. The successful completion of the routine must have been a hard-won victory. She ran to Bump to congratulate him. By now, her hair had come entirely loose. It streamed behind her as she skipped and jumped, laughing with delight. The whole scene possessed an aura of liveliness—something akin to the fresh tang of youth. Lor's heart beat right out of his chest. But as before, he didn't know if he were happy for the boy or worried for himself.

Moments later Stalwart looked in Lor's direction. He wanted to see the wire-walker's reaction. Lor's response was immediate. He saluted the boy for a job well done.

• • •

The day of Stalwart and Sara's premiere Lor dressed meticulously. The money bosses—tired of seeing half-empty stands and a malnourished money wagon—had scheduled a single performance that day. Lor had only one shot to give his all.

He peered into his mirror, wishing he could fit his whole body into the miniscule square. He wanted to see collectively his muscular physique, the rosin that dusted his slippers, the gloss of his tallowed hair, the sparkle of his leotard. But he could see only his face. Up close, he again noticed the signs of decaying beauty. It was only a matter of time, he realized, a few more years—five at the most—before the radiance of his younger days vanished completely. How much longer, he wondered, before age stole his agility too.

Lor flipped the mirror so the tain faced out.

Better, he thought.

He should have known not to bring himself down before a rehearsal. It was best to stay light. The air could sense weight: the heaviness of a tired mind, the oppression of worry.

Leaving his car, Lor walked swiftly to the back yard. He kept track of the show's progress by watching who came and went: acrobats, character clowns, equestrians, showgirls. He also listened to the sequence of the ringmaster's announcements, audible even outside the tent.

The first part of the show passed quickly, it seemed. In no time Barnacle had called out his name. Lor strutted into the big top, wondering how many seconds it would take for the intoxicating strobe of the spotlight to find him. When it did, he bowed deeply and stared into the crowd. Always at his moment and no other, he fell in love with the gillies. Their whoops and screams—all made him feel like a king.

When the roar died down, he began to ascend the incline cable. It stretched at a forty-five degree angle from the ground to the tent's summit. The exertion required to begin his act was enough to strain Lor's stamina. Hand over hand, he pulled his body into space. During rehearsals he sometimes looked down—testing his ability to defy fear, catching glimpses of the spotters below—but never during a performance. The gillies mustn't see his hesitation.

Upon reaching the high wire platform, Lor bowed again, this time to collect his breath. This season his routine on the wire was fairly simple: cartwheels and spins, and for good measure, a few forward and backward flips. Nothing tricky. Then again, the most famous wire-walkers always died during uncomplicated acts. Overconfidence bred carelessness, Lor supposed. He had chosen an easy routine because it was the end of the act, rather than the act itself, that was meant to thrill.

He completed three-quarters of his routine quickly and without much enthusiasm. Barnacle's voice again filled the electric confines of the big top.

"And now, ladies, gentleman, and children of all ages, Lor the Fabulous Wire-Walker will attempt something no other performer has ever dared. Something so dangerous, so outlandishly hazardous, so perfectly perilous that we ask you to please refrain from speaking. One whisper might disturb the Mighty Lor's concentration and send him plummeting *to his death*!"

A terrified hush replaced squeals of excitement.

Lor crossed the wire to the opposite platform, where a special pair of boots awaited him. He slid out of his slippers and donned the boots, tying them so tightly his toes ached. He checked the bottoms for a thick coat of rosin. Satisfied, he raised his right hand, a signal to the ringmaster that he was ready.

"Ladies and gentleman, the Bringlebright Traveling Circus thanks you for your silence. Now, see Lor the Fabulous Wire-Walker as you have never seen him before, as he attempts to ski down the incline wire with *no harness, no balancing pole, and no safety net*! His magnificent descent is called *The Slide of Death*!"

Lor looked among the legions of gillies. They appeared to him as a single throbbing mass. Many were unable to quell their anticipation. Their panting could be heard even at the rooftop of the world. Lor smiled and blew "farewell kisses"—Barnacle's idea. He wondered if the audience could see the white gleam of his teeth from such a distance.

Now there was nothing he could do but summon his courage and stay on course. He turned sideways, planting his feet on the wire: knees bent, heels facing in, toes pointing out. One more breath and he was off.

The whoosh of his feet, the wire whizzing precariously beneath him, the wind slapping his face—these sensations ended before he knew it. He could savor only the end: always, the mad applause of a delirious audience. His feet touched the floor. He wobbled for a moment, the way he imagined sailors wobbled about a ship before finding their sea legs. Then he bowed deeply, repeating chants in his head. He hoped through a magical conduit the audience would hear them too. "Behold the best!" "The one and only, the Marvelous Lor!" "Remember me, love me, dare not forget me!"

He basked only briefly in applause before walking with quick, deliberate steps out of the ring, straight to the back yard. Though charged up, he sat down to remove his boots. He winced when he touched the soles. They were still hot.

• • •

From the back yard Lor listened carefully. He knew when Stalwart and Sara would come on, immediately after the dressage riding act. Waiting there, mind thick with concern, Lor wondered if the brilliance of yesterday's rehearsal would be repeated in today's show.

His trembling hands told him that it would. As long as Stalwart and Sara held fast to their spontaneity, their performances would indeed be great. Technically, the two youngsters weren't any better than most of the kinkers. Yet they had elevated themselves into a higher category by way of their innocence. Theirs was a rare and special moment: the birth of celebrity. Lor remembered his own initiation—those first years at Bringlebright when he had looked in the mirror and seen stardust. He had radiated joy and anyone who had wandered within his corona had felt it too.

As time wore on, though, this euphoria had diminished. It had to, for the flares of first love are fleeting. Lor knew he would live out the rest of his life without ever again experiencing that moment when youth, talent, and happenstance collide. All he could do was watch someone else take a turn.

He heard the ringmaster announce the beginning of the next act. For a second time he entered the big top, this time with somber steps. He stood in the shadows, waiting for someone else—his son—to shine resplendent.

"The Bringlebright Circus discovered the next two performers on a talent search through the country. Young they may be, ladies and gentlemen. But these performers are staggering, indeed! Watch them tame a bloodthirsty tiger. Watch them command elephants into extraordinary positions. Watch them accomplish feats other trainers wouldn't *dream* of trying. It is my pleasure to introduce, in their first ever professional performance, Stalwart and Sara the Stupendous!"

The spotlight skipped playfully around the Center Ring, but did not find its target. Seconds passed and the gillies, hungry for a peek, began to squint, crane their necks, murmur to one another. Delays were uncommon in the circus—and never preplanned. Lor glanced at the ringmaster. But he seemed as baffled as the rest.

Two long minutes passed before Stalwart and Sara appeared. Lor couldn't be sure which entrance they had used. In fact, he couldn't be sure they had used an entrance at all. They had just materialized. Poof—like magic. Had they used magic to change their looks too, he wondered?

Sara wore a glamorous concoction that shimmered like the silver scales of a fish. Hers was a costume that would enchant anyone. But it was Stalwart who stole the gillies' attention. Lor's eyes roamed from his son's mask, to the debonair flourish of his cape, to the gloves that christened each of his hands. Safe in this extraordinary costume, the boy stood taller. He held his head high. His back ran straight as a perch pole. He gave the illusion of being a man, not a scrap of a lad, and certainly not one who had spent his whole life worried about his appearance.

Lor left the shadows for a better look. In disbelief he realized the full potential of Stalwart's transformation. He heard proof in the howling applause of the gillies. He saw it in the hundreds of spellbound eyes.

The gillies didn't blink for fear of missing something. Neither did Lor. The act began with Sara and the tiger in mock combat. Was it her piscine dress, the regal set of her hair? She appeared as both real-life conqueror and fictitious damsel-in-distress. The audience sighed in admiration. She knelt down, put her head in the tiger's mouth. The spotlight showcased her thin neck, which could be crushed in a single crunch. Somewhere in the audience a woman screamed bloody murder.

But Sara was already back on her feet. She and the tiger circled one another, like fighters before a brawl. The beast sprung. She jumped too, and they collided mid-air. Together, they rolled over, again and again, beast over girl, girl over beast. Everyone waited for Prince Charming, the masked man, to save her. But Sara herself seized control, shouting orders to the giant cat to halt, lie down at her feet, even lick her hand.

The masked man finally stepped into the spotlight. His very walk seemed virile—a hero's swagger. And although the beautiful girl had been captivating, the gillies couldn't wait to watch *him*—the more mysterious of the two. He positioned all three pachyderms side by side, a mountain of crinkly gray skin. Then he led the vanquished tiger toward them. He waved his arm, revealing a glimpse of the purple satin lining of his cape. The tiger responded by ascending a series of platforms. Another sweep of that astonishing cape and the tiger sprung onto the back of one of the elephants. Would a battle of claws and trunks ensue? But no, the tiger jumped from one elephant to the next, back and forth, finally springing into the air in an intense detonation of flying fur. The gillies scrambled out of their seats. They could no longer watch passively.

The masked man repositioned the elephants. Breathlessly, the audience members watched this circus staple: the Long Mount. They hoped for a twist on the old routine. And they weren't disappointed. Never had they seen elephants walk like this, like people, each step a rumbling miracle. Suddenly, the gillies wished they were on the floor, close enough to smell these startling new performers, to touch them, to caress the silky lining of that cape. And maybe, to peer under Stalwart's mask.

Lor scanned every face in the crowd. He looked for one person who hadn't been converted. But everyone had fallen, even the ringmaster. Barnacle stood thunderstruck, megaphone slack in hand, for once speechless.

• CHAPTER NINETEEN •

Stalwart knew at the end of their act, when the gillies began to roar loud as lions. Something had happened. It had happened that very first performance and it continued, unabated. He couldn't say exactly what it was, but the signs surrounded him. In the air, the smell of it: thin in the beginning, now heady. Its effect on his skin: a smooth, hot compress. Stalwart wondered if Sara felt it too. Did she also hear its song—melodic as a lullaby?

During one of their performances, weeks after their premiere, he watched her face as the gillies waved small Bringlebright flags—an undulating panorama of green and blue. Her delight actually sizzled. And finally, Stalwart understood what had happened: they had stepped into new skins.

The change lasted long after they left the ring. It lasted even when the show had ended and the kinkers hurried back to their tents and cars, to scrub off make-up and peel off costumes. Stalwart liked this rising belief in himself, this sensation of being pulled up and up, somewhere near the moon. He slept better, not as troubled by loneliness. He laughed more. He visualized himself and Sara on the circus posters, the same way he'd seen Lor Cole. In his cape he sneaked into the House of Mirrors. For the first time in his life he admired the way he looked.

One evening, Sara took him to an area beyond the back yard, where wild grasses and dandelions grew in abundance. She wanted to dance.

But the radio didn't pick up any signals, so they walked farther, and farther still. Before they knew it they had trekked three miles from the circus lot.

It felt good, Stalwart observed, to be away from the flurry of life for a while. He had become so focused on performing that even a simple reminder of ordinary existence—the crunch of twigs beneath his feet—had a stimulating effect.

The moonlight was bright, but even so, they decided to stop and make a fire. They picked a spot and Stalwart cleared a patch of ground while Sara hunted for tinder. She emerged ten minutes later, arms loaded. Although he offered to help, she insisted on arranging the assortment herself. She piled thin branches at the bottom, finer kindling and dried pine needles at the top. When she had finished, the structure resembled a tent.

"I don't have a light," Stalwart muttered, patting his pockets. Sara, however, held out a match.

"You always carry those around?" he asked.

"For cigarettes."

"I've never seen you smoke."

"Only when I'm angry."

"I've never seen you angry."

Sara smiled evasively. "We would've been able to build a fire without matches—using a bow and drill."

"Where did you learn that?"

"From my father of course."

When others floundered, Stalwart thought, Sara flourished. She'd survive no matter what the situation or where the place. He told her as much as she held a match to the woodpile.

"That's what you think," she answered.

She blew on the tiny flame until it spread, creating a full-fledged campfire. They settled down beside it and watched the warming glow.

"You ever think about how things have changed since we started performing?" he asked.

"How do you mean?"

"How everyone talks to us now. Take Barnacle. Did you see him after our first performance? He wanted to adopt us."

"That's nothing. He gets like that whenever he envisions higher sales."

"But don't you *feel* different?" Stalwart persisted.

"No. I feel exactly the same. All this praise, it puts a shiny coat on life. But it will wash off. That's why I'm not taking it seriously."

But Stalwart remembered her face. No one could fake that kind of rapture.

"It's not only the attention," he continued. "I mean, that's nice and all. But for me, it's the way the world has opened up. Suddenly I want to try new things. I feel—like I've opened up too."

Sara pulled a stick from beneath the burning pile. She stoked the fire until the flames blossomed higher. A frown marred her face. "I wish I felt that way, Bump. But I don't see myself trying new things. I don't want to leave the circus. I just—now that my father is gone, I want to stay close to what I know." She paused. "Besides, who would take care of the animals?"

"I didn't think about that," Stalwart admitted.

"Maybe you should have. You want to know what I really think of all this attention? I think it shuts the door to a person's heart."

She pulled her knees to her chest and hugged herself tightly. Stalwart, who felt much smaller than he had seconds before, grew quiet. Their silence left room for the sounds of night: insects buzzing, the crackling of their fire.

For a time they sat distanced from each other. Then Sara pulled closer, wrapping her arm around his waist. He returned the gesture, unsure of how to interpret it. Eventually their isolation receded and they held each other with an urgency that seemed to stop their lives from pivoting in chance directions. Stalwart had never felt so stable. Yet his heart beat so fast he was afraid it would give him away, reveal every secret, needful thought he had ever penned in his journal. So close, he could smell her hair—a day away from a wash, rich with flowery oils. He saw the zigzag of her part and wanted to trace it with his fingertip.

They embraced until the fire faltered. Stalwart, who could have sat there a lifetime, sighed when she told him they had better return to the train, get a good night's rest. He untangled his arms, pretended that the brush of his hand against her face was an accident.

"How do we put this out?" he asked her, nodding toward the fire.

Sara stood up, brushing off her bottom. She scooped up a handful of earth and sprinkled it on the flames. The blaze recoiled, visibly wounded. "You have to choke it," she explained. "That's the only way."

She continued to throw in more fistfuls until the fire fell low. Then she stomped the remaining embers with her shoes, bringing death to the same blissful light she had nourished moments before.

• • •

Since Stalwart and Sara's grand coup, a seamless transition into stardom, Lor had been unable to sleep. In the dead hours of night, he sometimes snatched a few desperate hours. But he inevitably awoke agitated. He awoke to see the downward slope of his career and the image of a man—himself—teetering at the edge. Even more disturbing, he had begun to talk when no one was around. He mostly addressed the boy. But these were speeches he would never have made if Stalwart were present.

"I won't deny I've made mistakes. If I would have known I'd spend half my life on the wire, never on the ground long enough to love anyone right, maybe I would have done things different. If I'd known the air runs thin on high, maybe I would have found a way to breathe easy. But I can't change what's past. You must know—it's too late. When I see people, I see them from the perspective of the wire. They look like ants. I don't know why they're scurrying about. I don't know why they all look the same." He paused. "Was it worth it—seeing the world from empty platforms all these years? Standing alone and apart? I can't answer that, boy. I don't know any other way."

Lor paused. His eyes were wet. He wiped away the unsprung tears, hating himself for his sudden frailty. He wasn't ready for this. He wasn't ready to renounce all he had become. And why should he have to? How did he know the doubts he had now were any more truthful than the unflappable confidence he'd had before?

He squared his shoulders. He couldn't stand to see a man slumped and defeated.

"Maybe life's dealing me a test," he said aloud, this time to himself. "Maybe it's testing me the same way it did when I had to walk on the moving train. I succeeded then, though I didn't know I would. And I'll succeed now, if I can shake these damn misgivings."

Lor knew he needed a distraction. If he could stop wallowing, even for a few hours, maybe he could build himself up to where he used to be.

With new resolve he ventured out of his car and into the train yard. Stars still flickered in the night sky, but dawn would begin soon. The first rays of sunlight rose languidly from the horizon. Everyone was asleep, except for the roustabouts. They had finished tear-down. Now they swarmed about the train, loading wagons and equipment. Lor decided to help. Maybe hard labor would cool his heated mind.

"Thought you'd still be prancing about in your leotard," Legman Jack chuckled, hustling Lor from behind. His breath wreaked of whiskey and sardines. "What're you doin' here?"

"Helping out. Had some time."

"We don't need no charity. Besides, your hands are soft as a woman's."

Not so. They were riddled with callouses, the result of climbing the incline wire every day.

"Whatever you say," Lor replied.

"I remember a time when you spat on this work. You were always running to the ringmaster, crying like a baby. 'I don't wanna be a roustabout! I wanna be with the Weitzmans!' A sorry sight you were."

Lor fought to uncurl his fists.

"But if you wanna help, I ain't gonna hold you back," Legman continued, belching. "Far be it from me to get in the way of *Lor the Fabulous Wire-Walker*."

It's all a test, Lor told himself. He nodded curtly to Legman and walked away.

Nearby, roustabouts and townies looking to make a buck were end-loading. The pull-over team, a pair of horses on the ground, hauled wagons atop the flatcars using ramps at the back of the train. Roustabouts helped the pull-over team draw the wagons forward, across the cars and the metal plates set between them. They hauled the wagons to the front, one by one, filling all available space. A poler remained ahead of each wagon, holding the wagon's tongue and guiding its front wheels with care.

Lor hopped aboard, joining a team of sweating, grunting men as they helped tug an overstuffed wagon down the chain of cars. Within minutes, he had broken a sweat. He felt his muscles stretch then contract. A pleasant soreness worked its way up his arms. As he toiled, his mind cleared. He thought of nothing of relevance, just the grease on his hands, the sharp smell radiating from his underarms, the breeze sweeping through his sweat-soaked shirt.

It took two hours to position all the wagons, then tie them down. When the workers had finished, one of them—a fellow Lor didn't recognize—handed him a cigarette. He patted Lor on the shoulder: a job well done. Lor answered the stranger with a smile. Minutes later Gus gave the "all aboard" signal. A sense of fulfillment enveloped Lor as he hurried back to his quarters. He locked the door behind him, stretched out on his bunk.

With his body exhausted, his mind had finally relaxed. His thoughts returned to the demons he'd earlier fought. They had diminished in size and clout, as he had suspected they would. He saw now what he had been too shaken to see before. He needn't feel shame nor indignity. What plagued him was not his disconnection with others, but his frustration with himself.

For the first time Lor realized he had no outside competition, not in Stalwart or in Sara. Perhaps he hadn't had it in Ranju either. No wire-walker at Bringlebright was as talented, no sky-dancer as powerful. And yet, Lor did have a rival. He had one in himself—in what he had become. He had turned into Sebastian Weitzman, the very man he had been hired to reform. He had stopped pushing himself with each passing season. He had turned smug.

Lor felt sick at the notion, but he could not deny its truth. This was the third consecutive year of The Slide of Death. In all that time he had not made a single variation or added any difficulty. He no longer approached the coming season with an eye toward innovation. He thought only of preserving his primacy.

He knew then what he had to do. He could achieve glory only if he took great risk. He had known this as a younger man, but somewhere along the way he'd forgotten. Stalwart, in his unexpected grandeur, had reminded him.

• • •

The next day Lor could hardly wait to begin rehearsing. He waded impatiently through the daily performance and a four-hour rehearsal with the Weitzmans. In the cookhouse he chewed and swallowed his food without tasting it. Every one of his senses was elsewhere, on the wire.

Finally, when most of the kinkers had finished for the day, Lor set to work. He entered the big top, eyes squinted in determination. There wasn't enough time left in the season to create an entirely new act. He would have to alter the existing one. Fortunately, The Slide of Death left a lot of room for experimentation.

Lor began to stretch: calves, shoulders, ankles, neck, back. Working each and every kink took him longer than it used to. When he was Stalwart's age, he hadn't bothered to stretch at all. But now his body resented the extreme strains of performing. Before bed he smoothed a muscle relaxant on his skin. Lucy Loon said he used so much he had depleted her supply.

A full hour later he was ready to climb the incline cable. He tied his sliding boots together by the laces and slung them around his neck. Then he pulled himself up. The climb was not easy. He toiled for every inch. Some days were like this: he simply lacked the strength. Fortunately, he could always compensate with sheer will. He gritted his teeth until he ground off the enamel. Worm-trails of perspiration slinked down his face, then splashed on the ground. Sweating was to be expected. But it was dangerous. Moist hands could slip. Sebastian Weitzman had warned him to wear gloves, but Lor preferred the raw friction of skin and metal.

At last he reached the top. Exhausted, he sat on the platform, legs dangling in the empty air as he caught his breath. He shouldn't have started his first practice so late in the day.

"Lor!" a voice called from below. "We're leaving now. Want us to stay and spot you?"

Al Fick, the equestrian director, and two of his underlings, the last kinkers still rehearsing, waved at him from forty feet down.

"No, Al," Lor shouted. "I'm all right."

The equestrians departed the big top, horses in tow. Lor watched the striped flap of canvas ripple, then still. His breathing had normalized, but his arms still quavered. He rubbed the muscles, feeling them tick and throb beneath his skin. He had an urge to return to the earth. But he would not be thwarted, not even by his own powers of reason.

Lor stood up. He made a decision, then crossed the wire quickly. Several times he journeyed across, back and forth, until he had forgotten about his sore arms and tender spirit. Eventually, he shed his slippers and untied the laces of his sliding boots. He donned one, but dropped the other on the platform.

Katarina's near-fall had required countless hours of rehearsals. But he didn't have the luxury of precaution, not with time imprinting its passing on his face. Then and there, Lor took a chance. He didn't founder in danger, or worse, in doubt. He stepped onto the incline cable.

Balancing on a single boot, he sensed the cable jerk and sway. But it was only his nerves capering. He let himself go, one foot grazing metal, the other bent precariously behind. He felt the usual charge of air, the acceleration of a vertiginous free-for-all. For several moments the cable, slim as a child's wrist, stayed faithful. Then it slipped from beneath. Lor reached up. He would catch himself as he always had. He would use his nimble hands, his God-given strength. But he wasn't in time. His fingertips only brushed the steel.

He heard the slamming of his body against the earth. At first he thought he had died. Death must feel like this: a collision of bones and dust. Looking up he saw the ceiling of the big top. It was much farther away than moments ago, when he'd noted the hasty needlework that hid the holes and splitting seams. The tent should have been replaced years ago. It was another expenditure Mr. Barnacle had delayed.

Lor groaned. He feared he wouldn't be found until morning. By then he would be cold to the touch. What an undignified end—to be discovered stiff and blue amid manure and tanbark.

Through the silence Lor heard himself speak. He was surprised by the words, clearly meant for Stalwart. He reached up to clench his own throat—to halt this deathbed confession. But the words came out anyway.

"Boy, I can tell you the glory was sweet. When the ringmaster told me I'd made it, I knew what he meant: fame at any cost, fame at the greatest price."

• CHAPTER TWENTY •

"I wouldn't have believed it, but there's not a thing wrong with you—not a damn thing."

Lor peered up to see Lucy Loon's round face bobbing over his.

"You're bruised—bruised bad—but that's all."

He swallowed a lump in his throat and wondered where he was. Was this the afterlife—an extension of the circus?

"You've been here twenty-four hours. Sleeping the whole time, like a baby. Meanwhile, I've had to endure a parade of people traipsing through *my* medical tent. You sure made a lot of people concerned. Mr. Weitzman, Mr. Fick, even Mr. Barnacle has been in. I've never seen the ringmaster so scared. His hands were shaking. I didn't give you a single thing. But I gave *him* a tranquilizer."

"Lucy?"

"Yes, Lor?"

"Do you mean to say I'm not dead?"

The quack snorted as she cleaned her tools with a rag and rubbing alcohol.

"Wish you were, do you? You should be dead after a fall like that. What were you thinking? Why did you leave your other boot on the platform? I suffer too many fools in this show."

"I have no right to be here," Lor whispered.

"That's true. Your fall wasn't much different than Cirella's. And look how she ended up. I guess it wasn't your time."

"Why Lucy, you always say you don't believe in providence."

The doctor sniffed. "I'm not sayin' I do. But being in this tent—seeing what I've seen—I can't deny that some things are beyond explanation. Of course, your situation is different. It's clear why you're still here."

"What do you mean?"

"I didn't see it for years," Lucy admitted. "I was staring at the wrong end of the string."

"What are you talking about?"

"Your secret."

Lor had never had such a conversation with Lucy Loon. He had never considered her a purveyor of wisdom. He had never considered her anything more than a mouthy crone. Just now, though, he dreaded her knowledge.

Lucy produced a small box from a drawer of medical supplies. Lor stared at it from the cot where he lay.

"What's this?"

"It's from the boy."

"What boy?"

"*Your* boy," Lucy chided.

He met her eyes. He expected accusation, but saw tenderness.

"A blessing that child is," she murmured.

"Lucy . . ."

"I've kept many secrets in my time, Lor Cole."

She deposited the box on the wire-walker's chest and exited the medical tent. Lor watched the package rise and fall in time with his frenetic breathing.

He took it in his hands. He recognized the ribbon that kept the lid in place—the same red cording that bound Stalwart's photographs of Cirella.

Untying the bow, Lor again halted his tears. The huge droplets weltered about his eyes. He opened the box and reached in. A note sat on the top.

Dear Lor,

Sometimes one happens across a friendship at exactly the right time. This is how I feel about ours. I keep the memory of the climbing tree close.

> How clever you were to show me that people, like trees, must reach boldly into the sky.
>
> Rest well and feel better soon. Your Friend, Bump
>
> P.S. I want you to have this. I've always thought that it suits you.

Tentatively, Lor reached into the bottom of the box. His fingers skimmed finely worked metal: Stalwart's watch.

• • •

Lucy Loon insisted that Lor stay another day in the medical tent. The bruises, some six inches in diameter, ached at the slightest movement. Yet Lor found immobility even worse than pain. With nothing to occupy his mind, he concentrated on his regrets. Augusta, Opal, Cirella, Stalwart—they visited him again and again. They spoke to him sweetly, with infinite patience. Lor lamented their tolerance.

At last the ghosts receded and a real visitor came. The green-eyed man sat by Lor's side. His slim fingers were woven together. His gaze was hard.

"The ringmaster is displeased, Mr. Cole. He believes your behavior was not in keeping with a star performer's image. He called your fall an amateur's mistake."

Lor looked beyond those clover-colored flecks. He studied the man's waxy skin, the pale impression of his lips. Lor could not guess his age.

"When is a man old?" he asked, surprised to realize he'd spoken the words aloud.

"I could not answer that, sir."

"Is it when he wishes he were young?"

"I don't know, sir."

Lor stretched his legs, instantly releasing arrows of pain. "This accident has loosened my tongue," he explained. On his face a grimace masqueraded as a smile.

The green-eyed man appeared at a loss. "Mr. Cole, the ringmaster wants to see you as soon as possible."

"What about?"

"That I cannot disclose."

The wire-walker sat up abruptly. His entire body protested the decision. "I'm ready now," he announced.

The man stood, startled. "If you insist."

Lucy had given Lor a pain-killer, but he swore the pill only enhanced his suffering. Standing sent tremors through his body. He limped miserably behind the green-eyed man. Together, they exited the medical tent and crossed the circus lot, which wound eventually to the train yard.

Lor felt as if he were participating in the world's shortest funeral procession. He was not mourning a lost life, however, but a demolished career. After his spectacular folly, the ringmaster might even let him go. This idea was so staggering, so unspeakably retched, Lor felt giddy.

"Wait here. Mr. Barnacle didn't know you would be ready so soon," the man explained. He thrust out his hand, but Lor had neither the will nor the strength to defy him. They faced one another stolidly before the assistant entered Barnacle's car.

When he had gone, Lor dropped to the ground. It wasn't an active decision, but a passive response. He sat in the dirt, soiling his clothes, his hands, and his pride for the second time. And yet, he didn't much care. He pulled his son's watch from his pocket and watched the minutes tick by with unnerving precision.

Eventually, the door to the ringmaster's car opened. Lor expected to see the assistant or Barnacle himself. Instead, three hearty-looking men stepped out. Lor recognized them, but he couldn't say from where.

"You all right, fella?" one asked. He reached down to offer Lor a hand, but the wire-walker refused. He found the strangers overconfident, maybe conceited, treading on Bringlebright's grounds as if they had a right. The man shrugged off Lor's rejection. "A kinker on his rump is a kinker in the dump," he said.

The others laughed at his pronouncement. They slapped his back with vigorous approval. Lor was relieved when they strode away.

The door opened again. This time the ringmaster appeared. He wore his top hat. It seemed out of place so far from the big top.

"Why, Lor, you look like a hobo. Has nothing changed since our first encounter?"

"I'd say quite a bit has changed."

Barnacle fingered his mustache. "And so it has."

Gathering his aching limbs, biting back the pain, Lor pulled himself to his feet. He followed the ringmaster inside.

"Have a seat," Barnacle indicated. Lor obeyed, then stared at Barnacle's desk. Toppling stacks of legal papers replaced the usual order.

"Spring cleaning?" he asked.

"I'm glad the fall didn't hurt your sense of humor, son. But may I remind you—spring is months away."

Barnacle settled behind his desk. He eyed the mess with grim acceptance before turning his attention to his guest.

"Tell me, son," he asked. "Were you trying to fly?"

"No, sir."

"Were you trying to kill yourself?"

"No, sir."

"Well, then, I'm fresh out of theories. Explain to me why you catapulted yourself into thin air."

"It was an accident, Mr. Barnacle."

"An accident borne of stupidity or misguided bravery?"

"I'm . . . I'm not sure."

"I'm about to make an important decision, son. I need to know if you're all there."

"I haven't gone crazy, sir."

"No? Have you ever seen a sane man try what you did?"

"Mr. Barnacle," Lor winced, "I haven't been performing up to expectations—up to *my* expectations. I wanted to prove to myself that I haven't lost what got me here in the first place."

Mr. Barnacle sighed. "Son, I thought your hubris was inexhaustible. Why now, after so many years, are you doubting yourself?"

Because my son is outpacing me. Because so much of my hair has turned gray I stole black dye from the costume tent. Because where before I dreamed of escaping my past, now I dream of revisiting it.

"I don't know."

Barnacle sighed again, this time more volubly. "There is something I need to tell you. Be warned: it won't be easy to hear."

Lor readied himself for his walking papers.

"Did you recognize the three men who left my car?"

Lor nodded. "Yes, but I couldn't place them."

"You've seen them in the papers, but probably never in the flesh. They are our mortal enemies, Lor. And I've just surrendered to them."

"You've what?"

"They were managers for the Ringling Brothers. They do cut a figure, don't they? Just like the original Ringlings used to. Who do you think I modeled this mustache after? We made a deal. Starting next season, the Bringlebright Traveling Circus will belong to them."

Lor had nothing to say. Surely the ringmaster was joking.

"We were their final rival—the last independent circus with any kind of clout. They never fancied us a real competitor. Frankly, even in our heyday—fifteen years ago—we didn't pull in the kind of cash in a season that they pulled in in a month. The age of the small circus has passed. We're entering a new era—an era of consolidation, of small businesses being gobbled by giant ones, of charming little shops merging into monsters of mediocrity. I've been dreading this for years. But there's no stopping change. Son, you can write that as my epitaph.

"I can tell by your eyes—you think I've made a killing on this deal. I haven't. I sold for mere pennies what was once worth a fortune. This has been a hard year for all shows. Even the Ringlings closed ahead of paper. But they still have reserves. And we don't. I've been in negotiations for two months," Barnacle revealed. "I've had to bear this burden alone. You're the first person I've told."

Lor wanted to respond, but wasn't sure how. "Sir, forgive me. I can't think straight."

"Nor can I. Want a drink?"

Without awaiting an answer, the ringmaster pulled a bottle of plum brandy from his desk. He fished for glasses, then, thinking better of the idea, handed the entire bottle to Lor.

"Drink up, son. I haven't told you the other half of the story."

"There's more?"

"Yes, quite a bit. You see, the managers won't take our personnel. They want our name, our brand, our customers, but not the nuts and bolts of our operations."

Lor uncorked the brandy. "What do you mean, Mr. Barnacle?"

"They asked for only one act—our very best act. And they left that decision to my discretion."

Even now, in the midst of sweeping change, Lor could not bring the bottle to his mouth like a common drunk. He couldn't forget that he was in Mr. Barnacle's car, a place as close to a palace as he'd ever see. He awaited the names. They would pass uncomfortably from the ringmaster's lips: Stalwart and Sara. It was only right. It was only fair. Barnacle had said it himself: there's no stopping change.

"I've decided you, Lor Cole, are still Bringlebright's most luminous asset. I want you where I can see you: in the spotlight."

Lor labored to understand Barnacle's meaning.

"Sir, you're saying I will be all that remains of Bringlebright?"

"Yes."

"What about the others—the Weitzmans, Al Fisk's group, the clowns, the showgirls? What of Stalwart and Sara?"

"Everyone must go—from the freaks to the circus band." The ringmaster paused to take another bottle from the desk. From this he drank heartily. "It breaks my heart, but there's no other way."

Lor supposed he should be delighted, or at least relieved. Here he had been given another chance, just as he'd entered a dark hour. Yet no grace penetrated his anguish.

"And you, Mr. Barnacle. What will you do?"

"I'm going into retirement, son. Not an old man's retirement—long, lazy days have never suited me. I'm going to travel with Mrs. Barnacle. She has always wanted to see the world. That's why she reads so much. She fascinated by new lands, new people. Me, I've always had the whole world crammed into the cars of this train. But I'm going to humor her. She is my wife, after all."

"You're done with the circus for good?"

The ringmaster took another slug. This he swallowed uncomfortably.

"I couldn't say, Lor," he murmured. "I couldn't say."

A pause ensued. The ringmaster continued to drink as Lor stared at the dark eye of the open brandy bottle. He could see the liquid below, bright, roily, trapped.

"Mine was a hard decision," Barnacle said at length. "You've seen for yourself that Stalwart and Sara have become major contenders."

"Yes."

"They rank a close second. But I couldn't dismiss you, Lor. In a way, you've come to symbolize this show."

Lor continued to stare at the bottle, gaze descending the long neck. Was a symbol the same thing as an icon, he wondered? Could one live forever as a symbol? He tilted the bottle and the liquid sloshed from side to side, creating tiny waves. Once, when he and Augusta had walked along the edge of New Haven Harbor, she had told him that waves don't end. They hit a shore, bounce back, and roll onward toward the next, becoming meeker with every mile traveled. Given enough time even the greatest wave would become a ripple, Augusta had said.

Lor imagined himself telling Stalwart this story: a life lesson disguised as an anecdote. They would walk, hand in hand, to the shore. They would feel cool saltwater lap their toes. They would gaze at something larger than even their dreams.

"Where will they go?" Lor asked. "The people who have spent their whole lives here—what will become of them?"

"I don't know, son. That is for them to decide."

Stalwart's foundation was the dusty floor of the big top. His ceiling: striped canvas. He shared this house with the only family he'd ever known: Sara, the animals, and memories of Ranju.

"What of the elephants?" Lor asked.

"A funny question, lad! I wouldn't think the elephants would be high on your list of priorities."

"Will you sell them?" Lor persisted.

"If I can make good money. If not, I'll dispose of them."

"But if you were to keep Stalwart and Sara, you would keep the elephants too?"

"Of course. But there is no point to these hypotheticals. Your act is *it*."

Something settled over Lor: a choice that was not quite a choice but a decision born of past errors, one he had already made, long before his recent accident, even before he had sat in the tree with the boy, a decision that transcended time and space, infinite in its necessity.

"I decline, Mr. Barnacle."

"What did you say?"

"I cannot go with another circus. I'm done with this life."

"Get yourself together, Lor! What else do you have? I'm handing you, on a silver platter, preservation. Take it!"

Lor corked his bottle and set it on Barnacle's desk. "I've made up my mind, sir. I'm past my prime. I'd prefer to go before people start reminding me."

Barnacle leaned forward. His eyes scratched and tore at Lor's conviction.

"What do you have on the Outside, son? I've never heard you speak a word about a woman, a home, a father or a mother. When I found you it was obvious you hadn't been cared for—not like you've been cared for here. This—the circus—is your rightful place."

"It was my place, but no longer."

"Where will you go?" Barnacle pried.

"I haven't decided."

Seeing the ringmaster's expression, furious with impotence, Lor did not reveal the truth. He knew exactly where he was going and why.

"You're making the biggest mistake of your life. Don't you know? A circus man collapses outside the ring."

Lor stood. He looked for the last time at Mr. Barnacle's sanctuary. The surfaces were more tactile than ever: buffed wood and soft brocade, buttery leather and glazed china. In these few minutes the car had already changed. It had receded into history. It had become a museum exhibit: unreachable behind a velvet cord, musty and stale from disuse. Finally, Lor looked at

Barnacle himself. He languished behind the desk: the proud monarch of a forgotten dynasty.

"Thanks, sir, but I'll take my chances."

November 6, 1937

Dear Journal,

It is appropriate that I write on your very last page. Mr. Barnacle called today "the end of an era." You, Journal, will coincide with this end, for I will never write in you again. When next I pick up a pen, I will have a new journal before me—and new stories to tell.

Don't be sad, loyal Journal, for you will always be my dearest book, my fondest collection of memories. I know this for certain, even though I don't yet know what my future holds.

The Bringlebright Traveling Circus has been disbanded. This I learned only hours ago. The ringmaster told us in the cookhouse. The curtain was gone for good. We—the kinkers—listened together with no partition to divide our ranks. Together we sat: Sara and I, Lucy Loon, Lor, Mrs. Barnacle, the hair-hangers and acrobats, the equestrians, the moneymen, Baby Jane and the freaks, Sebastian and Fifi Weitzman, the showgirls, the joeys, the bullmen, Legman Jack, Fat Stan, Rusty, Spider, and Bar None. We were strangely silent as Mr. Barnacle explained what had happened. The Ringling Brothers' circus has taken over. Bringlebright was bought out from under our noses. Mr. Barnacle explained that he had tried to reason with them. But the Ringlings are just as we always suspected them to be: ruthless and unsympathetic.

I don't know where everyone will go or what will become of their lives. Only Sara and I will continue on with the circus. The Ringlings asked that we, as well as the elephants, join the new show. We will be the only kinkers to uphold Bringlebright's legacy. Journal, I can't help thinking we are ill-equipped for the job. We don't have Lor's aplomb or the equestrians' long-standing record. Why we were chosen over the rest? There is only one explanation: we have a guardian angel.

After the announcement, Sara grabbed my hand under the table. She couldn't say anything, but I know what she was thinking. *Thank heavens we have a place to go. Thanks heavens we won't be leaving.* I was thinking the same, Journal. But I couldn't express my relief, not when everyone else was grieving.

We'll be finishing out the rest of the season, the ringmaster said. We'll receive our wages then. The end isn't far off—only a handful of shows remain.

When the ringmaster finished his speech, everyone left the cookhouse and reconvened in small bands and private circles. They rehashed the news in disbelief. I could hear the whispers everywhere. They drifted from the satellite tents and train window slats and big top.

Sara and I were our own group: a lonesome pair. We stood in front of the train and studied the artwork on its steel sides. Soon the painted blue-and-green flags would disappear behind new designs. Our past would be chipped away, fleck by fleck. Our remaining flyers would drift on rogue winds. New events would vanquish Bringlebright's memory, until only a few people remembered this day and how we felt as the realization bore down on us, icy and relentless.

Beside me Sara asked, "What of Suki and Maple?"

I didn't know how to answer. The casualties surrounded us. Soon everyone we knew would leave the circus lot forever. They would step tentatively into the Outside and wonder what kind of life would befall them. The animals had it no better. Maybe they had it worse.

"Talk to the ringmaster," I said, putting my arms around her shoulders. "Maybe he can do something."

"You heard him. He has no power now."

I didn't believe that. During Mr. Barnacle's speech I had looked at Lor. He had returned my stare with a tenderness that made me blush. I saw in his eyes something I had not seen in anyone else's: fulfillment. Which made me think there was more to Bringlebright's end than the ringmaster had let on.

"Talk to him," I repeated.

• • •

Lor had all his belongings packed in a single trunk. He had left his costumes behind. He wouldn't need them where he was going. He stood on the platform of the railway station, waiting for the train to New Haven. He had money in his pocket: not a lot, but enough. On the opposite platform the Bringlebright Traveling Circus train stood ready for departure. Lor smiled softly. He remembered the last time he had gazed so intently on a train. He had been a boy, Stalwart's age, loitering at the New Haven Railway Station. He had watched the faces in the windows, squinting with concentration as he tried to guess where each passenger was going.

Those days seemed so faraway. They were the stuff of a simpler world.

Waiting, ticket in hand, he tried not to imagine what lay ahead. But the possibilities trundled about his head, and he was helpless to their momentum. In his mind he visited his mother's grave laden with flowers. He hugged Woodrow hungrily. He strolled along the shoreline and breathed in the ocean. He found Opal hanging clothes on a line. Her back was turned and she was speaking to a young man, handsome and possessed of many dreams. Lor recognized her strong shoulders, her wind-swept skirts. He called out her name. She turned very slowly. Lor stared at her face. It was weathered and no longer beautiful. He stared, but could not read her expression. It was blurred by the time that separated them, thousands of days blown past in an instant.

Below his feet, the platform rattled tellingly. His train was nearly here.

BIOGRAPHICAL NOTE

Chandra Prasad finished *Death of a Circus* only after extensive research of early twentieth century circuses and interviews with dozens of circus performers and historians. She is the editor of—and a contributor to—*Mixed: An Anthology of Short Fiction on the Multiracial Experience* (W.W. Norton), which includes original pieces by Ruth Ozeki, Danzy Senna, Peter Ho Davies, Cristina Garcia, Wayde Compton, Rebecca Walker, and Diana Abu-Jaber. She is also the author of *Outwitting the Job Market* (Globe Pequot), as well as numerous articles on diversity and the workplace, which have been published in the *Wall Street Journal*, *India Abroad*, *India New England*, and Vault.com, among others. In 2007, Atria, an imprint of Simon & Schuster, will publish her latest book, a novel about a girl who poses as a male student at Yale University in the 1930s.